HOME RUN

A Texas Heat Romance

CAMILLA STEVENS

ABOUT THE AUTHOR

Camilla Stevens lives in New York City. At night you can find her typing away, often with a glass of wine, getting all the steamy, humorous, Happily Ever After stories out of her head and down on the page. You can usually find tulips, her favorite flower, making an appearance in most of her novels.

SIGN UP FOR HER NEWSLETTER:
http://eepurl.com/cbc3BD

AMAZON AUTHOR PAGE:
amazon.com/author/camillastevens

Want to Join the ARC Team? Sign up Here:

http://eepurl.com/cvJzfP

Next page for more!
www.camillastevens.com
author@camillastevens.com

ALSO BY CAMILLA STEVENS

HOME RUN

Thwack!

It was the sound that would change their lives forever.

Carter Fox is the powerful home run hitter for the Houston Sluggers.

Baseball was the only good thing in his life.

Then *she* winds up with one of his home run balls in her hand.

Jordan Douglas has three priorities in life: Law school. Graduation. Job.

There is absolutely no room for a playboy baller.

Then she winds up with one of his home run balls in her hand.

An overt show of bravado.

A case of misread intentions.

A slanted news piece that gets picked up nationally.

Pretty soon all of Houston is talking.

Damage control leads to something deeper...

...until a tiny, little curve ball is thrown into both their lives.

Now the game is changed forever.

This is a **Stand Alone**, BWWM Romance in the *Texas Heat Romance Books,* with an **Unexpected Baby**.

WARNING: Due to quite a few extra steamy scenes, and Adult language 18+ only!!

"That was the second out!"

Jordan Douglas nearly dropped her hot dog.

"Jesus, Ben!" she mumbled under the bun she brought back to her mouth.

"Sorry," her cousin muttered.

She gave him a wary look as she bit off the end and chewed. He was going to ask her to get up again, she knew it.

Ben stared at her, his lips contorted in a mixture of impatience and guilt.

He couldn't hold himself back any longer. "It's just that...one more out and Carter's up at bat!"

"I just got this thing," she reminded him, lifting the hot dog, extra mustard.

There had finally been a wonderful window of opportunity, where the guy selling hot dogs had actually been in the vicinity of their seats, and Carter wasn't about to take the bat. Jordan had seized the moment.

Then, *bam*, the Rockies had managed to get two outs, quick as lightning.

"But it's a draw, 4-4. This could be the last inning, especially if he hits a home run!" Ben pleaded.

"Can I just finish it first? I'm starving!" she pleaded.

Her 12-year-old cousin pressed his lips together, torn between not wanting to be a nuisance and his desire for the thing he wanted even more: one of Carter Fox's home run baseballs.

She gave him as much of a glare as she could muster, hoping it might help him decide.

He shot right back with those puppy dog eyes. She knew for a fact they had materialized just to guilt-trip her into putting on his mitt and heading down to the bottom of the stands in their section yet again. It was a battle of stares.

Jordan couldn't help herself any longer and began to laugh, punching him lightly in the arm. She took another quick bite of the dog and handed it to Ben, switching it out for the catcher's mitt in his lap.

"Don't get your hopes up, kiddo," she mumbled with her mouth full. She stood up to go down as she fitted the mitt to her hand.

"Jordan!" he called out.

What now? She turned around, one hand on her hip.

"You have some mustard on your upper lip." He pointed to his face to show her where it was, holding back a smile.

"Thanks a lot, cuz," she said, running her tongue over her upper lip to lap up the tangy smear. "At least now when I *miss* catching that ball, I won't look like a complete idiot."

She could see he wanted to laugh, but thought better of it. No sense in pressing his luck.

Smart kid.

Considering how often she had done this, it was a good thing they were sitting on the end of the row, mostly because of Ben's condition. He had been hit by a drunk driver while riding his bike a while ago, which had shattered his left leg, leaving him in a full leg cast.

Ben patently refused to sit in the special needs area, even though it offered a much better view of the game. After all, that section was not between second and third, where Carter Fox's home runs usually ended up. That just wouldn't do, especially when Ben had an older cousin to pop out of her seat every other inning to try and catch one of those balls.

Smart kid. Maybe too smart.

This would be the fifth time today Jordan had left her seat, hand securely mitted, to head down to the bottom of their section with the other hopeful fans.

She frowned, just as she had each time she made her way down. Carter Fox had been known to pay a hefty sum for his home run balls, so the crowd was substantial, and very agitated. This was bound to be as unpleasant as the last few times.

Even though she had almost twelve years on him, she and Ben got along as really good friends. So when he wanted, more than anything, to go to the Houston Sluggers game, she offered to take him, even though she had zero interest in the sport.

Ben practically idolized Carter Fox, who had almost single-handedly brought notoriety to the fairly new National League upstart ballclub thanks to his home run streak. In fact, everyone in Houston seemed to have Slugger Fever, which was unfortunate for the other home team, the Astros.

If her cousin wanted that home run ball, she would make a valiant, if statistically futile, attempt to catch it for him. Even if it meant dealing with the worst attendees of the game.

"Back again?"

It was the same obnoxious man with a tiny, douche-patch right below his bottom lip, who spent less time looking out for the ball than he did eyeing Jordan's legs or trying to look down the front of her tank top, despite her meager offerings up there.

Jordan wished she had worn something that covered her up a bit more, especially since the Sluggers' stadium was covered, complete with air conditioning. To hold a game any other way in the middle of summer in Houston would have been suicide in terms of ticket sales, even for the most hard core fan.

Ben had decked himself out in Sluggers' gear in honor of his favorite team. Jordan's royal blue tank top, that fit perhaps a bit too snugly against her chest, was the only piece of clothing she had brought with her from law school this summer that matched his gung-ho team spirit.

"Just make sure you stay out of my way," he continued, a leery smile appearing between those ruddy cheeks. "This may be his last hit of the game and that ball is mine."

Jordan just ignored him. All the same, she took a few steps back up the stairs so that she was away from the bulk of the crowd. It probably meant she wouldn't get the ball, since Carter Fox had never hit a home run this far up into the stands. This was evidenced by the complete lack of hopefuls around her. She tempered her mild guilt by reminding herself that she had a better chance of being hit by an asteroid than catching that ball. Seriously, who could predict exactly where it would land anyway?

She crossed one arm over her stomach and dangled the other one, which felt heavy with the mitt on it. With her hair up in a ponytail, the cool air of the stadium hit her neck. During the summer it was impossible to keep her relaxed hair straight. Instead, she would wash it, braid it, and let the resulting wavy curls do their thing. In some ways, she preferred it like that, since it suited her heart-shaped face and the deep dimples she sometimes found a bit too precious. It made her feel like a less cool version of Donna Summer.

She looked out on the field as the players just stood there waiting for the play to begin.

Why couldn't Ben be into something that moved a bit faster, like basketball or football? Baseball had far too many lulls to hold Jordan's interest. But he loved the stats, he said. Baseball was a "thinking man's game," whatever that meant.

Jordan just wanted to get back to her hot dog. That was the one good thing about coming to a baseball game.

Finally, a player for the Rockies was tagged out at second and Jordan perked up, trying to at least make an attempt to seem ready for action. The teams switched out as Jordan stifled a yawn.

The Rockies took the field, and the first batter up for the Sluggers headed out of the dugout. Ben's favorite player:

#47, Carter Fox.

Jordan watched with sudden interest as his muscular physique walked toward home base while the other team took their places on the field. The crowd went crazy with anticipation as he gave a few test swings away from the plate. Even Jordan could feel herself getting a tiny, adrenaline-fueled buzz as she watched him in action. Maybe baseball wasn't entirely boring.

The huge screen at the end of the field zoomed in on Carter as he finally took up position at home plate. He removed his batting helmet to wipe his forehead with one very nicely developed forearm. His wavy, blond hair was a tousled mess that she had an urge to reach out and run her fingers through. Perhaps hot dogs weren't the only good thing about baseball.

He placed his helmet back on his head and got back into position. The camera focused on his face again. A brief sizzle of pleasure went through Jordan, just as it had the last few times she saw that face up close. The green eyes blazed with intense determination. His strong jaw looked so taut, she wouldn't have been surprised if a few of his teeth were currently being crushed. She noted the arm and shoulder that faced the field. The man was huge!

Looking at the package as a whole, it was no wonder Carter Fox got so much play off the field. Jordan was well aware of his reputation. You didn't spend even a little time in Houston and not know about the Sluggers' star player, no matter how indifferent you were to the sport. One had to wonder how he even had time to practice, when he seemed to spend most of it hosting parties at his River Oaks mansion or out on the town with the flavor of the week.

She snapped to attention when she felt the hush of the crowd. Carter Fox was poised and ready. The pitcher was taking his signals from the catcher.

A shake of the head. No.

Another shake of the head. No.

Finally, there was a nod and he threw his arm back to pitch the ball.

He didn't stand a chance.

Carter hit it with a smack that she was positive she could hear even this far up in the stands. She braced herself as she saw it heading toward the usual area between second and third base. It didn't hurt to be prepared...just in case.

Her eyes widened and then began to blink rapidly as she saw the trajectory.

Oh no.

Oh, no, no... NO!

The arc was way too high for the crowd below her to have any hope of being where it landed. In fact, it looked as though the ball was heading straight up to her. Jordan's breath caught in her throat as she thrust her gloved hand into the air. She wasn't sure if she was more terrified of the ball spiraling toward her head, or the horde below her that had just discovered they were standing at the incorrect latitude to catch it.

She focused on the approaching baseball, angling her arm, mostly to prevent getting knocked in the head. Before the throng of people below her could clamor up the steps in a stampede, she felt the *thunk* as the ball actually fell into her glove. Despite the protective mitt, her palm immediately began to sting.

"Oww!" she yelped, wincing.

Then her eyes grew wide as she realized what had just happened. Despite the soreness radiating through her hand, an amazed smile grew on her face as she pressed the precious ball to her chest and jumped up and down. She saw herself on the jumbo screen, giddy with excitement as her face beamed with joy. The next moment it was on Carter Fox's face as his lips formed an O of appreciation, then mouthed the words, *very nice*.

Jordan had only a moment to get a bit feverish over that, before she was knocked straight on her ass by the crowd from below. The very man she had been trying to avoid earlier was front and center. Jordan protectively hugged the mitt holding the ball to her chest as she was crushed into the steps from his huge body slamming down on top of her. He was followed by a few more who couldn't stop their momentum.

She felt the breath rush out of her lungs as the mass of people scrambling on top of her compressed her chest. The edge of the stair dug into her back and she began to panic.

Oh my God, I'm going to die holding one of Carter Fox's balls in my hand.

Hands grabbed at her glove, and arm, and pretty much everywhere. She felt a fist hit her jaw, but still she held on to the ball for dear life. Just as the hands of the man on top of her were about to pry her glove open, she felt him being lifted off her.

As the pressure eased off her body, she gasped for precious air. She saw that security and a few people from the stands had come in to break up the pile-up. Mr. Douche-Patch swung a fist at one of the men holding him back, and the man swung right back at him. Jordan scrambled up the steps like a crab, still holding on to the ball. By now, there were at least ten people punching and yelling. Thankfully, most of them had forgotten about her and the home run ball.

Jordan made it back to her seat to find Ben looking at her the way a 5-year-old would if they had just discovered Santa Claus emerging from the fireplace.

"I hope you appreciate this," she said, removing the offending glove and ball and placing it in his lap.

"That. Was. Awesome!" Ben wheezed, barely able to catch his breath.

He grabbed the ball and looked at it with a mixture of joy and awe.

"Says the guy who didn't just get trampled by about twenty people," she said with a touch of snark, but couldn't stop the smile that came to her face as she saw how ecstatic her cousin was. Frankly, she was a bit heady with elation herself. What were the odds she'd actually catch that ball?

"Jeez, they're still at it!" he said shifting his focus to the brawl below them. "Leave it to my cousin to cause a riot at a baseball game," he laughed.

"Ha, ha," she retorted. "Let me see that thing."

Ben instinctively put a protective hand over the ball, worried that his cousin would do something drastic.

"Don't worry, I'm not going to lose it. Though, I should throw it back down there considering how much sympathy and thanks I'm getting from you."

Appropriately chastised, he ceded the ball. "I'm sorry, you're right. Are you okay?"

Jordan touched the side of her jaw that was already feeling tender. "Yeah, it wasn't too bad. Who knew baseball was such a violent sport?"

Ben looked at her with a guilty frown on his face. She didn't want to ruin what was probably the best moment in his life with the little scuffle she had just been involved in.

"Really, I'm fine, Ben."

He gave her a smile. "Oh, and by the way, Jordan. Thank you, thank you, thank you!!"

Jordan laughed at his excitement, then threw an arm around his shoulders with the idea that sprung to her head. "Hey, how'd you like me to get him to sign it for you?"

She laughed even harder as she saw his expression, thinking that his eyes couldn't have grown any bigger. God, she loved this guy.

"I'm going to try and get him to come meet you too, maybe take a few photos. After what I just went through, I think it's the least he can do."

"You know what?" Ben said, looking at her with adoration, "You're pretty cool,"

"You know what? I *am* pretty cool," she said with a faux air of importance, then she laughed. "Now where's the rest of my hot dog?"

2

Thwack!

That was the sound he loved. There was no greater rush Carter Fox got than from the sound of wood hitting cowhide.

There were five tools in baseball: speed; arm strength; fielding ability; hitting for average; and hitting for power. Carter, was good at most of them, but he *excelled* at exactly one of these. His powerful hitting was what had brought at least half the fans to the stadium today.

As he sped toward first base, Carter knew before the ball had even made the top of the arc that it was another home run. His 30th. He was halfway there.

Almost there, Babe.

Babe Ruth was his idol. Sure, there had been plenty of players who had hit more single-season home runs, but something about reaching Babe's nice round number of 60—a record which he had held for 34 years, and during an era with fewer games per season to boot—plucked a chord inside Carter that hit that perfect note of nostalgia and pride.

More importantly, he was about to score another Sluggers' win for his team. The icing on top of this home run cake was the nudge pushing them closer to making it to the post season.

Once it was clear to Carter that the ball was headed to the stands, he relaxed. No need to rush off to third base. Let the moment linger.

He loved it. Baseball was the one—the *only*—good thing in his life. The feel of his bat connecting with the ball. The crowds. The lights. His teammates. Most of all being out here on the diamond.

His eyes wandered up to the screen. For once it wasn't mirroring his face back to him. It was broadcasting something far more enjoyable to look at. He slowed down, appreciating the image of the woman who had apparently caught his ball. The shorts and tank top—royal blue, he was pleased to note—revealed smooth, cinnamon skin that he had an instant desire to feel underneath his hands. Huge, brown eyes with amazingly thick lashes beamed down at him. As her full lips broadened into an excited smile, deep dimples dotted both of her cheeks.

God, this woman was gorgeous.

She was definitely doing something to him as he rounded the bases. He could feel his groin start to swell. Maybe he'd make a point of personally trying to get that ball back. He mouthed his appreciation, his lips forming a very impressed O. The screen switched to his face at the very moment that O continued on to form the words: *very nice.*

Whoever was in charge of the cameras was smart enough to switch right back to the one focused on the woman in the stands. If she was on Carter Fox's radar, she was worth a second look.

That was when the blood rushing to his cock reversed direction and went straight to his head. By now, he was rounding third base and slowed down just enough to see the woman get tackled to the ground. The blood in Carter's head began to boil. He could feel his fists tightening into boulders, wanting to slam both of them into the face of the man who had just assaulted her. What kind of animal was this guy?

Carter may have been labeled a playboy by the media, and he, more often than not, lived up to that image, but he would never, *ever*, hurt a woman.

For some reason, watching this particular woman get attacked made him see red more than he normally would have. Carter had the desire to both punch this guy's lights out, and shield the woman from the danger around her with his own massive body.

Maybe it was because she was currently—hopefully, still—in possession of his 30th home run ball. Maybe it was because she was the sexiest thing he'd seen all day. Maybe it was both.

He crossed home plate and his mind fell back into the game as he was mobbed by his teammates celebrating their win and congratulating him on his home run. Based on the roar of the crowd, he wasn't so sure the fans weren't about to do the same. No need to finish out the inning. Carter had done it. Another win for the Sluggers. He should be happy, and he was—*thrilled*, actually.

Still, his mind kept going back to the woman on the screen.

The reporters were already swarming by the time the team was headed back to the clubhouse. The fans would be crowding him on the way out outside. He wondered if he'd see the woman on the screen again, this time in person.

"Carter, a word?"

"Hey Fox, can we ask a few questions?

"Carter, how does it feel to have your 30th home run of the season?"

"Carter, what do you have to say to those who feel your home run stats are too impressive for you not to be doping?"

That one stopped him cold. He looked around to see who the offender was and saw a new face in the crowd of reporters. He was a short man with a slight build, glasses, and a face that seemed to have a permanent smirk. That smirk grew wider when he saw that *he'd* been the one to get Carter Fox to stop in his tracks.

Carter stormed over to him so aggressively that even those standing near the man took an anxious step back. Despite obviously wanting to maintain a composed front, Carter saw him flinch slightly. Then that smug smirk reappeared.

"What the hell did you just say?" Carter growled. "Who are you anyway?"

"Lucas Grabow, writer for the sports news blog, LoneStarStateBaseball.com."

Carter searched his brain. He'd never heard of the site, but he looked down and saw the press badge. Apparently, anyone could get one these days

"I hope you have some evidence to back that up," Carter continued. "Otherwise, you might just find my fist putting those words right back in your mouth."

There were rumors of course. No player who scored as many home runs as Carter did could avoid them. But no one had ever offered any evidence of Carter Fox doping. That was because there was no evidence to be found. Carter was just naturally strong. Combine that with an arm he'd been swinging a bat with since grade school, and he didn't need enhancement drugs. Thus, most reporters stayed off the topic, not wanting to be sued, or worse, have a not so friendly meeting with Carter Fox's fist. Obviously, this guy hadn't got the memo.

"Can I quote you on that?" Grabow said, the shit-eating grin still on his face. "I never said I had evidence, I'm just wondering what your response is to the *rumors*. Obviously, if you're clean, then you could just deny it." He gave an exaggeratedly sheepish shrug in the hopes that it would set Carter off.

"There's nothing to deny," Carter said in a dangerously even tone of voice, not taking the bait. "They aren't rumors, they're lies. And you're nothing more than a sleazy, bottom-feeding *blogger*"—he spat the word —"who probably wouldn't even have a site if it wasn't for the Sluggers."

The reporters around Grabow snickered and the smile on his face faltered. Carter walked away, ignoring the rest of them. He was in no mood for a media blitz. He had just scored his 30th home run, his team had just won, and this asshole had just flipped his switch from elated to pissed off.

By the time Carter left the clubhouse, most of the fire from his interaction with Lucas Grabow had been extinguished. A nice hot shower and the camaraderie of his teammates had helped.

There was a smallish crowd of die-hard fans and a few reporters still waiting as he walked out. Usually, he enjoyed this part after a game: that final bit of post-game congratulations. Today, he couldn't help but wonder how many of them thought he was actually juicing. He cursed Lucas Grabow once again.

Then he saw her.

There was the usual throng of groupies screaming his name, hoping to catch his attention. Any other day his eye would have immediately gravitated toward them. Today, he had eyes only for one woman.

Carter had a better opportunity to check her out now that she was standing there in person. She had the sort of long, cinnamon legs that curved in and out perfectly at all the right places: narrow ankles, nicely rounded calves, a dip inward at the knee, *very* nicely rounded thighs. She shifted from side to side as she leaned on one foot then the other, which made him notice the rest of her body. She had that sort of pear-shape he loved: all dangerous curves on the bottom and demure and small up top.

It was the face that did it for him, though. The face on the screen was nothing compared to the live version. He saw the small bruise on her chin, and the fury at the man responsible for it overcame him again. Hopefully, the asshole was in jail right now.

The anger was quelled by the perfect lips, those dimples, and the lashes fluttering around those bright, brown eyes. A man could sink into those deep brown pools and forget to come up for air.

She was standing there with the ball in her hand—his ball—smiling and talking to some man who was obviously admiring the ball...or was it the body that the ball was in front of? Those dimples re-appeared as she smiled up at him. Carter's primal jealousy took over and he wanted nothing more than to make her forget about this guy, and every other man on earth. He had to impress this woman, and there was one thing that had always served him well in the past: money.

3

"It's just a small bruise."

Jordan had been waiting for well over an hour for Carter Fox to make an appearance. She couldn't believe people actually did this after every game, especially out of the comfort of the environmentally controlled stadium. Even this late in the day it was humid and hot, so the families with younger kids had long since given up.

The guy standing next to her was nice enough, but she had an idea it wasn't the ball he was eyeing. She lowered the hand holding it until she saw his eyes follow it right down to her crotch.

She *really* wished Carter would hurry it up.

"Still," he said, his eyes flicking back and forth between her eyes and—presumably—the ball, "it takes a certain kind of man to punch a woman, even for Carter Fox's 30th home run ball."

Jordan just smiled and nodded in agreement. Texas men were so macho. At times it was endearing: holding doors open, always adding ma'am to the end of a sentence. Other times it was a bit patronizing.

"Hey, beautiful."

She turned at the cocky voice and saw Carter Fox heading straight for her. She nearly gasped at the size of him as he made the final approach. It wasn't even that he was overly large, he just had a *presence*.

Her heart skipped a beat as those green eyes of his blazed down at her with a wicked twinkle. Standing this close to him, she noticed that he had a tiny little indentation at the end of his long, straight nose. It would have been almost adorable...if it hadn't been in between those devilish eyes and even more sinful grin. She could smell the fresh scent of whatever he had used to shower with, but also the musky undertone of pure, animalistic heat. It was intoxicating. *He* was intoxicating.

She realized Carter and everyone else around her were waiting for a response. The look he gave her was expectant, as though he was used to a certain type of response to his attentions. After the remaining butterflies in her stomach fluttered away, Jordan came back to herself. She wasn't about to be another one of Carter Fox's notorious conquests. She was just here to get this ball signed and maybe get him to come inside and meet with Ben.

Just as she was about to ask, that wicked grin flashed again.

"I'll give you $10,000 for that right now," he said, his eyes wandering down her body.

She blinked in surprise and the crowd around her whistled, oohing and ahhing at the number.

It took her a moment to remember the ball in her hand.

$10,000? For a ball? Certainly, that amount was probably nothing to Carter Fox, but it was still just a ball. It would probably be worthless when he hit another home run at his next game. Then she remembered that this wasn't even her ball to bargain with.

"I can't really—"

"$50,000 then."

Now she was in literal shock. So was the crowd around her, finally awed into silence. That was more than an entire year of her law school tuition!

Ohhh Ben, you're lucky I like you so much.

Jordan had just enough pep left in her despite the craziness of the day to plaster on her most flattering smile, batting her eyelashes prettily as she went right into her spiel. Might as well stroke his male ego a bit, strictly for Ben's sake of course.

"It's not really my ball to sell. I caught it for my cousin. But if you could sign it, that would be great!"

He grinned and she felt herself get feverish just as she had during the game. It was a bit surreal, having Carter Fox's attention all on her.

"Actually," she continued, "I was wondering if you wouldn't mind coming with me once you're done here with your fans. My cousin absolutely adores you. Perhaps you could hang out with us a bit?"

He stared at her with a somewhat confused smile, as though trying to understand what she had just said.

"Wait a second," he said, and then he leaned in closer with a lowered voice. "Is this like a...*ménage* thing you're trying to set up?"

Jordan's smile was frozen on her face, while her brain tried to catch up with what her ears were hearing. It was just long enough for Carter to assume a threesome was exactly what she was offering up.

"Well, hell, I'm game," he continued. "Especially, if she's as gorgeous as you are."

Jordan's brain finally got the memo. *She?...Gorgeous?...Ben?*

Carter had no idea her cousin was a 12-year-old boy. Why would he? He apparently only had sex on the brain. She heard the, mostly male, crowd around her start to chuckle. Her face burned with embarrassment.

"That's...*ew!* What in the hell is the matter with you?" She gave him a withering look of revulsion, which was only mildly tempered by the fact that it made that stupid grin on his face disappear.

"A *ménage a trois?* You really are a disgusting jerk. You have no idea how to treat your fans, and *zero* respect for women. All I wanted was your damn signature on your damn ball, and for my cousin to meet his idol." She noted with satisfaction the flash of confusion in his eyes at the word "his."

"But obviously, the *amazing* Carter Fox is too much of a womanizing perv to bother meeting his *true* fans, unless, of course, they come packaged with the right amount of T & A for his personal enjoyment. Maybe it's time Houston woke up and realized that for once.

"As for the ball, I'd toss it into the gutter, where your mind obviously is, before selling it to you, even if you offered fifty *million* dollars. Unfortunately, it's not mine to throw out. Keep your damn money."

Now his face was a mixture of stunned amusement, which only pissed her off even more. He wasn't even taking this seriously.

She had a strong urge to slap him, but that would probably only make him grin again. Instead, she just walked away.

Jordan felt completely tainted as she walked back inside where she had left Ben in the comfort of the air conditioned front area.

The man had literally suggested a *ménage a trois*—in front of everyone! Who did that? He definitely lived up to the playboy image she'd seen in the media, she just hadn't expected to be confronted with it so...*blatantly*. She shuddered with disgust, realizing *this* was the man that Ben looked up to.

Seeing Carter in person, she could see why people had a tendency to idol-worship him, even beyond his notorious home run streak. He was even more imposing up close and personal than he had been on the huge screen in the stadium. He had towered over her 5'7" height like a mountain, muscles blatantly flexing. She didn't need to touch them to know that they were hard as granite. Hard enough to hit 30 home runs so far this season.

She shook it off as she saw Ben sitting where she had left him. Not knowing how long it would take for Carter to actually make an appearance, she hadn't wanted Ben spending all that time leaning on his crutches in the heat. Now she was glad she'd left him there.

As she approached him, Jordan realized that she had completely neglected to get the ball signed. In fact, she had even threatened to throw the damned thing into a sewer. She frowned, trying to think up an excuse.

She certainly wasn't going to mention the *ménage*.

"Hey Ben," she said tossing the ball up in the air. "Sorry, but I couldn't get him to sign it. He kind of just rushed off before I had a chance to talk to him."

Looking at the disappointment in his face, she felt bad. It made her that much more pissed off at Carter Fox. If he hadn't been such a manwhore, then she wouldn't have been too flustered to remember to get the signature despite what he'd said.

"Excuse me miss?"

She turned around at the sound of the voice behind her. It belonged to a lanky, short man with a press badge around his neck, wearing wire-rimmed glasses and a slightly smug smile look on his face. For some reason, when he saw Ben, the smile grew to one that could compete with that of a kid in a candy store.

"Lucas Grabow, journalist, for *Lone Star State Baseball*," he pointed to the press badge on his chest. "I was just wondering if I could do a profile on the lucky person who caught Carter Fox's 30th home run ball."

That was the last thing Jordan wanted, especially after the riot act she'd just read the man who'd hit that ball. In retrospect, it probably hadn't been the smartest move. Especially not for someone who wanted to get a permanent position at *Morris & Gibson* next year. She was working at the law firm as an associate this summer before her third and final year.

She took a closer look at the badge. It certainly seemed legit.

"Cool!" Ben exclaimed. "An actual interview!"

"Actually, we should probably get going."

Lucas just continued, taking his cue from Ben instead of Jordan. "You two wouldn't happen to be related, would you? I can certainly see the resemblance."

"Yeah, she's my cousin," Ben piped, before Jordan could stop him. "She caught the ball for me since I couldn't." He awkwardly lifted his leg up to show Lucas the obvious.

Lucas gave an appreciative chuckle.

"Well, this would make a perfect story. A girl, er, woman," he gave a meaningful grin toward Jordan, which didn't give off the female empowerment vibe he was probably going for, "manages to catch Carter Fox's 30th home run ball, while fighting off an army of attackers, all for her younger cousin who is..."

He wrinkled his brow at Ben. "Say, what *is* the deal with the crutches?"

"*Excuse* me?" she exclaimed.

"I was hit by a drunk driver while I was riding my bike." Ben didn't seem too perturbed by the question, despite the blunt manner in which it had been asked. It had been well over a month since the accident, which had left the entire family traumatized at the time. By now he was used to people asking about the full-leg cast, even enjoying the attention a bit.

"You know, it's been a long day and we're just trying to get home now," Jordan said, already feeling the weight of the day wearing on her.

"It would make a nice little memento of this day for you," Lucas offered.

Which was the last thing Jordan wanted.

And the very thing Ben wanted.

"Come on Jordan! This would be almost as cool as Carter signing the ball!" Ben said, a pleading look in his eyes as he turned to his cousin.

Oh, Ben!

He was still young enough to be thrilled with the idea of being famous. Unfortunately, now the journalist had her name.

Ben just plowed right on, oblivious to the ambivalence his older cousin was feeling about this whole thing. "Could you get our picture too? I'm going to print it out and frame it next to the ball in my room."

"Absolutely, buddy!" Lucas seemed even more thrilled with that idea than Ben was.

"Awesome!"

"Absolutely not," Jordan said. The last thing she needed was a picture cementing everything she was now regretting about this day.

"Oh come on, Jordan," Ben begged, using those damn puppy-dog eyes on her that had been working all day. "I could show all my friends and they'd think it's the coolest."

For heaven's sake, the boy could make Tiny Tim seem like Ebenezer Scrooge. The crutches certainly helped. It reminded her of the shitty year he'd had so far. She had disappointed Ben once already today, she might as well give him this.

"Okay, fine," she sighed. After all, it was just a harmless little puff piece about catching the home run ball.

"Perfect! Now, why don't you stand up so you're next to your pretty cousin, Mr...?"

"Ben. Ben Douglas. And this is Jordan Douglas," Ben said, happy to be as accommodating as possible.

"Got it," Lucas said, writing their names down. "And how old are you, buddy?"

"Twelve," Ben said proudly. "And Jordan is twenty-four."

Which was something she didn't feel was particularly relevant. Before she could give Ben a good what for, Lucas was on to the photography.

"So let's make sure to get that cast in the photo so we can show everyone what a trouper you are."

Jordan had the vague idea that the man was being particularly exploitative of Ben's condition, but Ben was just eating it up. Lucas positioned him just so, making sure the crutches and cast were glaringly obvious, and then snapped a few photos.

"Great!" Lucas exclaimed. "Perfect. I'll be posting today. Make sure to be on the lookout for it! LoneStarStateBaseball.com."

Jordan frowned. She had missed the "dot com" at the end of the name the first time around. All the same, she breathed a sigh of relief when he finally jogged away from them.

"That was cool!" Ben said, beaming. "We got our own interview. I can't wait to see it!"

Jordan was glad that Ben was enjoying it all. She had a sneaking suspicion she had just made a huge mistake.

❦ 4 ❧

"**D**ammit, Carter! The kid's a damn *cripple,* for cryin' out loud!"

Carter scowled at the offensive word. It wasn't just the crass nature of the term, it was a reminder that he had screwed up. *Seriously* screwed up.

Somehow Lucas Grabow had not only documented the tirade of the woman who'd caught Carter's ball, but he'd also managed to get a nice little photo of her with her cousin, who as it turned out, wasn't "as sexy as she was." It all painted a pretty bad picture. Scratch that, it painted a career-tainting, endorsement-canceling, fanbase-diminishing picture.

How the hell was Carter supposed to know that her cousin was a 12-year-old boy—a 12-year-old boy on crutches? He mentally winced at the entire episode. No wonder she had called him a disgusting jerk.

In retrospect, he couldn't even say why he'd said what he did. The moment she'd mentioned her cousin, the little brain between his legs had immediately taken over. What man could think straight in the face of those damn dimples and those damn legs of hers?

He'd actually been surprised when he thought she was offering up a threesome. He couldn't put his finger on why, but she hadn't seemed like the type. As he very quickly found out, she wasn't.

A few fans had recorded the episode for YouTube posterity. Then, a couple of sites had picked up the complete story from LoneStarStateBaseball.com; Carter Fox's comeuppance made great fodder for the highlight reel of the week. Now, it had officially made its way to legitimacy via the *Houston Chronicle* and ESPN.

Lucas *fucking* Grabow.

Jordan *fucking* Douglas.

Carter shifted in his seat, remembering those curvy legs and brown eyes. It would do him no good to use the word "fucking" in the same sentence as Jordan Douglas.

"Are you even listening to me?"

Carter shot an irritated glare at the Sluggers' General Manager. It was pretty bad when you had both the Manager, who coached the team on the field, *and* the General Manager sitting in front of you. Michael Snyder currently had a tiny vein on his forehead that was visibly throbbing in time to his angry words.

At least Miles Derrick, the team's manager seemed to be taking it in stride. In fact, Carter could swear there was a hint of a smile at the wringer he was being sent through. Miles was a huge fan of his players getting their life lessons the hard way. Well, Carter Fox was certainly learning today.

How the hell had he missed Lucas Grabow in the crowd of fans outside the stadium that day?

He knew how, and she went by the name Jordan Douglas. Jordan Douglas, who wasn't some Sluggers ball girl hoping for a wink and a smile. Jordan Douglas, who, as it turned out, was in the top 10% of her class at UT Law. Jordan Douglas, who thought Carter Fox was "a disgusting jerk."

Carter couldn't deny much of that assessment.

Disgusting? Based on the thoughts he was having about her even now, despite himself: Check.

Jerk? In retrospect: Check.

Jordan Douglas. Brains and beauty in one fiery, little package. It made him all the more interested in her.

"We've kept you on a long leash because it brings the fans in. When the fans start getting angry, it's time to rein you in."

Carter snapped back to attention. He shouldn't have to take this crap. He was a 6-foot-4 mass of muscle, and he was being talked down to by a man half his size. A man half his size, who made his salary partially off the arm that Carter used to serve up those home runs that fans filled those stadium seats for.

"You proposition a woman, and not one of your little groupies, a fucking *law student*—which was a *particularly* fun little twist—and then suggest a *ménage a trois* with her 12-year-old cousin, who just *happens* to be on a pair of goddamned crutches. Oh, and the best part is—they're both *black*!"

Carter wanted to point out that that wasn't exactly how it had gone down. But people heard what they wanted to hear, and read what they wanted to read, the more scandalous, the better.

"Do you have any idea how many damn groups we've had up our ass since your little incident? The feminazis, the Jesse Jackson crowd, some cripple org. Parents all over the city are gunning for your head. Thank God neither of them was *gay!*"

"Well, it certainly doesn't help when you go around using terms like 'cripple,'" Carter growled.

He couldn't help himself, poking the rabid dog. Even Miles gave a slight smile, but subtly shook his head in preparation for the violent reaction Snyder was about to have.

"Don't you get smart with me right now, Carter. The only thing saving your ass is that swing of yours. I can't speak to what Gatorade and Nike are going to do, but I wouldn't get my hopes up if I were you."

"So go ahead and terminate my contract. Trade me to another team if you want." Carter shrugged, knowing the owners would do no such thing. "Maybe the fans are angry right now, but they'll keep coming to see me play."

Snyder just glared at him. "There's a term called 'compounding effect' Carter. You might want to look it up. And *this*, this shit right here that we're dealing with? It's compounding with interest."

Might want to look it up?

So the man thought he was just a dumb jock.

"Actually, the *interest* is what gets compounded, Snyder," he said leaning forward across the desk. "And the compounding effect works both ways. I think the *interest* earned from Carter Fox has compounded enough to weather this *market downturn*."

Snyder just gaped, the vein in his forehead pumping like a turbo engine. Carter could see Miles suppressing a smile to his left. No one was a fan of the team's General Manager.

Up until now, the owners had been fine with his "bad boy" image, even subtly encouraging it, mostly because the fans ate it up. The parties that had his neighbors in River Oaks getting their panties in a bunch. The blonde/brunette/redhead—sometimes all three—on his arm at some club every other weekend. The cash he liberally threw around everywhere he went. Men wanted to be him. Women just wanted him. A lot of it was for show these days, maintaining the image. The thrill of it all was beginning to wear off. This meeting certainly wasn't helping.

"You're going to fix this, Carter," Snyder continued, slightly chastened. "You may think you can just go on as usual, but the team owners don't agree. We've got a press conference set up next week. You are going to offer a *sincere* apology for your statements. Then you are going to personally invite this cripp"—he paused as he saw the dark look on

Carter's face—"this *boy* for a one-on-one with you. We'll make sure there are plenty of press around to see it."

Carter just shrugged. The meeting hadn't gone nearly as badly as he had expected. They just wanted damage control.

Aye-fucking-aye, captain.

Houston Sluggers' Star Hitter Strikes Out Big Time With Fan

Carter Fox may be well on his way to breaking the in-season world record *for home run hits, but when it comes to his fans, the "star" batter just struck out big time. In an incident that some may find amusing, others may find offensive, but everyone can agree was a major league foul, Carter found himself confronted with someone who may not be a Sluggers fan for long.*

Attendees at the Sluggers-Rockies game on July 23rd may remember Jordan Douglas as the face that launched a thousand punches—or at least a few dozen. Douglas was the woman lucky enough to catch Carter Fox's 30th home run ball, but perhaps she was not so lucky after all. A brawl ensued, as a few of Carter Fox's fans brutally attacked the defenseless woman in an attempt to steal the ball from her. After the game, evidence of the savage attack was still visible on Ms. Douglas's face in the form of a large bruise on her chin.

Undaunted by her experience, Jordan Douglas remained focused on her ultimate goal: get Carter Fox to sign the ball for her beloved younger cousin, Ben Douglas, who was unable to obtain the signature himself. Ben is a 12-year-old boy who, earlier this year suffered the heart-wrenching experience of being hit by a drunk driver, leaving him in a full leg cast and thus unable to vie for the *home run ball himself. Anyone lucky enough to meet the plucky, young Sluggers fan, would be relieved to learn that Ben was waiting patiently inside the stadium due to his condition. The alternative would have had this minor exposed to Carter Fox's borderline obscene language as he first, offered to pay Ms. Douglas $50,000 for his ball, right before happily inquiring about a ménage a trois with Jordan and her cousin, all in front of a large crowd of Sluggers' fans.*

In all fairness to Fox, he had no way of knowing that Ben Douglas was merely a child. Still, one has to wonder:

Is Carter Fox the sort of role model we want for our children?

Ms. Douglas pretty much summed it up in her statement regarding the Sluggers' home run star: "All I wanted was [his] damn signature on [his] damn ball, and for my cousin to meet his idol," she proclaimed, struggling to keep her emotions in check. "But obviously, the amazing Carter Fox is too much of a womanizing perv to bother meeting his true fans, unless, of course, they come packaged with the right amount of T & A for his personal enjoyment."

Her words certainly provide concerned parents of Houston's Sluggers fans a healthy serving of food for thought.

～

Jordan sat in her office and stared at the screen. This was probably the 50th time she had read the article by Lucas Grabow, if you could even call it an article. It looked more like a hatchet job. If she had known the man was nothing more than a blogger hoping for fodder for this sleazy piece, she would have put a complete nix on the "interview."

Everything on the screen in front of her was completely twisted to make her seem like some whimpering damsel in distress and then some sort of prudish harpy. She certainly hadn't "struggled to keep her emotions in check." That was a laugh. It would take a tougher man than Carter Fox to break her.

Grabow hadn't been very generous to the Sluggers' player either. There was a definite personal bias going on there. Jordan almost felt sorry for Carter Fox...almost. It wasn't his fault that the jerk in the stands had attacked her. In her more generous moments, she was also willing to concede that Carter certainly didn't know that her cousin wasn't "as sexy as she was."

"Don't tell me you're reading that thing again," Tiffany Pittman said from the other side of the office.

Jordan spun around in her chair to find her officemate already looking in her direction. The two of them had been thrown together to share an office since they both focused on corporate law. As spoiled as summer associates were at *Morris & Gibson*, the generosity seemed to end at giving them each their own office.

Both of them being ambitious females, and working in the same environment for extended hours, they had developed a sort of affinity toward one another. It was nice to have someone to commiserate with, even in areas outside of law. Of course, her friend didn't seem to be doing much commiserating these days.

"*What?*" Tiffany shrugged in response to Jordan's expression. "You always make this sighing noise when you read it."

Jordan frowned as Tiffany began her mock imitation of her, one hand going up to her forehead in an overly dramatic fashion.

"*Ugh,* it totally sucks that I caught Carter Fox's home run ball.

"*Ugh*, I can't believe he offered me $50,000....*Worst day ever!*

"*Ugh*, my life is so awful because the hottest guy on the Houston Sluggers wants to screw me."

She laughed as she brought her face down to look at Jordan, who wasn't at all amused.

"Seriously Jordan, if Carter Fox offered me $50,000 and the opportunity to have sex him, you wouldn't find me complaining. He's so damn *hot*."

"Well, feel free," Jordan said. "You're probably just his type."

Tiffany was tall, blonde, and had the body of a runway model. She was pretty much a carbon copy of every woman Jordan had seen pictures of Carter Fox with. She had all the associates here—and a few partners—going gaga. Jordan was more than happy to let her steal the limelight. Especially in light of recent events, she had zero desire to be the center of attention.

It had been bad enough this first week back at the firm. It was either embarrassed looks or amused smirks from other associates. The worst had been the female partner who had taken Jordan aside to give her a "wee bit of advice": It's hard enough being a female—a *black* female—trying to make partner one day, don't shoot yourself in the foot by making ill-advised comments in front of the press.

Duly noted.

The article—*blog*—had just been the start of it all. YouTube had several videos of her confrontation with Carter, which only fanned the flames. Jordan and Roy and Pat, Ben's parents, had been hounded non-stop this week by the media. Ben's mom had curtailed it on their end, and Jordan had refused all offers for an interview on hers. That hadn't stopped the media from figuring out everything about her: where she went to law school; where she was working this summer; where she was staying with her parents. Someone had even published her class rank at UT! How did these people get this stuff?

It was terrifying, mostly because a lot of perfect strangers seemed to have an opinion on the matter. Unfortunately, a good portion of it wasn't very favorable to Jordan. The internet being what it was, the comments ranged from mean-spirited to just plain vile:

This is what happens when girls try to catch the ball, leave it to the men, ladies...

Maybe if she hadn't been showing so much T & A herself, then...

If Carter Fox gets traded out because of some dumb...

She can hold on to my balls any day! In fact, I'd let her...

Jordan decided then and there to stop indulging any and all forms of media related to Carter Fox. She just hoped Ben was doing the same.

She kept thinking back to that day and how it would have been completely different if one tiny thing had been altered. Maybe if she'd stayed down at the bottom of the stands with the rest of the crowd. Maybe if she'd held her glove a little bit lower and missed catching it. Maybe if she'd just let it hit her in the damn head; she would probably have less of a headache right now.

Jordan closed out the page on LoneStarStateBaseball.com and pulled up the case she was supposed to be researching. It was better than torturing herself any further with that damn blog.

❧ 6 ❧

G one was the snug t-shirt that showed off the tattoos and muscles. Gone were the faded jeans that left only a *little* to the imagination. Gone were the worn out cowboy boots. Gone was the 2-day old stubble that gave him a rough edge. Most of all, gone was the smug, fuck-me smirk that drove the ladies crazy.

The new Carter Fox had donned the official *mea culpa* uniform of every sinner, hat in hand, begging the public for forgiveness: a plain, light blue dress shirt (that covered each and every tattoo); gray slacks (leaving *everything* to the imagination); brown loafers (*loafers*, for Christ's sake!); and a clean shaven face. As instructed by the higher ups and the P.R. team, his face was set in a permanent expression of remorse.

The last part hadn't been too hard to achieve. If he could, Carter would have gone back in time and never hit that damn home run, if only to avoid this circus.

But Carter Fox had made the bed, now he was lying in it, and rightfully, so. He was here to play a role after all: reformed bad boy. Or at least until the public screamed for the old Carter Fox back. Eventually, they would.

Bad boys always finished first.

The room finally settled down as the P.R. rep for the team stood in front to urge everyone to quiet down.

"Carter Fox will be making a brief statement, then we will open the floor up to questions."

The rep nodded to him and Carter relayed the statement that had been etched into his brain, lest he forget even a single line.

"Most of you are aware of the unfortunate incident that happened on July 23rd after the game against the Rockies. I won't go into details, but I made an inappropriate remark to a young woman who was only trying to get me to meet with her cousin and get an autograph. My comments to Miss Jordan Douglas were completely out of line and inexcusable, and I offer my most sincere apology to both her and her cousin, Ben Douglas, as well as any fans who happened to have heard my remarks.

"Miss Douglas, my words do not reflect the opinions of the Sluggers' franchise, players, managers, or owners toward their female fans." They had made damn sure to include that little tidbit. "Ben Douglas, I'm sorry that I didn't get a chance to meet with you, especially after learning how much of a fan you are.

"I would like to make it very clear that I value each and every one of my fans. Without them, I would not have a career. I especially value those fans who take time out to meet with me personally.

"Again, I regret what happened that day. Since I did not get a chance to meet with Ben Douglas after the game that day, I am offering a personal invitation to meet with him at the Sluggers' Stadium. I know this will not erase, or make up for what happened on the day in question, but I hope it will at least make it so that the Sluggers haven't lost a fan. I look forward to finally meeting you, Ben Douglas."

Carter lifted his eyes to the crowd below him and moved in closer to the microphone.

"I also look forward to meeting Miss Jordan Douglas again, if she's willing to give me another shot as well." He couldn't help the shit-eating smirk that came over his face. The old Carter Fox wasn't entirely gone.

"Thank you. I'll now take questions."

That last bit was an ad-lib on his part, and he'd probably get raked over the coals for it. He truly did want to meet Ben. Carter loved kids and nothing thrilled him more than seeing some boy or girl in the Sluggers' royal blue hat and jersey.

He couldn't deny that it wouldn't hurt to have Ben's cousin along for the ride. After all, Carter loved women too.

Of course there were questions. There were always questions. Hopefully, they would stay on point. The good news was, this time around Lucas Grabow did *not* get a press pass.

Carter pointed to Mason Ward of Channel 4.

"Carter, how do you respond to some of the offensive comments written online about the incident by some of your fans?"

Carter had read enough of the online forums to get a picture of what Mason was talking about. He had felt the same rage as he had when he'd seen Jordan get physically attacked. Now she was getting attacked via social media and he felt, in some small way, responsible.

"I'd like to first make it very clear that anyone who uses sexist, racist, or any other offensive language might as well stop being a fan of mine right now. I don't condone, nor do I screw around that sort of talk. I'd also like to make it clear that Miss Jordan Douglas is in no way, shape, or form responsible for any repercussions on my part. I'm the one in the wrong here."

He'd probably get heat for telling people they could stop being fans, but Carter didn't care. It made him sick some of the things people had said. At the very least, he didn't want the likes of that tainting his image. There was a fine line between bad boy and degenerate scum.

Next up was Connie Ortiz of Fox 11 News. "Carter, to date you've had a reputation for being a bad boy and a bit of a playboy. Is today the start of a reformed Carter Fox?" It was all very tongue-in-cheek, perfect for a light-hearted wrap-up in the evening news.

"Who knows, Connie," he said grinning, happy to play along, "I may have just found the woman to cure me of my wicked ways."

There was an appreciative laugh from the reporters.

There was one person in the back who wasn't laughing.

"I don't know why you insist on pushing the envelope all the damn time, Carter."

Madison Grant, her maiden name, thank you very much, was not pleased. The 5'9", former *Miss Brazos County* with a head of flaming red hair—which may or may not be dyed, don't you dare inquire—was sitting beside him in his truck. One lit Marlboro was tucked securely between two perfectly red lacquered fingernails. Carter wished she would quit those damn things.

He was driving her back to her Houston condo in his pick-up truck. They were going to have dinner at her place. In her words, she "just wanted to spend an evening having dinner with the son, whom she hardly ever gets to see."

Carter found it interesting that her dismay at hardly ever seeing him only seemed to materialize when one of his *particularly* scandalous escapades hit the tabloids. Madison liked to "strategize," a term that meant that Carter might as well clear his schedule for the evening. What in the world did he have an agent for, when his mother took control of everything?

There wasn't a woman on earth that could bend Carter Fox to their will—save this one, even at 26 years old. At some point, he'd have to renegotiate exactly what their mother-son relationship should be like. The thought made him exhausted. It was easier to just let his mother have her occasional intrusions into his life than sit her down for a *come to Jesus* talk. No wonder he'd never had a long-term girlfriend, let alone a wife. One controlling woman in his life was enough.

Carter supposed he put up with it for so long mostly out of guilt. She had raised him well, and for damn near all of it, single-handedly. He certainly hadn't made it easy for her. A good deal of his adolescence had been spent sneaking in and out of girls' windows and chugging beers with friends lifted from their parents' fridges in empty parking lots. He had the natural talent and an obviously amazing swing, but that would have gone to waste before he even finished high school if she hadn't kept a firm hand on things. Eventually, he'd managed a scholarship to Texas A&M. Carter had mostly her to thank for what his life was now.

Heaven knew his "dad" had had little to do with it.

"This is not some bimbo you're dealing with here," she went on. "She could cause serious problems. And there you are—*in front of reporters*—still making passes at her. If you're lucky, she won't take you up on this offer to join this cousin of hers when you finally meet with him. You need to stay focused on this kid, not salivating over his cousin."

Carter suppressed a smile. His mother knew him too well. He thought back to the woman in the royal blue tank top and shorts. For probably the hundredth time, he wondered what she would look like underneath all those clothes.

The smile broke through.

"Dammit Carter, you don't stop do you?"

He turned to see his mother casting a scrutinizing glare at him. Leave it to her to read his mind. Yeah, it was probably for the best if Jordan Douglas didn't take him up on his offer.

7

"The secret is in the grip."

Carter adjusted Ben's hands around the baseball. He was on the field at the Sluggers' stadium with Ben Douglas—sans his older cousin. The other players warmed up in the outfield and the two of them momentarily had the diamond to themselves. Carter was fulfilling his promise to him by giving the boy some time before tonight's game. Thanks to the higher ups, there were more than a few members of the press and the team's official P.R. rep in the stands taking note of everything they did. Ben's parents were standing in front of the dugout watching as Carter instructed their son on how to throw a proper pitch.

Ben was in a wheel chair, which had originally thrown Carter off. But as he had explained it, he wanted to "try and pitch a few balls. My friends are gonna go apeshit when they hear about it."

"Ben!" his mother had scolded.

Ben had given her a dutiful look of remorse, then secretly grinned at Carter.

It was a feeling Carter could empathize with. Moms.

They had spent the morning touring the stadium and meeting the other team members. Now they were on the field so Ben could get the full VIP experience.

"See how both the fingers and the thumb are on the seam? That helps you keep a firmer grip until release."

Ben just smiled and nodded, probably only caring that Carter Fox was actually touching his hand.

Carter had to admit that the smile was addictive. He hadn't relished the thought of playing tour guide, even to a kid. Especially, when that kid had failed to bring his hot older cousin. But this kid knew his baseball. He'd been able to rattle off the stats for every player. It was refreshing to see a fan who hadn't just jumped on the Sluggers bandwagon, but actually appreciated the sport.

"Got it," Ben said, fixing his fingers firmly around the ball. "This has been great, Carter, best day of my life."

That made Carter almost embarrassedly pleased. "Maybe you could pass that on to your older cousin," he suggested with a wink as he back-walked toward home plate.

"Oh no, Jordan is *supposedly* on a Carter Fox blackout." Ben rolled his eyes.

That stopped Carter in his tracks. "Really?"

Ben gave him a speculative look, then gave a sly smile. "*Yeah.*"

He could obviously read Carter's interest in her like a book. He was annoyed to find that it was so glaringly obvious. He could get any woman he wanted and one 12-year-old was making him feel like a damn teenager with a high school crush.

"But I think she secretly likes you," Ben confessed, rolling his eyes again. "You know how girls are."

Carter had no idea how girls were—did any guy?—but he was no longer back-walking at this point. Instead, he took a few steps right back toward Ben, his curiosity officially piqued.

"What makes you say that?" he asked with a half grin.

"She keeps telling everyone not to talk about you. But then she keeps bringing you up."

Carter's smile grew. So little Ms. Douglas also had a crush on Carter Fox.

Then an idea struck him.

"You know...I haven't had a chance to express my sincere apology to her in person yet. I'd really love to, maybe even over the phone?" He raised his eyebrows at his new confidant, hoping he'd take the bait.

Ben didn't need a road map, but he hesitated. "She'd kill me if I gave you her number."

"I can respect that," Carter said, nodding solemnly. "Maybe you could give her *my* number instead."

Where the hell had that come from? He never—*ever*—gave women his number. That was a recipe for disaster. Fortunately, Ben saved him from himself.

"She'd *never* call you," he retorted, actually laughing.

Now Carter found himself feeling slightly offended. What woman wouldn't jump at the opportunity for Carter Fox's personal number?

Ben saw his expression and gave him an empathetic look. "The thing is, I like my cousin. A *lot*. She's really cool. Not like most girls."

Carter nodded again, with a small smile.

"No, I mean *really*," Ben said, maintaining the serious expression on his face. "I don't want to do anything to hurt her."

Carter came in closer and knelt next to Ben.

"Listen, I have no intention of disrespecting your cousin. You're right, she's...something else." Carter removed his baseball cap and brought it down to his chest in a grand gesture. "And with your permission, sir, I would formally like to ask her out to dinner."

Ben reacted to the over-the-top formality by laughing, the way Carter hoped he would.

"Okay, let's just say that my phone just *happens* to be in the left pocket of the backpack on the back of my chair, and Jordan's number just *happens* to be in the contact list," Ben said. "If she threatens to kill me, I'm blaming everything on you."

"Way to cover your ass," Carter teased, laughing. Then, he went ahead and reached into the pocket. Ben even made a show of idly looking in the opposite direction as he did it.

As Carter cemented the ten-digit number to memory he thought to himself that at least there was on ally on his side.

8

It was all Ben's doing.

The entire family, gathered at her parents' house, had watched Carter play an abysmal game. Jordan was staying there for the summer to save money thanks to her exorbitant student loans. She didn't even have to be a fan to know that Carter had pretty much sucked that night. The Sluggers had lost 3-7.

After the game, Ben gave her a slightly pleading look.

"If he happens to call you, can you maybe just go out with him if he asks?"

"If he happens to call? Wait a sec, how would he *happen* have my number?"

"Uh, well..."

"Why you *little*..."

"Don't get mad. I just thought it would be really cool if my cousin was dating Carter Fox."

"So you just gave it to him?" she said, actually laughing in disbelief.

"So you'll go out with him?" Ben said, getting hopeful.

She didn't answer, making him wait as a small form of punishment. Then she sighed.

"*If* he calls, I'll *think* about it." The whole idea of going out with Carter Fox was absurd.

Jordan hadn't watched his press conference herself, sticking to her Carter Fox media blackout. From what she could piece together from others, he had actually given a rather sincere apology. In fact, a tiny part of her had been a bit flattered at some of the tidbits she'd heard he'd said regarding her.

But by now he had surely moved on to the next bright young thing to catch his eye.

"He'll call," Ben said, countering her doubt with firm assuredness. "You bring good luck."

"*What?*" She laughed, giving him a skeptical look.

"Just look at how great this summer has been for *me* since you came back," he had said,

Now he was just grasping at straws. "Yeah, and not so great for me," she said, chuckling.

"Maybe you two can be good for each other?"

"Like I said, I'll *think* about it," she said noncommittally.

Ben was smart enough to realize that was the best he would be getting.

Jordan was smart enough to know someone like Carter Fox would never call her.

She was jolted awake in a panic by the loud noise coming from the nightstand right next to her head.

Why hadn't she put her phone on vibrate? Why had she chosen the blaring, old-timey phone as her ringtone?

It dinga-linga-linged again and again as she blindly reached for it. Her hand groped empty air until she accidentally knocked the phone off the nightstand.

Crap.

She quickly slid over and bent down to grab it, only to hit her head on the edge of her nightstand.

"Oww!" she yelped grabbing her forehead with one hand.

She saw the lit phone lying on the floor just out of her grasp and she struggled to reach for it, only to tumble right out of bed. She fell with a thud and another yelp of pain.

She finally snatched the phone of the floor with a frustrated grunt. Looking at the number, she had no idea who it was, but at this time of the night she didn't want to take any chances. Hopefully, it was just a wrong number.

"Hello?" she said with exasperation.

"Jordan? It's Carter, Carter Fox."

She blinked in surprise. Then she brought her phone around to look at the time, and her, admittedly pleased surprise turned to annoyance. "What the heck...do you know what time it is?"

"Oh..." he paused on the other end, no doubt using this moment to actually look at the clock.

"Oh shi—sorry. Did I wake you?" he asked.

Jordan let out a brief, sharp laugh. The question was so absurd she couldn't help but be slightly amused. "That would be a definite yes."

"Sorry about that. I just had this strong urge to call after the game tonight, but I guess I just wasn't factoring in the time."

"Did you and Ben form some sort of cosmic connection?" she joked, smiling suspiciously into the phone.

"Pardon?"

"Never mind," she said, giggling. She was up now, and the pain in her forehead was beginning to dull, so she might as well have a bit of fun on his account. Her sleep fogged brain wasn't quite sharp enough to be mad at Carter Fox at this hour of the night—or rather, morning.

"So, would you be interested in going out to dinner with me, Jordan?"

Blunt and to the point. She could appreciate that—especially at this hour. She actually chuckled into the phone.

"Is that a yes then?" Carter asked.

Jordan backpedaled right into all her doubts and concerns again.

"Listen, I appreciate the apology at your press conference. I know it was just a stupid mistake on your part that got blown out of proportion. Though, I certainly hope you have a bit more respect for your female fans now." She had to at least get that little dig at him.

She could hear him chuckling on the other end. "That's for damn sure," he mumbled into the phone.

"But, I'm not even a baseball fan," she continued. "I was only there that day because of Ben. It's just that…I've just got a lot going on right now in my life with law school and this summer associate job, and…."

She had no idea how to just say no.

"And that means no dating?" She could actually hear the grin in his voice.

No dating. Now that she was rolling it around in her head, it seemed ridiculous. Of course she could date!

But Carter Fox of all people?

Oh, what the heck.

"Sure," she said impulsively.

A date with Carter Fox. God, this was so surreal.

Coral.

It was a good color on her, especially when she got as brown as she did in the summer. Definitely coral.

Or maybe the white dress. It showed less skin. Did she want to show less skin? She didn't want to look like a virgin. White gave the wrong impression.

No, coral. It was a good color on her.

She looked at herself in the mirror again. Coral sleeveless sundress. She'd bring a sweater just in case.

Definitely the coral.

Her summer curls were flat ironed and tucked behind a white headband. No telling how long that would hold up. Her feet were tucked into white sandals.

Definitely the coral. It looked good on her.

It was almost pick-up time.

She had wanted to meet him at the restaurant. He had firmly said no to that. So had her family, all of whom were waiting downstairs for her —scratch that—for *him*.

It was a bit embarrassing having him pick her up at her parents' house like she was still in high school, but then she remembered the $800 she had spent last semester for books alone, which wasn't even factored into tuition. Better to save that rent money than try to save face. Besides, why not do something fun for the family, like introduce them to her famous date for the night?

She sighed and opened the door to face the eager crowd waiting downstairs. Walking down the steps felt like prom night all over again.

They were all standing there looking up at her proudly. All because of Carter Fox.

"You look nice, Jordan," Ben said, grinning up at her.

"Yes, very nice Jordan," Ralph, her dad, said, beaming.

"It's just a date, y'all," she reminded them.

The doorbell rang, startling her. She could feel her heart beating faster. God, why was she so nervous? It was one silly date. With Carter Fox.

She saw her dad heading over to open the door and she rushed to preempt him. This was *not* going to turn into a big deal. He frowned down at her as she grabbed the knob.

"Carter!" she squeaked a little too brightly. She saw the bouquet of pink tulips in his hand and looked at them with an almost puzzled expression. Who brought flowers on a date anymore?

It filled her with something warm and pleasurable.

He obviously wasn't expecting such a pleasant welcome and gave her a broad grin. Then he eyed her coral dress with open appreciation.

Yes, definitely the coral.

"These are for you," he drawled, handing over the flowers.

She took them and stood there in the doorway in dumfounded paralysis. Her eyes wandered over the muscles that lingered just beneath the surface of his blue dress shirt. Then there were his jeans, not too tight and certainly not too loose.

"Jordan don't be rude, let the man inside!" her father said impatiently.

She blinked and raised her eyes to see Carter smirking down at her. He'd seen exactly where her eyes had ended up. She frowned and opened the door wider waving him in. He gave a satisfied smile as he passed the threshold.

"Mr. Douglas? It's very nice to meet you, sir," he said offering his hand.

Her father was only too pleased to shake it, holding onto it as he placed the other hand on Carter's broad back to lead him further in to meet everyone else. Jordan just stood by the doorway to watch, hoping that this whole family meet and greet would be over quickly.

Carter made the rounds, shaking everyone's hand, chatting with Ben, and making small talk with his parents. He was even able to charm her mother, who seemed surprisingly less than enthusiastic about all of this.

"Let's get a photo," her father said. The camera was already sitting on the living room coffee table.

This was the part that had made Jordan cringe internally. "You don't have to, Carter."

Before her dad could protest, Carter saved him the trouble.

"Nonsense," he said, a grin appearing on his face. "I would love to take photos."

Her dad gave her a satisfied smile as he went to pick up the camera.

Carter came in close to her and positioned himself slightly behind her as he placed an arm around her bare shoulders. The feel of that hand on her shoulder, touching her skin, sent an immediate shiver through her body. She only hoped he hadn't noticed.

Standing next to him was like standing up against a brick wall. It made her feel rather feminine and tiny, in a frustrating sort of way. She could feel every pec, every ab, and the hard thighs underneath his jeans, not to mention....

Good God!

"*Smile*, Jordan!" her father urged.

She gave a tight, surprised smile. As soon as she heard the shutter click she pulled herself away, giving him a glare. He just gave her an unreadable smile, then turned to focus on her family.

"How about one with you Ben?" he offered.

"Cool!" Ben said, only too happy to get another photo op with his idol.

Jordan watched as Carter wrapped one huge arm around her cousin and smiled as her dad snapped the photo.

"What about with my mom and dad?" Ben asked, taking full advantage of the opportunity.

"Ben!" Jordan said with exasperation.

"Not a problem, little man," Carter said.

It went on and on. By the time all was said and done at least twenty photos had been taken. He'd even managed to charm the seemingly reluctant Mrs. Douglas into posing for one.

"It was very nice to meet y'all, especially you Mrs. Douglas. I can see where Jordan gets her brains and beauty from."

Jordan knew that the brains part was enough to earn him a grudging smile. Her mother was harder on Jordan when it came to school than she was on herself. With Deborah Douglas it was all school and work, work and school, when it came to her daughter.

"We should get going, Carter," Jordan urged, hoping her family would take the hint. Not leaving anything to chance she grabbed his hand and led him back to the door. Even though he was twice her size he let her tug him away, enjoying himself a little too much.

Jordan pushed him out first, then leaned back inside, pulling the door closed just a crack. She stuck her head through and gave each of them a direct look.

"Don't you *dare* wait up for us," she warned them, hoping it was low enough that Carter didn't catch it.

She could hear them laughing as she closed the door shut and turned to face her date with a relieved sigh.

"Nice performance in there, Carter," she said, giving him an amused chuckle. "You certainly charmed everyone."

"What do you mean?"

"You know what I mean. This whole"— she waved a hand at him

—"amicable meet the family thing. Is this part of the plan to repair your image?"

He frowned at her. "Hey now. I may be a lot of things, but rude I am not. Your family was considerate and nice enough to invite me into their home. I returned the hospitality. You should appreciate having a family that cares enough about you to go through all this, even if it does embarrass you. I wish I had half as much."

That left her speechless.

"Now, shall we go Ms. Douglas?" he asked, giving her a questioning look and offering his arm.

She paused, giving him a long, searching look, then nodded and took his arm as he led her to the passenger side door. Maybe there *was* more to Carter Fox than met the eye.

9

The dinner had been lovely...for all of about one minute.

They were at Lupe Tortilla, one of her favorite restaurants. Carter had let her pick the place. He had picked her up at her house. He had met her parents. He had even opened the car door for her. He had brought flowers for heaven's sake!

The trip downhill had started with the sudden silence as soon as they were seated in the middle of the restaurant. The stares. The smiles. The whispers. The intrusions.

Jordan had ordered a margarita. A large margarita.

"So Ben is a great kid," Carter said. It was the right foot to start on. The one thing they actually had in common was the fact that they both liked Ben.

"Yeah, he had a really good time last weekend. Thanks for that," she said, taking a sip of the margarita once it finally arrived.

"No problem. I can see why you went to so much trouble for him, getting that ball."

He smirked, and she just averted her eyes, both of them remembering *the incident*.

She took another sip.

"Hey, great game today!"

It was a couple. The guy actually reached out to pat Carter Fox on the back. The woman just stared at him, cast a quick, curious glance to Jordan, then back to Carter Fox.

Jordan took another long sip.

"Thanks," said Carter, obviously used to such intrusions.

They walked off.

The waiter came. A boisterous focus on Carter Fox. "Can I take your order?"

They paused to give their food orders and then Carter brought his full attention back to her.

"So you're not a baseball fan?" Carter asked, giving her a grin.

"Sorry, it's boring," she confessed.

"I think once you understand the stats, it's actually pretty interesting."

"Hey, sorry to bother you, but would you mind if my son got a picture with you?"

A dad. A dad with a tow-headed, snaggletoothed son who couldn't have been older than six. Carter looked in her direction questioningly.

How could she possibly refuse? She smiled, giving a shrug in acquiescence, then took another sip of her margarita as she was patently ignored.

She watched his large arm envelope the minuscule, preadolescent shoulders. A flash. A gleeful jumping up and down on the boy's part. A shake of the hand between two men.

Jordan took another sip of margarita.

So this is what it was like to date Carter Fox.

"Where were we?" he asked, ever the gentleman.

But it was too late. The momentum had begun.

"Do you think we could get a shot with you as well?"

"Actually, folks—" Carter began, giving them an apologetic look.

"Of course you can," Jordan interrupted. This time it was not one, but two kids. A once in a lifetime chance for them, and she wasn't about to ruin it with her silly date. Baseball talk could wait. The smiles on their faces made it worthwhile.

Carter just gave her a half smile then went through the motions all over again, making sure to tousle the heads of the two boys afterward, making them laugh.

At the very least, it was one of the more interesting dates she'd been on.

They were rescued by their meal.

Carter was the one to eventually put a stop to it all.

"Hey, I'd love to, but I'm actually here with a date, and we'd really like to just enjoy our meal. Sorry folks."

This time it was a double date that didn't look too happy. Especially the two leggy brunettes who gave Jordan the *what-has-she-got-that-we-don't* look. She didn't feel so bad about this one.

By then, Jordan had finished her margarita. It was definitely time for another one.

"So we are now third in our regional division. There are three divisions, East, Central, and West. The Sluggers are West, in the National League." They were finishing up their meal, mostly in peace.

Jordan nodded along, barely grasping his words.

He gave her a thoughtful look and smiled. "You aren't absorbing any of this are you?"

She smiled into her second margarita. "Sorry, Ben's the one you want here not me."

"One of these days, you'll appreciate it," he said, taking a bite of his carne asada. "Sorry about tonight. I guess we haven't really had a chance to actually talk."

"I probably should have known better," Jordan said shrugging with a smile. "All the same, it's been...well, it's been an experience. At least I have something to talk about when I go back to law school."

He looked at her a moment longer, as though considering something. "Actually, I have an idea."

Jordan's eyes got wide with curiosity. Were they not done here? Had he not fulfilled his obligatory date duties?

"I barely got a chance to talk to you tonight," he said in answer to the unspoken question. "If you think I'm letting you get away this fast, you're sorely mistaken."

It made her smile into the last of her margarita.

❦ 10 ❧

In retrospect, Carter should have warned her how the date would probably go.

In his defense, it had been a while since he had been on a bona fide date. And make no mistake, folks, this was a date, complete with meeting the parents. Carter smiled at the memory of it.

The flowers had been a sudden spark of inspiration. He liked the way tulips looked and thought it might just nudge him closer to Jordan's good side. He had a feeling it had worked.

Despite his over the top performance, Carter really had enjoyed himself with Jordan's family. It was refreshing to see all the sentiment he'd only ever seen in movies and TV actually come to life in front of him. Good natured teasing. Inside joking. Laughter. Love. Even the critical scrutiny of her mother had given him the warm fuzzies. Jordan had grown up with the sort of family Carter could only dream about. In the 20 minutes he had spent in their presence they had made him feel more at home than he had ever felt with any of his own family members.

He couldn't remember the last "date" he'd actually been on. College?

High school? Once he had hit the majors, girls—women—just seemed to be a little "fly by night." Obviously, more than a few had tried to get him to wife them up, but he had always been far more interested in looking for the next best thing.

He'd meet them in bars, nightclubs, strip clubs, maybe take them back to his huge house in River Oaks, if that was where the night was going —and it usually was.

Right now would usually be about the time he should be thinking about what was around the corner—after hitting it and finding a way to finesse out of it. But all he could do was focus on those big, brown eyes and dimples that made an appearance every time someone dropped by the table to congratulate him or shake his hand, which had been all night.

And now he was reluctant to let her go.

Beat that.

The craziest part was that he wasn't even thinking about sex. Well, that was a lie. Of course he was thinking about sex. But, there was something more here.

They were walking back to his truck. As he opened the door for her, she turned to him with a smile that advertised just how many margaritas she'd had.

A wee bit tipsy there, aren't we sweetheart?

"Well, thank you for dinner Carter."

"Like I said, we're not done yet."

She blinked rapidly in response. He duly noted her eyes flit down to his crotch and then back up to his face with a note of panic in them.

He laughed.

"No, not that," he said. Then he leaned in, crowding her into the passenger side of his pick-up truck. "Unless of course you want to come back to my place."

Her expression changed. *"See,* there you go. And it was going *so* nicely—"

"Hold your horses," he said, laughing again. He grabbed her gently by the shoulders and reversed her escape into his truck. "As much as the idea appeals to me," he couldn't stop his eyes from roaming down the sundress she had worn tonight, "I have something else in mind. It'll give us a chance to actually talk. Trust me."

She considered him for a moment, then shrugged. He let go of her shoulders and watched as she stepped up into the truck. As she bent forward to duck in, he had a lovely view of her round backside underneath the thin, pinkish-orange fabric of her dress.

Oh sweet Jordan Douglas.

No sense going down that road...*yet.*

He closed the door after her and jogged around to his side of the truck and got in.

The idea had struck him as soon as they were finishing up their meal. Jordan in that dress was just killing him. Those dimples of hers were killing him even more. There was no way he wanted to let her go so soon. Other than his place, which he obviously would have been more than happy to take her, the only other idea that sprung to mind was one that had been put on the shelf long ago. He figured this one would be an easier sell.

"So, are you going to leave me in suspense?" she asked, actually giving in to a smile as he started the ignition.

"I think I might," he said, grinning back at her.

"Should I be scared of you?" A tiny edge of trepidation crept into her voice.

"Always, darlin'."

She was just on the right side of tipsy to laugh at that.

They sat in silence as he made his way back onto US-59. When he finally exited, Jordan looked around.

"The museum?" she asked, looking at the clock in his front panel. It was well after 11:30 p.m. "I think it's closed."

"Close, but no cigar," he said, making his way around the curve to the parking lot for Hermann Park.

"What's going on? Where are we going?"

"Boy, you just don't like surprises do you?"

"Depends on what kind," she responded, that trepidation creeping in just a bit more.

Carter pulled the truck into the near empty lot and turned off the engine. He reached in back and grabbed the extra-large, clean towel he packed in case he preferred to shower at home instead of in the Sluggers' clubhouse and didn't want to get the seat of his truck funky.

He responded to Jordan's confused look with a smile as he walked around to open her door for her. He crooked his elbow, offering it to her, ever the gentleman. Might as well go full throttle on this little ride he was taking her.

Jordan rolled her eyes with a smile. Then she took his arm and bowed her head graciously, playing along with it. They both laughed as he led her toward the huge grassy hill on the other side of the Miller Outdoor Theatre seating area. Any concert that had been there was long over and they had the area mostly to themselves.

The inspiration for this adventure had happened purely by coincidence after some charity event a year ago at the Museum of Natural Science, which was right next to the park. After his obligatory round of schmoozing and hand-shaking, Carter had just wanted some alone time. It had been a dark night so he had been able to wander around outside anonymously. Strolling along, hands in the pocket of his tuxedo, he had seen a couple lying there on a blanket looking up at the sky. They were completely oblivious to him, and he'd watched them for a good 10 minutes while they stared up and smiled, heads together, whispering to one another. He was a professional athlete with a 4-year $25 million contract, doing exactly what he loved most for a living...and he'd never been so envious in his life. Nothing but the night sky and a beautiful woman lying next to you.

He hoped Jordan was worth it.

He unfurled the towel onto the grass. The towel was meant for two people but when you were Carter Fox's size it got a bit crowded, even when he made a point of positioning himself right on the edge, long legs stretched out as he leaned back on his hands. He patted the space next to him, encouraging her to take a seat. He watched the debate play out in her cautious eyes before they came to a decision and had her shrugging as she finally plopped down next to him, tucking her legs underneath her in an endearingly ladylike fashion.

"So what's this?" she asked, giving a small laugh and looking around as she sat facing him, leaning on one arm. "You want to make out in the park?"

"Well, my intention was to get to know you a little better, but if you want to get down and dirty," he leaned over and shoved his stubble covered chin into her neck.

"Carter!" she yelped in surprise. He felt her laugh and cringe away from the prickliness of his chin.

"Jeez! you really are bad," she laughed, slapping him on the chest and shaking her head.

"That's why they love me."

She just kept shaking her head as she looked away toward the museums across the street. He noted that the smile remained on her face. That was a good sign.

"So what did you want to know about me?" she finally asked.

"What makes Jordan Douglas tick?" he asked his voice laced with a hint of mockery.

"Oh come on! What a lame question, and so cliché. I mean, how would you answer if a reporter asked you a question like that?"

"Baseball," he said simply. He lay back down on the towel, resting his body on one elbow as he faced her. "It's the one thing I'm good at."

"I have my doubts about that," she said. "You seem pretty capable in a few other areas."

He just chuckled as he took that in. "But really, tell me something about Jordan Douglas that might surprise me."

He sensed a pause and then a sigh. "Really? Work and school, school and work. Like you, my life orbits around a tiny sphere of things I'm really good at."

"I too have my doubts about that," he replied.

She gave a small chuckle, then she squinted one eye giving him a thoughtful look. That tongue of hers rolled around in her cheek. Perhaps it was the margaritas, but eventually, the choice to speak her mind won out.

"Okay, but you have to promise not to laugh," she finally said. "Actually, you have to promise *to* laugh."

"Now I'm just confused, but go ahead and tell me anyway."

"Off-color jokes," she said in a huff. "Not too dirty of course, but, well, I've got a bunch of them."

That was the last thing he would have ever expected and blurted out a loud laugh.

She laughed and slapped him on the arm. "I haven't even told one yet!"

"Okay fine, shoot."

She did a little wriggle of anticipation—which caused a part of him to wriggle with anticipation as well—then took a deep breath.

"What do you call babies born in a whorehouse?"

Carter twisted his lips with thought, having no idea what the punchline was. He grinned and gave her a shrug. "What?"

"Brothel Sprouts."

It was so bad he couldn't help but laugh, throwing his head back with a steady stream of guffaws.

"Oh come on," she chided, not sure if he was teasing or legitimately laughing at the joke. He couldn't have told her one way or the other.

"Okay," he said, recovering. "That wasn't even in the universe of dirty. You want dirty I can show you dirty."

"I'll bet," she said, a little sauce in her tone.

Carter filed that one away for later. "But I'll give it to you, you did make me laugh. Though I'm not sure if it's with you or at you."

"I said they'd be dirty, not good," she replied, matter-of-factly.

"You can do better than that," he goaded.

Jordan pursed her lips—which only made him want to suck on them— as she debated it, then chuckled. "Okay. How many perverts does it take to screw in a light bulb?"

A slow smile came to Carter's face and he shrugged.

"Only one, but it takes an entire ER team to get it back out."

This time his laugh was for real, and Jordan joined him.

"Okay, dirty and funny," he said after his laughter died down. "You win that one."

"Speaking of which, what's your super-secret thing, mister?"

Instead of answering, he fell onto his back and once again patted the towel next to him.

"Come lie down here next to me."

She just looked down at him with a wary expression.

"I promise I won't try anything."

She bit back a smile then fell back next to him with a dramatic plop. Her body felt tiny next to his. He brought one large arm around and nudged her head until she finally lifted it so he could place it under her head. Then he brought her closer so it was resting on his shoulder instead.

"There, now isn't that better?" he drawled.

"Just don't try anything, tough guy," she warned.

"Relax, I'm not going to try anything. I just want to show you something."

She laughed lightly against his chest and it felt like heaven. He wondered what those two love birds that were the inspiration for tonight's little imitation had talked about. Were they just beginning to get to know each other as well?

"Look up at the sky. See that bright white dot there?" he pointed to it.

"The star?" she asked after a moment.

"It's not a star. It's Venus. Goddess of Love." He nudged the back of her head with his shoulder as he said it and was rewarded with a small chuckle. "Did you know that it spins in the opposite direction from the other planets? It also rotates so slowly that a day on the planet is longer than a year."

There was a short silence from her before she spoke up.

"How do you know so much about Venus?" she asked and he was pleased to note the admiration in her voice.

"What little boy grows up in the home of NASA, and doesn't want to be an astronaut? I used to devour books about space, still do. I even have a telescope in my bedroom at home."

"Tell me some more facts about space," she prodded, snuggling in closer to him.

Carter smiled, loving the fact that she was curious about something he loved. "Well, space is huge, beyond what you can even imagine. Just to show you, the sun is big enough to hold over a million Earth-sized planets inside of it...and some of those stars you see up there are big enough to hold a million suns...and some of the largest known stars in the universe are big enough to hold a million of *those* stars."

He heard her give a heavy sigh. It was something he could fully appreciate, the enormity of everything he'd just said. Here they were, Carter and Jordan, two tiny little blips on the map of the universe. It could make even a man his size feel small.

"It's all so amazing," she breathed with wonder, moving in even closer.

"It is," he agreed.

They stared up at the blanket of lights above them in silence.

Oh yeah, Jordan was definitely worth this.

After a group of teenagers had interrupted their astrological observance, the two of them had reluctantly returned to Carter's truck.

They were now sitting in the car on the street of her parents' house. They had been sitting here talking for the past ten minutes, and she was very much enjoying herself. She found that a Jordan that wasn't so anally retentive was actually kind of fun. No thinking about law school or work or work or law school.

Two large margaritas. Jordan should have remembered how much tequila affected her.

And now, here she was, right down the street from her parents' house in a man's car. Not just any car, a *pick-up truck*. This was something she never could have done in school. It was home by 9 p.m., mom waiting up with the lights on. Pretending she was in high school made her feel absurdly naughty.

Carter had parked at the dead end of the street her parents lived on. The dead end, where the street lights faded to black.

Nice move there, Slugger, she thought.

"So why do you live with your parents?" he asked her.

"It seemed stupid to rent an apartment for just three months while I'm here. More importantly, I have student loans. About $97,000 when all is said and done."

Carter whistled in surprise.

"My thoughts exactly," Jordan laughed. "Mom's a high school teacher, Dad's an Air Traffic Controller. It was all on me and Sallie Mae, but it was worth it. I think....I *hope*. In the meantime, yes I'm still living at home, at least for the summer. Even in law school, I have a roommate." her head fell against the head rest. "I seriously can't *wait* to have a place all to myself."

She turned to him, with a squinty-eyed look. "And you? How did you become a Slugger?"

"Well, I was at Texas A&M—"

"You're an *Aggie*?" she interrupted.

He turned to her with a grin. "Ah yes, I forgot you were a UT gal. Makes us kinda like Romeo and Juliet, huh?"

"Hmm, the alumni families would certainly disapprove of this union," she said, playing along, then added in a lofty voice, "the tragic tale of the Longhorns and the Aggies."

He laughed. "Well, if it makes you feel any better, I was picked up by the Sluggers before graduation. I don't even have a class ring, which I think is heresy for an actual Aggie."

"Ohhh," she pouted, "that just makes you a little bit less excitingly inappropriate. In fact—"

Carter leaned in to kiss her. His lips were soft but firmly planted. Hers had no choice but to follow his lead as he worked both of their mouths slightly open. One large hand came up to cup the back of her head.

Jordan closed her eyes and moaned under his lips.

The moan turned into a frustrated groan when he abruptly pulled away.

"Sorry. I should have asked. I forgot how irate you get at unsolicited sexual advances."

Jordan was still recovering and her eyes flew open. She found him looking down at her with a teasing smirk.

"Shut up and kiss me again, Slugger," she murmured.

Carter chuckled and leaned in again. This time his tongue darted inside, and she felt her pelvis clench when the intrusion flitted against her own tongue. God, he was making her wet with just a kiss.

"Do you want me to stop?" he mumbled against her lips, obviously misinterpreting her intense moans against his mouth.

She just whimpered in response. Then she felt his hand come down to rest on the thigh of her skirt. It was a simple, cotton, sun dress with a flared skirt; a skirt that offered little in the way of obstruction for wandering hands.

He waited a moment before sliding it down toward her knee. Even through the fabric of the dress, she felt the hand leave a tingling sensation in its path.

She let the hand wander.

Eventually, it reached the hem of the skirt. The callused palms felt like sandpaper against her smooth thigh. It reminded her that she spent her days sitting in an air conditioned office staring at a computer. Carter Fox spent his days getting sweaty on the baseball field. The rushing heat inside of her intensified.

Her hand wandered up his arm, feeling the result of hours upon hours of swinging bats and throwing balls. He was so big.

His hand wandered under the hem of her skirt and she shuddered, reflexively squeezing his hard bicep.

He mistook that as a sign he should stop and immediately lifted his palm from her thigh. She groaned in disappointment and brought her hand down to his, leading it all the way to the lower part of her inner thigh.

You know what to do Carter.

And he did. The rough fingers felt even more scandalous against the softer skin between her legs. Her breathing intensified under his mouth and she wasn't so sure that she wasn't soaking herself right through her dress onto his seat. It had been forever since she'd done something like this. She might as well have been in a convent rather than law school these past two years.

She gasped as the fingers met the cotton fabric of her panties, running a finger along her slit through the damp fabric.

"Naughty girl," he mumbled with a smile against her lips.

She just gripped his arm harder in response, parting her legs for him.

His fingers crept under the edge of her underwear, pushing it roughly aside. She momentarily thanked herself for having the foresight to get waxed this morning. Not that she had been planning anything like this —at all.

The blood rushing through her body made every single nerve-ending between her legs even more sensitive. She groaned, trembling against him as his fingers slid along the slick outer lips. He hadn't even penetrated her and already he was making her come.

Carter caught her with his other arm, reaching it over the center console and wrapping it around her back protectively. She felt small in his embrace.

So big and strong.

Sweet Lord, he was turning her into some kind of wilting violet!

The fingers began to probe, eventually finding the tiny little bundle of nerves. She literally jumped out of her seat just from the first feathery touch. The rough finger came back around, circling it gently. She had to wrap her arms around his neck to stay upright. The stimulation continued and she pulled her lips away from his, unable to breathe any longer.

"Look at me," he instructed.

She brought her breathing under control, despite his continued massaging of her clit. Then she looked directly into his piercing, green eyes. They stared back at her with just as much intensity.

"Open your legs wider. I want to feel every part of you."

She twisted in her seat to face him, then spread her right leg open as wide as she could. She kept her arms around his neck as his fingers slid down further into her underwear. Her eyes grew wide when he guided, first one, then two fingers inside of her. As they wandered up, twisting and stroking, his thumb stayed focused on her clit. The mixture of sensations drove her wild, and she could feel the swelling of the orgasmic wave that was about to hit her.

"*Carter...*" she whimpered, struggling to keep her eyes on him as he instructed.

"You can scream out if you want to," he said softly. "It's just us here."

That brought Jordan around to where she was. On the street where her parents lived. On the street of the neighbors she'd grown up next to. In a man's car—a *truck*! And not just any man, but Carter Fox...who had his fingers inside of her.

Even as an adult it was scandalous, maybe even more so. Teenagers could be excused for being this reckless. Grown-ass women should be ashamed of themselves.

That was all the encouragement she needed to send her over the edge. She threw her head back and cried out, not caring if anyone heard. Her body convulsed around his fingers, while her own dug into his back.

When she brought her head back down to face him, he had broken out into a broad smile. He pulled his fingers out from her underwear, the sensation causing ripples of pleasure to run through her body all over again. He brought them up to his face, right under his nose. Then he put the tips into his mouth to taste her juices.

It was a shocking display and Jordan stared at him like a stunned rabbit.

"You taste amazing," he growled.

He brought his fingers close to her and she could smell her heated sex instantly. Something about it caused her to shudder with prurient delight. As if under his spell, she obediently parted her lips so he could place his fingertips inside. She felt the rough fingers on her tongue as it partook of the slightly tangy taste. She lapped his fingers like a kitten savoring a bowl of cream.

"Nice," he purred.

When there was nothing left to taste, he pulled his fingers out.

Jordan looked down at her lap and studiously began to smooth her skirt down. The practical part of her brain knew there was no way anyone could have seen what they had done. Another scandalized part of her secretly wondered, and not without a hint of excitement, at the prospect.

What was this man doing to her?

"I should probably go inside now," she said.

"I've got you," he said, quickly opening his door.

He had circled around the truck and was at her door before she could even release the handle.

"It's only proper that I walk you to the door. I am a gentleman after all," he grinned down at her and she could feel her body getting warm with embarrassment. No gentleman would have led her down the path they had just gone.

But who the hell wanted a gentleman?

Jordan smiled to herself as she let him walk her the short way up the street to the front door of her house.

She was surprised to find the lights on inside. The residual effect of two margaritas made her fumble in her attempt to find the key in her purse. When she finally pulled it out, her body was still so gelatinous she could barely guide the key into the hole. Carter released the key from her quivering grip and steadily slid it into the lock.

When she opened the door she found her mother in the living room reading a book.

"Mom!" she exclaimed, a little too excitedly. "You're still up?"

"I couldn't sleep," her mother said mildly. Her eyes slid over to appraise the man standing next to her.

"Mrs. Douglas," Carter said respectfully. "It's very nice to see you again."

Her mother stared at him a moment then offered a tight smile to accompany the brief nod she gave him. She didn't bother to return the verbal greeting, instead choosing to cast a glance in her daughter's direction.

Jordan just stared at her in disbelief, unable to process the fact that her mother was actually waiting up for her. She was completely mortified.

"Thank you Carter," Jordan said, turning to him and eagerly guiding him out the front door. "I had a—a lovely time."

"I'll call you," he said in a rush.

"Yes, that would be great. I really did have a wonderful time. Thank you," she said in a rush, then closed the door on him. It was rude, but she had more important fish to fry.

She spun on her mother. "Okay, do you feel like explaining this? Or have you forgotten I'm 24-years-old?"

Deborah just stared placidly, then she patted the couch next to her and asked, "Can we talk?"

Jordan stared back for a moment. "Are we going to talk, or is this going to be a lecture?"

"I just want to explain. I think you're ready to," she gave a sigh, "understand why I am the way I am with you."

Jordan's anger went down a notch but she didn't move.

"Please?" her mother implored.

Finally, Jordan nodded and sat next to her mother.

Deborah looked past her out the window, waiting a breath before she started.

"I never told you this before because you never really dated in high school and didn't seem too serious about anyone in college. I guess that's my fault, pushing you so hard with your studies and all."

Jordan waited, wondering where her mother was going with all of this.

Deborah gave a heavy sigh. "I was actually engaged before your father."

Jordan's mouth fell open. She blinked rapidly at the news. Her mother? With someone before her dad? It seemed like a completely foreign idea to her. They fit so perfectly together, in a sort of yin and yang way. Her dad was easy going and quick with a joke. Deborah was more stoic and slower to thaw.

Her mother saw her expression and gave her an empathetic smile. "I know, it's hard to believe, but it's true. I was young, still in college in fact.

"Jay was perfect. Smart. Handsome. Charming. He was a junior, and he had me hooked my freshman year. He was going to be a doctor, and I was going to be his perfect little wife.

"You know, originally I wanted to be a lawyer, like you. We were both at Cornell. He applied and applied and the only medical school he made it into was Baylor, here in Houston. I was still a junior but he eventually wore me down into following him and I transferred to the University of Houston. At that point, I figured I would end up marrying him and I focused my attentions on him and his goals. I even gave up trying to get into law school."

Jordan fell back against the couch processing all of this new information.

"Mom," she sighed, "I'm not giving up law school or my career for Carter Fox. For Pete's sake, we've been on one date! It's just, I don't know...*fun?*"

Deborah simply smiled again. "It started out fun with Jay as well."

Jordan sighed. "Mom—"

"And then the first slap came."

Jordan gasped.

"It was when it was too late, when I had given everything up for him. He knew I was trapped."

Jordan sat straight up and looked her mother in the face. "Carter has never *once*—"

"They never do...until they *do*."

"That's not fair, Mom. You don't even know him."

"Perhaps," her mother said giving a slight nod, "and I'm not accusing him, but...he does have a reputation."

"And now you believe everything you read in the papers?" Jordan asked skeptically.

"All I want for you," Deborah said, bringing the conversation back around, "is to be able to make it on your own, not by depending on someone else. You have no idea how hard it is to get out when you don't feel you have any options.

"It took me years, and Jay nearly killing me, before I was finally strong enough to leave. I got my teaching certificate and made it on my own before I eventually—*thankfully*—found your father. Now I'm with him, not because I *have* to be, but because I *want* to be.

"That's all I want for you Jordan. To be with someone because you want to be, not because you're impressed with their lifestyle or money or fame or whatever. I want to see you succeed in your own right, be independent, know that you can make it on your own. *Then* find someone to be with."

It all made sense now. The dating—or lack thereof—when she was still in high school. The push to be successful. Jordan couldn't even be sure that law school was actually what *she* wanted, or some idea that her mother had planted in her head. She was doing well, and there were even aspects that she loved, like the legal clinics. But what would she be doing if her life hadn't been guided by the controlling hand of Deborah Douglas?

"Mom, I love you and I know you're just looking out for me. So far, I like Carter and for once this summer I'm having a bit of fun. This doesn't mean I'm giving up everything I've worked so hard for to run off and be a ball player's wife."

"I just—"

"No. I'm going to bed now. This discussion is over."

Deborah just pursed her lips.

"Goodnight, Mom."

"Goodnight, sweetheart."

Thankfully, this was the last time she'd be living at home. Next year this time, she'd have her law firm job and could rent one of the nice luxury apartments in midtown. Then, she wouldn't have to make out with men in trucks.

She smiled at the thought. On second thought, perhaps not *everything* would have to change.

T*hwack!*

Carter watched as his 31st home run ball went into the stands. *Finally.* They were at an away game in Tampa Bay so the crowd was slightly less enthusiastic than the hometown crowd for this home run.

Perhaps Jordan was his good luck charm. He smiled as he thought of their one and only date. He could still feel that smooth skin under his hands. The feel of her next to him as they lay there looking up at the sky. Even the dirty jokes.

She had told him that she had to head back to Austin for school, which meant they probably wouldn't see each other before then. It disappointed him more than he cared to admit. On the other hand, Austin was only about a three-hour drive away....

As he entered the dugout, he high-fived the rest of his team, accepted a few pats on the ass, and sat back on the bench to watch the inning unfold.

The Sluggers beat the Rays 7-2.

〜

"Congratulations. You have no idea how excited Ben is, even if his ball is pretty much worthless now."

Carter was in his hotel room on the phone to Jordan as promised. It was good to hear her voice, especially after such a spectacular game.

"Well, we're still third in the division. Not great, but if this keeps up we can probably eek it out as a wild card."

"I have no idea what that even means," she laughed.

"One of these days I'm going to have to teach you about baseball."

"Is that a threat?" she teased.

The phone buzzed as another call came through on his end. He took a brief look to see who it was. The number was one he—thankfully—hadn't seen in quite some time.

"Shit," he mumbled, under his breath.

"Was that another call?" Jordan asked. "I can let you go."

He wasn't about to break up this conversation, especially for this particular caller.

"Nonsense. I can call them back."

"No, no. It's late, and I have to be at work bright and early. It's my last week. Gotta make a good last impression." She sighed. He could hear her yawning. "Take your call."

"Alright then," he said with resignation. He enjoyed hearing her voice, especially when it got sleepy like this. It made him feel like she was in bed next to him. One day he would have to get her there. He smiled into the phone. "I'll call again tomorrow, and we can finish where we left off, maybe with a happy ending this time."

She gave a small laugh. "Don't make promises your mouth can't keep."

"Mmm, that sounds like an interesting challenge" he teased.

Jordan laughed as she realized what she had just said.

"Seriously," he continued. "I'll call you."

"Mmm-hmm," she mused. "Okay then. I'll be ready and waiting. Good night, Carter Fox."

"Good night, Jordan Douglas."

He hung up the phone and looked at the call that had tried to come through during their conversation. There was a message left but he didn't need to click it to know that it wouldn't have much in the way of information. No, he would have to call back. He always had to call back.

He sat staring at the phone, debating what to do. He should leave it, let it go. He knew from experience—too much experience—that it would only lead to bad news. But if he didn't take it, it would hang over his head until he dealt with it.

Carter took a deep breath and hit return for the number. He brought the phone up to his ear and waited. It was answered on the second ring.

"*Sonny boy!*" Bobby Joe Fox's voice rang out a bit too cheerfully on the other end of the line.

"Don't call me that."

"How are things, Carter?" the voice said without so much as a pause. "How's the lovely Madison Grant treatin' ya these days? Still ridin' your ass?" A cackle broke out on the other side.

"Cut the shit, Bobby. What do you want this time?"

"I'm just tryin' to get to know my son a little—"

"I'm this close to hanging up the phone," Carter interrupted.

The fact that Bobby Joe Fox had the nerve to refer to him as a son was enough to push him over the edge. The man hadn't been a "father" since Carter was 10 years old, and he'd walked out of his life forever. Or at least until Carter had signed on with the Sluggers.

Bobby Joe gave a deep sigh on the other end of the line.

"Alright son—"

"*Don't* call me son," Carter growled.

Bobby Joe paused before continuing, knowing when to leave well enough alone.

"Well, s—Carter—your old man got himself into a bit of a pickle. You see, there was this great plan. Solar panels! It's the wave of the future. And this company in—"

"How much?"

Bobby Joe Fox had a way of spinning tales. If he hadn't spent his entire life chasing down the next get-rich-quick scheme, he might have actually made a pretty decent living as a salesman or maybe even a writer. But both of those professions required a degree of actual work ethic and responsibility. Two things Bobby Joe Fox seriously lacked.

"$20,000, but it would be an investme—"

"Don't."

"Fine, but you just don't know Carte—"

"Who to?"

"Well if you make the check out to—actually it would have to be a cashier's check, you see—but you could make it out to me and I'll make sure that—"

"I'm hanging up."

"*No!*" Bobby Joe said in a panic. "No...*dammit* Carter! Haven't I paid enough? Every damn time I call, I try to make up for—"

"I'm hanging up."

"Dammit!" Bobby Joe yelled on the other end. After a moment, he sighed again then continued. "Fine. There are a couple of...*associates* I had to borrow from to invest in this project. How the fuck was I supposed to know it would take 10 damn years to— Anyway, I'll give you the names and address. They're gonna need it pretty quickly son—

er—Carter. Your old man's in a bit of hot water here and it's reachin' its boilin' point. These guys, well they're getting pretty impatient." He cackled on the other end again, though there was no humor in it this time.

Carter sighed. There were always guys who were "impatient." People who were patient didn't loan money to the likes of Bobby Joe Fox. People who cut off fingers and charged a thousand times the standard interest rates loaned money to the likes of Bobby Joe Fox.

"This is the last time," Carter said.

"I understand. I promise I'll pay you ba—"

"Send me the information. This is the *last* time."

"I know. Thanks, Carter. You know, I love ya so—"

Carter hung up.

As he tossed the phone on his nightstand he looked at it and knew with absolute certainty: this was the last time.

❧ 13 ❧

Jordan lugged the rolling suitcase up over the last step. She nearly dropped the box of clothes tucked under her other arm from the effort. She paused to hitch it on her hip a little more securely before heading down the hallway.

She had driven back to Austin. *Morris & Gibson* had *finally* offered her a position, and her family had sent her off with a nice little Tex-Mex themed congratulatory party.

It had left little time for Carter and Jordan to get together. But he had hinted at maybe coming up to see her at some point.

Jordan and her roommate, April, had sublet their apartment for the summer and the key had been sent back to her last week. April wasn't supposed to be back until next week so she'd have the place to herself for a while. She was actually looking forward to that. After such an eventful summer, with literally *everyone* knowing her business, a bit of alone time was refreshing.

She shoved the key into the lock and used the elbow holding the box of clothes to push the door in.

"Oh shit!"

It was the first thing she heard and it caused her to drop the box of clothes and jump in panic. It took a few moments to register what she was looking at. A very naked April Palomino was sitting astride her boyfriend—a similarly very naked Matt Dueker—in the middle of the living room floor.

"Oh my God, oh my God, *ohmygod!*" Jordan screamed, quickly swiveling her body to face the hallway.

She heard the scramble behind her and waited until the frantic noises subsided.

"Are you decent?" she asked after a while.

There was a bit more whispering then she heard April's voice, "Um...yeah?"

Jordan waited a moment longer, then slowly turned around. Matt was M.I.A. and April was exiting her bedroom with her bed sheet wrapped around her like an impromptu toga costume.

"What the *hell*, Jordan!" she said accusingly. "I thought you weren't going to be back until Friday."

"You said *you* weren't coming back until Saturday!" Jordan responded.

April's eyes went to the ceiling in recollection. "Oh...yeah, well sorry." She laughed. "Guess you caught us."

Jordan picked her box up from the floor and rolled her suitcase in. April had a perfectly good bed to do the do in. Why in the world would she be in the living room of all places?

Says the woman who got to third base in a truck outside her parents' house.

At least someone was getting their rocks off here in Austin. It made her think of Carter Fox and how they had yet to go that far. Frustrating to say the least.

"If you just give me a chance to drop my stuff off I can leave you to it.

"Thanks, and sorry about that," April laughed. "Welcome back, I guess!"

"Yeah."

Jordan unloaded the last of her luggage and boxes in her bedroom. They were both sitting awkwardly in the living room, waiting, by the time she was done.

Matt at least had the decency to look somewhat embarrassed by the whole incident. April just seemed to think it was hilarious. Between Jordan and her roommate, April had always been the more libertine of the two of them. Frankly, it was a wonder that she and Matt had been together as long as they had.

"Sorry about that. It's just that...well, you're kinda *always* here, Jordan" April explained. "At least at night. And weekends. And pretty much any time you're not at school. I thought I'd take advantage of the few days I had the place to myself."

"Well, I'm done here, so have at it!" Jordan said with a grand gesture.

"Oh, hey!" April said brightly. "I heard about that thing with Carter Fox! Did he really offer to do a threesome with you? Next time hit a girl up!"

Jordan looked at her in surprise. She cast a quick glance to Matt who just gave a small laugh.

"Oh, we're totally cool. Besides, Matt would absolutely let me hit it with Carter Fox."

Well, that explained a lot. If it hadn't been for a mutual need to split the rent, she wondered how in the world April and she would have ever ended up together. As it had turned out, other than mismatched social lives, they meshed pretty well as roommates.

"So...?" April looked at her expectantly. Matt seemed to be a little too interested as well.

"*Really?*" Jordan asked, giving her roommate a *get real* stare. "No, of course I didn't have a threesome with Carter Fox, or anything else for that matter!"

For some reason, she had no desire for her roommate—for *anyone*—to know about her and Carter. That first bit of public fanfare was something she didn't need a repeat of. Better that her roommate thought she was some boring, anti-social prude.

"Don't worry, I'll be gone a while so you two love birds can get back to having fun."

Jordan sat in the car honestly wondering what to do. It was August, still too damn hot for this. She could go to Starbucks, or the public library maybe. How much time did April and Matt really need? She looked at the clock. Almost 3:30.

The Sluggers weren't even playing tonight, so there was no point in going to a bar to watch Carter from afar.

Her phone buzzed and she was pleased to see it was Carter.

"What are you up to?" he asked as soon as she answered.

"Melting in my car," she answered with a laugh.

"How would you like to melt in my arms instead?"

14

"Hey there Slugger, care to give a gal a ride?"

Carter looked at Jordan smiling into the passenger side window of his truck as he idled in the parking lot of her apartment building. He had actually driven the 180 or so miles up from Houston to see her. What in the world did that indicate?

He had spent the entire drive up letting the answer to that bounce around the back of his mind. Now, seeing her standing there, smiling up at him, he didn't even have to ask himself why.

He whistled. "If I knew they grew 'em like you here at UT Austin, I would have seriously reconsidered my academic choices. And wearing my favorite outfit to boot!"

Jordan looked down at the royal blue tank top she was wearing, then laughed as though she just realized she was wearing it.

"Well, isn't this kismet? But speaking of academic choices, it's a bit scandalous for me to be standin' here leaning into the truck, conversatin' with a former Aggie right smack in the middle of Longhorn territory," she drawled, matching his vibe.

"Well, I guess you better hop on in and protect that virtue of yours."

Jordan giggled and hopped in. Then she turned to him with a skeptical smile. "So you drove all the way up here just to see lil' ole me? That certainly puts a lot of pressure on a gal."

"Well, maybe a certain gal could make it up to a certain guy by letting him take her out." He leaned in. "Besides, those dimples are worth the gas money alone."

Jordan laughed, bringing out those dimples in all their glory.

Carter leaned in even closer.

Jordan leaned back, giving him a playful smile.

He just came in closer. "You gonna make me work this hard, even after I drove all day to see you?"

She rolled her eyes up to the side with a mischievous smile. "Well, I suppose I could—"

Carter brought his hand around and placed it on the back of her neck, pulling her in for a kiss before she could finish. After a tiny squeak of surprise, she melted into it.

It was good; nice and warm like a comforting meal after a long day of work. When she brought her arms around his neck, it caused a slow, but intense burn in him.

He pulled away and looked at her. "Mmm, yeah, definitely worth it."

"I'm glad you came," she said, her fingers making trails at the base of his neck, which was turning that burn inside him into a bonfire. "So what's the plan?"

"Well, this is your town. I guess I have to let you pick the place again."

"Oh no," she laughed. "I learned my lesson last time. No restaurants."

"We could grab a drink at a bar?"

"Do you have any idea what lushes law students are? We'd be outted for sure. Ixnay on that, especially anything on 6th Street."

Carter had no idea what the reference to the street had to do with anything, but he did know she was gradually eliminating any obvious choice for a typical date. "Movie?"

"Hmm," she said looking up thoughtfully. "I suppose once we got past the ogling crowd and settled in it would be nice and quiet and cool. But we couldn't really talk."

Carter just laughed. "Well, since you're so quick to shoot down all my ideas, what did you have in mind, missy."

She gave him an exasperated look. "Are you really gonna make me suggest it?"

He was completely clueless at first. Then he kicked himself in the head. This woman really was making him lose it. "I don't know, the last time I suggested something like that, you read me the damn riot act."

That got a laugh out of her, then she tilted her head to the side and gave him an endearing smile that turned her dimples into perfect abysses. Carter felt himself sinking right into them, all while another part of him was rising rapidly.

"Fair enough," she said. "Okay then Mr. Fox, why don't we get ourselves a hotel room?"

"I thought you'd never ask, Ms. Douglas."

She had picked a place called the Driskill simply because she had heard how great it was, but had never stayed there. Whatever she wanted, he was more than happy to oblige. It *was* a nice hotel, in an old-fashioned sort of way. The lobby was sparsely populated, which made checking in hassle-free, even though neither of them had anything in the way of luggage. No need to draw a map for that one, but the staff was professional about it. It helped that he wasn't exactly in Slugger Fever territory.

Jordan was looking out the window onto the balcony overlooking the street below them. Carter came up behind her and wrapped his arms around her, leaning in to whisper in her ear. "So, you have any other suggestions as to what we should do?"

She turned around in his arms to face him. Her face crinkled and she scrunched her nose. "Well, I just got done moving in and you just got done driving for three hours. I think it's obvious."

Carter laughed. "Message received...happily, I might add."

She gave him a sly smirk as she pushed him back inside, pulling his shirt out of his jeans as he went. He followed her lead, tugging that royal blue tank top over her head.

By the time they made it to the bathroom they were naked. In their eagerness to get undressed they had barely taken time to notice the novelty of seeing each other fully unclothed for the first time.

Carter certainly enjoyed what he was looking at. Jordan had small, ripe breasts that rose from her chest like the perfect halves of a small orange. Her waist flared out into hips that were perfect for holding onto as you braced yourself against her. Carter could already feel his hands itching to do just that. Her legs were the same gorgeous stretch of curves that had drawn him to her in the first place.

Based on the way she was subtly eyeing him, she was just as impressed.

He grinned as he reached in to turn on the shower. Then he looked at the top of her head. "You worried about your hair?"

Her nervous smile disappeared and transitioned to open shock. "How the heck do you know anything about black hair?"

"Jordan, like I said, I haven't actually dated in a long time. But, first of all, a third of my team is black. Second of all, I've, well, *been with* enough black women to know, you don't mess with their hair."

"Ew," she said, wrinkling her nose, but she laughed all the same. "Well thank you for looking out for my hair, Carter," she said with a pert hand on her hips. "But I'll be fine...I have my ways of fixing it after. So are we gonna do this or not?"

By now the steam from the shower was warming them in the air conditioned room. She didn't have to ask him twice. He let her in first and followed, enjoying the back of her just as much as the front.

As he watched the water cascade over her head and make rivers down her body, he felt that warmth inside of him again. If every shower could be like this, he would probably never leave.

He grabbed the soap and began lathering his hands. She did the same when he was done. From there it was a long, leisurely process as they explored each other's bodies with soapy hands, which was really the best way to go about it.

His hands eventually found their way between her legs once again.

"Carter," she moaned, closing her eyes and throwing her head back as his index finger found the right button.

Meanwhile, her small hand was wrapped around his dick, making it impossibly harder than it already was. If he didn't stop her soon, he'd finish right there on the shower floor instead of in bed as he originally intended.

He pulled in closer to her, still massaging her clit. Reaching behind her, he shut off the water.

"Let's go to bed."

15

M*y God, he's huge!*
Jordan followed Carter's broad back out of the shower. Her hair was a mess, but she ran a few fingers through it, hoping it wouldn't get too tangled before she could re-wet it and braid it as usual.

Those thoughts disappeared as she realized what was about to happen. Sex with Carter, finally! As they dried themselves off, she took surreptitious glances at his tattooed chest, arms, and abs. Her breathing got heavier and she quickly focused on drying herself off.

"You are allowed to look, you know," he teased, having caught her.

She just laughed, feeling silly. "I don't want to make you feel like a piece of meat is all," she teased right back.

He came over and picked her up. She laughed in surprise but wrapped her legs around him as he carried her back into the bedroom. It helped relax her, this playfulness.

He tossed her on the bed. She giggled as she bounced on the mattress. "Carter!"

"Prepare to have your mind blown," he said, standing above her with his fists on his hips in a Superman pose.

It was so silly she laughed. Then she caught sight of his fully erect penis and a sobering rush of heat pulsated through her. It was so thick, and long, and veiny that she could feel both her mouth and her insides salivating to take it in. Jordan crawled over and reached out to take it in her hands.

"Uh-uh," he said backing away. "There's no way I'm letting those hands get anywhere near this thing again. I'm liable to finish before we've even started!"

She twisted her lips. "Don't you believe in foreplay?"

"Hon, I've been rarin' to go since I first got in my car," he assured her. "Now let's see about getting you going."

"Maybe it gets me off to stroke you," she retorted.

He leaned down on the bed on his hands crawling toward her. "Well, that is some *very* good information to have," he grinned. "But the point remains."

He crawled further and further toward her until he was practically on top of her. She fell back with a laugh and he crawled over her until he was straddling her on all fours over her prone body. She looked up into his intense eyes and saw the same hunger that was filling her.

"Very nice," he purred, looking down the length of her body beneath him.

"I like it when you say that," she smiled, remembering the first time she'd ever seen him mouth those exact words up on the big screen at the Sluggers' game.

"I'll say it every damn minute if it gets you underneath me lookin' like this," he said, grinning.

"Very nice," he said again, smirking down at her. "But we forgot one small thing."

He jumped off the bed, surprising her. He grabbed his jeans and dug inside, pulling out a condom. He ripped it open with his teeth. Just as he was about to roll it down his cock she reached up and grabbed his hand.

"Let me," she insisted. "I want to feel you in my hands."

He smiled and handed her the condom, resuming the position above her on all fours again. Jordan watched his face as she stroked the dark, pink head with the round piece of latex. She smiled as his forehead creased and he groaned with pleasure.

"Good God, woman," he growled. "Are you trying to make me come before we even get started?"

She gave him a break and placed the condom on the tip, then slowly ,but firmly slid it down his length, making him groan even deeper. When it was finally in place, he gave her a hungry look and shifted his legs, so that one knee forced itself between her legs, the other following suit. The size of them forced her legs far apart, and she was spread open wide to him. The feeling as the open air hit her wetness caused her to bite her lip with a moan, as her clit tingled from the chilly caress.

He pushed himself off of her and back onto his heels as he appraised her, lying wide open for him. One hand went between her sex and she felt a thick finger slide between her wet lips stimulating her all over again.

"It looks like you don't need much foreplay either," he teased.

"Oh God, Carter," she cried, finally resorting to begging. "Please, just fuck me already."

He winked at her. "You don't have to ask twice, Jordan," he said.

He grabbed her thighs and pulled her up toward him so that they straddled his hips. Then he leaned forward again positioning himself above her, as his hand went down to guide his cock into her eager wetness.

She felt the large head press against her much smaller hole. She bit her lip awaiting the feel as it popped through to penetrate her. When it came she grunted with the impact and moaned as it pressed against every single part of her inside.

She relished the feel of it. Jordan had never felt so completely and totally full as she did with him inside of her. It was like every other sexual experience she had encountered had only been training for the real thing. Carter Fox was the real thing.

Her legs clamped around his waist and she reached up to grab his ass, forcing him deeper and deeper into her, even though she knew it was impossible for him to go any further. All she was sure of was that she wanted him completely and totally inside of her. Filling her. Penetrating her. Stretching her. She didn't care if she was ruined for all other men. All she wanted was Carter Fox.

"Yes, yes," she urged even though he was thrusting with the power and force of a turbojet.

"Jesus, Jordan, you feel so damn good," he groaned as he fell down to his elbows on top of her.

The feeling of his hard, chiseled chest, just barely touching hers as he rocked his hips into her made her moan. Her hands slid up from his ass and her fingers curled into the flesh of his upper back, her fingernails digging crescents as she felt the coming waves of pleasure fill her body.

As the ocean of ecstasy began to swell, she arched her back in anticipation, squeezing her thighs harder around his sides. Her fingers dug firmly into the secure stronghold of his broad back as she held on tightly, letting the first wave crash deep inside of her. The walls of her sex spasmed around his cock as the swell of ripples ran through her body.

"Oh, God Carter, yes, yes, yes!" she cried out as the tide ebbed and flowed inside of her.

The already sensitive parts of her were reignited as he continued on, coming to the edge himself. Her limp body recovered and she pressed herself around him once again, cheerleading him on.

"That's right," she urged. "Use my body. I wanna feel you come for me."

It was all the encouragement he needed. One moment later she felt him stiffen, arching his back as though electricity was running through his veins. With an ear-piercing groan, she felt his girth convulsing against the walls of her pussy. She embraced it, watching his pleasure unfold with adoration. Finally, he fell on top of her in exhaustion.

They lay there like that, sticky with a sheen of sweat covering their bodies. Eventually, Carter rolled off of her, still breathing heavily.

"Well, that was definitely worth the drive up," he teased, chuckling.

Jordan laughed, slapping him on the chest as she rolled onto her side to cuddle up against him.

"So how is this going to go?" she asked.

They had taken another shower. This time she had taken the trouble to do her hair, braiding it around her head like a crown. Once it was dry she'd wear the wavy curls to survive the last of the Texas summer heat. Carter had called her Chocolate Swiss Miss, which made her laugh.

Now they were on the balcony, eating the room service they had ordered.

"How's what gonna go?" he asked

"Don't be coy," she admonished. "You know what I mean. Me in Austin. You in Houston. Me in law school. You playing baseball."

"Are you asking if I intend to see you again?"

She shrugged, looking out onto the street. She felt the anxious anticipation of his answer set in.

Carter reached across the table to take her hand, bringing her back around to face him.

Hey, Jordan," he said with a sincere look on his face. "I like you, a lot. And I'd really like to see where this goes. Even if that means we have to text, and facetime, and Skype, and talk on the phone until you come back to Houston then so be it."

Jordan felt her heart fill with something so warm and fierce she thought she might just break down crying.

"But I have to say this, even if it means breaking the speed limit and you cutting a class or two, we are going to have a repeat of today between now and then, little lady."

Jordan just laughed.

Venus. Goddess of Love.

Carter was in his bedroom. His sanctuary. It didn't stop the music from below from penetrating the walls and floor. It was almost morning and they were still at it downstairs.

It was the annual holiday party he hosted at his place after each baseball season. It was usually only attended by the bachelors and single male friends of the Sluggers, for very good reason. That was because it was also usually very well attended by a flock of females.

He bent his head down to look through the telescope again. As bright as Venus was this time of year, he didn't really need a telescope to see it. He just wanted it up close and personal.

It reminded him of someone special.

The long distance thing with Jordan had ended up being mostly texts and phone calls, with the *very* occasional conjugal visit, due to both their busy schedules. She would be back in Houston for the holidays, and a full week was dedicated to just the two of them.

It made his dick begin to twitch. Frankly, her graduation and permanent move back to Houston couldn't come soon enough.

Usually by this time at his party, Carter would be in the downstairs bedroom at the other end of the house enjoying his own happy ending to the party. It was designed with the very sexually active bachelor in mind.

One day these parties would have to end. More and more of his teammates had managed to get themselves hitched. Wives knew what went on at these parties. No married man would ever expose himself to the ire that would ensue should he dare make so much as an appearance at a Carter Fox party.

He heard the commotion downstairs make an abrupt shift. The music still blared. But now there was a louder, more angry ruckus going on.

"Dammit," Carter muttered to himself, figuring an anthill of a spat had turned into a mountain of a fight between a few the players, probably over some girl. His house, his responsibility. He sighed and made his way downstairs.

He stopped at the bottom of the stairs as soon as he saw the real reason for the change in the mood of the party.

"Well, there's the man of the hour," Bobby Joe Fox yelled. "The boy who can't even answer the phone when his daddy calls."

Carter had made good on his promise that the last payment to whomever, was indeed the last. Which meant, yes, ignoring his "daddy's" phone calls. Eventually, they stopped coming, Bobby Joe finally taking the hint. And Carter hadn't regretted it a bit. Good riddance.

Now it seemed like the old man was changing tactics. If Carter wouldn't take his calls, he'd just show up in person.

Carter managed to keep his cool, but his fists tightened at his sides. Several of his teammates stood ready at the sides, while the women just looked on in startled fright.

"What the hell are you doing here, Bobby?" Carter asked, as if he didn't already know the answer.

"What? A father can't come to see his son durin' the holidays?" Bobby Joe said, with a sinister grin. "You won't take my calls, so I thought I'd drop in. Wish you a Merry Christmas personally."

He looked around and his eye fell on a ginger-haired bombshell in a silver dress that looked like duct tape wrapped around her generous curves.

"It looks like I came at just the right time," he growled, ambling toward the woman, whose eyes grew large once she saw the direct route he was making her way. "I always did have a weakness for redheads."

Bobby Joe wasn't a bad looking man. Anyone looking at the two of them could see he had contributed to Carter's daring green eyes and full head of wavy blond hair. If the years of alcohol, and God knew what else, hadn't muddled the edges, he would still have it. Now he was just a pathetic loser chasing after one pie in the sky after another.

Carter was the first to reach him, taking three long strides, even as two of his teammates stepped in to block the way.

"I don't think so," he said grabbing the man by the arm.

Carter had also been gifted his height from Bobby Joe, who stood eye to eye with his son. Once upon a time, he might have been able to hold his own, strength-wise, against Carter. Years of Carter playing in the majors had ended that, and now Bobby Joe simply struggled helplessly under the one hand that held him firmly in place.

Bobby Joe gave his son a look that suggested murder. "Don't you put your hands on me, boy! You forget who taught you how to swing that bat?"

Carter said nothing, simply holding him in place.

"Well, since we're getting all intimate, let me show you what your daddy had to go through thanks to his good for nothing, ungrateful son."

Bobby Joe pulled up the sleeve to the arm Carter was holding. A series of what looked like cigarette burns, ten in total, ran up his forearm. It was enough to cause Carter to loosen his grip in surprise. He had known there would be consequences to his inaction, but it was a bit of a shock to see it in person. He could hear a few of the women gasp behind him.

"That's what they called 'getting off lightly,'" Bobby Joe growled. "Only because I assured them that my dear, sweet son would step up to the plate."

"Bobby," Carter sighed. It was time to end this.

"But, *noooo*," Bobby Joe continued. "My ungrateful bastard of a—"

"Enough!" Carter said, getting angry again. It wasn't his fault his dad couldn't keep his nose out of trouble. It certainly wasn't his responsibility to bail him out every time. Not anymore.

He began dragging Bobby Joe back toward the front door. That's when the man took a hard swing at his son, busting his lip wide open. It was enough to shock Carter into letting go. Bobby Joe took the opportunity to pull away in a rage, only to run at his son again, swinging for his face.

Carter backed away quickly enough to avoid the brunt of it, but the knuckle managed to get his nose hard enough to draw more blood. Thankfully there was no indication it was broken. That's when his teammates came running into help out, grabbing the man and holding him back.

His fellow Sluggers held Bobby Joe in place as he struggled. They looked at Carter questioningly waiting for his direction on what to do with him.

Carter strode over and grabbed Bobby Joe by the collar of his shirt and pulled him out of the hands of his teammates, literally dragging him to the front door. His father kicked and screamed the whole way. With one hand, Carter opened the door and dragged Bobby Joe outside.

He did a quick scan of the large circular driveway in front of his house, searching for the car that was most likely tied to the man in his hands. He'd left the front gates open so he wouldn't have to buzz in every attendee. In the sea of Escalades, BMWs, and brand new pick-up trucks, the dirty, beat up, 10-year-old truck wasn't too hard to find.

The only thing saving Bobby Joe from a trip to jail was the fact that Carter was sure the man wasn't drunk. Carter was quite familiar with a drunk Bobby Joe, and there was a distinctly sharp lucidity in the man's eyes that belied having had a sip at all tonight, oddly enough. Perhaps the man wanted to be sober enough to actually remember giving it to Carter the way he had.

Carter could taste the blood on his tongue, and it only served to piss him off. Carter pulled him up by his collar and slammed him against the driver's side of his truck and held him there.

"You listen to me, and you listen good," he growled in his face. "I don't ever want to see your damn face or hear your damn voice again, you hear me? No phone calls, no text messages, no contact whatsoever. We are done!"

Bobby Joe just gave his son a sullen look.

"You got off lucky tonight," Carter continued. "Next time I'll beat your ass to a bloody pulp. Understand?"

Bobby Joe struggled underneath him, pressing his hands into Carter's bloody face to push him away. Carter was more than happy to oblige, twisting away but waiting until the man was actually in his truck. He waited while the man fiddled around inside, looking for his keys or whatever. He wasn't going to go back inside until he was sure the man was gone. Carter jumped back in surprise as Bobby Joe started the ignition and squealed out of the driveway in a hurry.

Carter took a moment to cool off in the chilly morning darkness.

Merry fucking Christmas.

Jordan wound her way around the quiet, wide streets of River
Oaks, carefully following the directions Google Maps had given
her to Carter's place. This would be her first time actually
seeing it.

The Douglas family Christmas and New Year's tradition always
entailed a trip to Shreveport, Louisiana to visit Jordan's grandparents.
Jordan had nearly a month off between semesters and had no problem
spending most of it in Houston.

Especially since a week of it would be with Carter.

By now, both her parents were aware of her long-distance relationship
with him. Even her mother had managed to come around, grudgingly.

She had on a pair of stretch pants, riding boots, and a long, black
cashmere sweater that she had received for Christmas. By the time she
finished the waxing appointment she had scheduled and enjoyed a late
lunch, it was almost 3 o'clock.

When she finally found the right number on the right street, she
stopped and stared for a moment at the sprawling white house set
back behind a wrought iron fence with a line of shrubs hiding it from

view. She pulled up to the gate and pressed the buzzer for the intercom.

As though he'd been waiting for her, Carter answered almost before she could pull her finger away.

"Hey, beautiful, come on in."

She smiled as the gates opened up and she drove her car into the open circular driveway. She turned off the engine and got out of the car. Now that she was behind the wall she had a better view of the house and grounds. Taking it all in she realized that "house" was a major understatement. Estate was more like it, especially since the entire thing could hold two—no, three of the house her parents lived in.

It was a cream colored, classic home with a dark tiled roof. There was a huge balcony overlooking the perfectly manicured lawn in front. The lawn actually looked more like a miniature park, or at least it would when the sculptured shrubs and trees grew their leaves back in.

"Hey there, Juliet," she heard his voice say from above her.

She looked up toward the balcony that had been empty a second ago, and smiled at Carter leaning over the edge.

"I think you have the locations reversed, Romeo," she said, smiling in response.

He just laughed. "Hold on a sec, I'll be right down."

She held on. She held her breath. Then she blew it out her mouth. She took one last long look around at his property, then made her way to the trunk of her car just as he was opening the front door.

"I got that," he said rushing over as she was pulling her suitcase out.

Instead of taking the suitcase he grabbed her around the waist and swung her around in a hug.

"Carter!" she laughed, then wrapped her arms and legs around him.

Carter leaned in to kiss her and she smiled against it.

He pulled away, smiling. "It's good to see you, Jordan."

"It's good to see you too, Carter."

With that, he let her slide to the ground then grabbed her bag, carrying it in with one hand instead of rolling it inside. She shut the trunk of her car and followed him in. The floor of the front foyer was covered in white marble. Her boots tapped noisily against it as she followed him. It opened up into a huge living room. There was a gorgeously large Christmas tree, decorated with white ornaments.

She walked forward a bit and turned around and saw the staircases that rounded down on either side of the entrance. Above her was a huge chandelier. She couldn't believe people actually lived in places like this.

"So, welcome to Casa de Carter," he said, resting her bag by the stairs. "Let me give you the grand tour."

"Should I take my boots off or something?" she asked.

He smiled. "You can take anything you want off."

She hit him on the chest playfully.

"I'm going to take my boots off, and only my boots...for now," she added with a teasing smile. The house was far too nice for her to feel comfortable treading around in them.

As she walked over to one of the couches, she could see the backyard through the windows. It was a larger version of the front, but with a grand pool and hot tub as the centerpiece. To the left was a huge grill area and patio with a seating area.

"The hot tub is ready to go anytime you are Ms. Douglas," Carter said, sliding his body up behind hers and surrounding her with his large arms.

"In winter? It's a bit chilly, no?"

"That's the point," he said laughing. "Plus, I've got something else that can warm you up."

She laughed and turned around in his arms. "I wanna see the rest of this place."

He gave an exaggerated sigh and let her go, taking her hand instead.

Other than the large living room, the first floor housed a large workout room, a small home theater, a large formal dining room, a smaller cozier eating area right off the kitchen, and one room he refused to show her.

"Now I'm really curious," she said with a wicked grin. "What is the notorious Carter Fox hiding in there?"

"Trust me, you don't want to know," he said, trying to pull her away.

"Come on, how bad could it be?" she insisted, keeping her feet firmly planted.

He cringed and grabbed the back of his neck. "Okay, fine. But don't say I didn't warn you."

He reached over and opened the door. Jordan eagerly peeked in...and cringed.

"It looks like—it looks like one of those hotels that—"

"Yeah," he said, grimacing. "I'm going to have to get a decorator in there ASAP."

He reached out and shut the door on her. "Okay, on to the upper floor."

She followed him slowly, pondering what she had just seen. She knew Carter Fox had a reputation but that was weird. There were no chains hanging from the ceiling, or a wall of sex toys, but that was a room that pretty much screamed SEX!

She shook it off as he led her upstairs, one hand holding hers.

"First of all, let me show you where you'll be sleeping," he said, leading her around a walkway that circled the foyer below. He pushed the double doors in and led her to what had to be the master bedroom.

Unlike the travesty downstairs, this one was beautifully decorated in muted, neutral colors. Right in front of them was a large picture window with a balcony looking into the backyard, and a spectacular view of downtown Houston. To the left was a large master bathroom flanked by two huge, walk-in closets with more space than any man should have.

He led her to the right toward the bedroom area. The bed was centrally located in a spacious room with another picture window view of the backyard and downtown Houston to the left and a cozy seating area and fireplace to the right. It was the kind of room that you never wanted to leave.

"It's beautiful," she said in awe. Then she turned to him. "It doesn't seem like you at all," she said laughing.

"Looks can be deceiving," he said with a grin. He walked over to the bed and plopped down on it. "Should we break it in?" he asked.

She swished her hips as she walked over to him. "Now there's the Christmas present I'd been hoping for."

"Well, let me help you unwrap it," he said, furiously pulling his shirt off.

Jordan laughed as she followed, just as eagerly removing her clothes.

❧ 18 ❦

The sex had been fast and furious, as only two people who had gone far too long between sessions could accomplish.

Jordan's body curled up against Carter's and he noted how perfectly she fit: her leg draped over his thigh, her stomach against his hip, her breasts pressed up against his ribs and her head securely in the crook of his shoulder. It was like two pieces of a puzzle sliding right into each other.

"These sheets are so smooth," she murmured. "It's like sleeping on melted butter. I could stay here forever."

Her eyes got drowsy. She was falling asleep against him, apparently worn out by their session. 1020 thread-count, Egyptian cotton could do that to a person. Eventually, he heard the steadied breathing and knew she had escaped into a nap.

He hugged her closer to him, happy to just lie there like that.

"What do you think you're doing?" Carter asked as Jordan slid off the bed and began picking up her sweater.

She had woken up, bright-eyed and bushy-tailed, even though it was now dark outside.

"Getting your Christmas gifts. They're in my bag downstairs."

"Oh no," he said sliding off the bed. "If it means you getting dressed again, I'll be the one to bring your bag up. Besides, I have to get yours from under the tree as well."

"Okay then, mister, get to it!" Jordan said, laughing as she fell back on the bed, naked as everything and making him forget all about those damn presents for a good hot second.

He two-timed it down the stairs, not bothering to get dressed himself. Already he was eager for round two of what they had just done.

There was only one present under the tree. The only family he would be likely to buy presents for usually took off for warmer climates during the holiday season, all expenses paid by her loving son.

He saw Jordan's suitcase by the front door and recalled that he hadn't set the alarm. After completing that task, he grabbed his present and her suitcase and hurriedly carried both upstairs.

He'd had the present wrapped professionally with a thick, white on white, flocked brocade paper. There was a wide, black velvet ribbon tied around each side, meeting right beneath a large bow in the middle which held two silk roses.

"It's beautiful, Carter!" Jordan exclaimed as soon as she saw it. She hadn't got dressed, but she had pulled the sheets up to cover her chest as she leaned against the headboard.

"Well, there's more to it than that," he said, laughing as he sat on the bed near her, handing it over.

She reached over to give him a soft punch, then examined the box again. "I can't rip this open. It's like a work of art."

"Remind me to keep that in mind next year. It'll save me a few bucks."

She gave him a scolding smirk, then carefully removed the roses and untied the bow. It took her almost five minutes of gently peeling the taped paper, all while Carter groaned and moaned, before she finally got to the box underneath.

Inside was a black leather briefcase. As Jordan ran her hand over it with awe, even he had to admit it was impressive looking. It was sleek and sophisticated, with two handles to carry it on the arm. There was an attachable shoulder strap as well. She fingered the gold embellishments and clasp as she opened it.

"I had no idea what to get you so—I just know you want to be a lawyer. I hope you don't mind it being practical instead of romantic."

"This? This is better than any sappy romantic thing," she gushed, then reached over to hug him.

She pulled away and looked at him, beaming.

"Your turn," she said, getting up off the bed and running over to her suitcase.

"I hope *you* don't mind," she said. "I had to wrap my own gifts. Blame my dad, he likes corny wrapping paper."

He smiled as he looked down at the green paper covered in multicolored Christmas stockings. "I'm too curious to be considerate of your wrapping," he said.

She shrugged and waved a hand telling him to have at it.

He ripped the big, store-bought bow off the small flat present and shredded the paper to pieces. He was truly curious. When he got to the white box beneath, he looked up with a grin.

Jordan was biting her lip anxiously as she watched him. He found it oddly endearing.

"I had a star named after you. I figured out too late that it's only symbolic—in fact I think maybe even fraud on the part of the company I bought it from, but the little certificate looks nice. You mentioned you had a telescope in your room so now, when you look up through it, you can pretend it's yours."

She was rambling. It made him smile. The gift made him smile even more. He knew only NASA had the right to officially name stars but the certificate was nice and—more importantly—she'd remembered his love of space. He was genuinely touched and looked over at her with a smile.

"It's terrific," he said.

He placed the certificate carefully on the side table next to the bed so that she would know he actually cared about it. Then he moved on to the next gift. Before he could finish opening it, she was at it again.

"It's the DVD set, *Cosmos*? With Neil deGrasse Tyson. It's supposed to be really good and, well, I thought you'd like it. Although in retrospect you probably already have it. What to get the guy who has everything, huh?" She smiled and shrugged.

He reached a long arm around her head and brought her in for a kiss. "It's perfect," he mumbled into her mouth. He could feel her smile underneath him and he moved in closer.

"So, what now?"

"Well, I do have the perfect gift and a big TV right in front of us to enjoy it with. And I recall you saying something about staying in bed forever, which is fine with me."

Jordan laughed. "Sounds like a plan."

They watched *Cosmos* until they fell asleep again.

The blackout shades were open. The late morning sun that still lingered behind downtown Houston cast a hazy glow through the room as it filtered through the light curtains that were still drawn.

Jordan was facing away from the window, curled in a tiny bundle at Carter's much larger side. As the light permeated the room, the brightness eventually found its way to her eyelids and they squinted tighter, before fluttering open. She did that sleepy morning grimace as she adjusted to waking up, then her eyes found his face looking down at her.

"Morning, sunshine," he said.

She gave a lazy smile in return and reached up to rub her eyes.

"So, that was a nice cozy little night," she said, her smile getting bigger as she snuggled further into him.

"Yeah. Something I could get used to" Carter replied.

Jordan left that one alone for the moment but didn't miss the happy little thrill that went through her.

"What time is it?" Jordan asked.

He reached over to pick up his phone from the nightstand. "A little after 10:30."

"Hmm," she said nodding. She looked up at him with one eye squinted shut. "Hungry?"

The question immediately made his stomach grumble. They hadn't even eaten last night, at least not as far as food went.

"Yeah, I guess I am. So, should we scramble up something?" he asked.

She shifted so her head was lying back on his chest as she looked up at the ceiling. "Actually, scrambling is about the only thing I'm capable of. I'm not the world's greatest cook. It's my one fatal flaw."

"Wait, what?" he exclaimed.

"Sorry," she laughed. "I'd make a terrible wife."

"So we're already having that discussion are we?" he teased,

Jordan's face winced with embarrassment. "You know what I mean."

"Yeah, yeah," he said, hugging her closer playfully. "But, this presents a problem, because I sure as hell don't cook. I suppose we could go out somewhere."

"Hmm, but that would mean getting dressed," she mused, pursing her lips.

"Yeah, scratch that," he said, and she watched his eyes slide down her cleavage as she pressed up against him.

"Perv," she said, twisting his nipple lightly.

"Ow!" he yelped, twitching in response. "So, I think between the two of us, we can manage something...without suffering the torment of you covering those lovely legs of yours."

"Well let's get at it, I'm starving."

"Mind if I borrow a shirt?"

"I insist," he responded.

She ran over to his closet and picked a t-shirt that probably normally clung to his muscles like a second skin. On her it looked like a short nightgown, reaching just past her behind.

"Mmm, I hope you're not wearing anything underneath that," he insisted.

"Oh, maybe," she said raising her hands in a stretch, her arms rising high enough over her head that she easily gave him proof of her strict adherence to that order. She smiled as she leaned against the wall to watch him. "As for you, I wouldn't mind you just the way you are."

"You want me to cook *naked?*"

She looked at him speculatively. "Hmm, you're right. I wouldn't want my favorite part of you out of commission."

"So you admit you're just using me for my body then," he said, stretching out on his massive bed.

"Well, it's such a nice body," she replied walking over and crawling over the covers to straddle him. She walked her fingers up his chest as she smiled down at him. "But no, you have my *temporary* permission to cover your naughty bits."

"On second thought." He reached up and grabbed her around her waist, lifting both himself and her off the bed. She yelped in surprise as he swung her easily around and carried her sideways against his hip out the door and around the walkway to the stairs.

"Put me down!" she screamed, her fists pummeling his lower back and firm behind. She could feel the shirt sliding right up past her ass, giving him quite the view. It was oddly thrilling in a humiliating sort of way. She hoped he couldn't see too much because it was making her wildly wet.

"Keep that up and you'll get a spanking," he warned as she continued to slam her fist against him while he carried her down the stairs.

The thought sent a spasm of pleasure through her.

Spanking, huh? I'll show you, Carter Fox.

She gave him a nice little pinch on his right cheek

"Ouch, woman!" he yelped. He gave her quick, sharp pat on the ass.

Jordan yelped in surprise, but kind of enjoyed the lingering tingle from that first sting.

She gave him another pinch in response.

"Keep it up, Jordan," he warned. "You have no idea how much I love the feel of your ass on my hand," he said as he gave her another little slap.

She wriggled in his arms, knowing exactly what she was doing to him. She'd never been manhandled like this. Of course, she'd never dated anyone as big as Carter. It was embarrassing having her entire lower half completely exposed and on view for his pleasure as he carried her like a sack of potatoes down the stairs.

It was also incredibly erotic.

But she wasn't about to let him get off easy without at least a little bit of putting him firmly back in his place. When he reached the kitchen he finally set her down and she quickly pulled the shirt back past her lower half with a frown on her face.

Just as she was about to go into attack mode, she stopped and stared and laughed.

He followed her eyes to his cock which had reached about 9 o'clock already.

Now, it was his turn to frown. "What the hell is so funny?" he grumbled, crossing his arms over his chest.

Jordan saw his expression and stopped laughing, knowing full well what fragile egos men had when it came to their junk. Still, she couldn't keep the grin from her face.

"I don't know. It's just so in your face, sticking straight out like that. Not that I'm complaining," she said coming closer to him with enticing eyes. "It's very impressive."

She pulled away, remembering her priorities. "Wait a second. I'm supposed to be mad at you." She crossed her arms and gave him an evil look, but couldn't hide the glimpses down toward his "in your face" dick.

"How about you let me make it up to you?" He picked her up to place her on the island.

"Hey!" she yelped. She was silenced as he parted her legs, his rough fingers sliding down her inner thighs.

Oh...this I can tolerate.

"Carter" she breathed, laying back to accept what was about to happen

He grabbed her legs and slid her forward so her ass was right on the edge of the counter. He pressed his face forward and she could feel his hot breath against her wide open wetness. It sent a painful shudder through her body.

He reached his thumb up to stroke the hood of her clit away and reveal the tiny pink button. A gasp and a shudder went through her. She sighed a moan as he circled it with his lips, his tongue darting out to flick and swirl around it.

That's when the doorbell rang.

〜 2 0 〜

Carter was the first to react. He angrily pulled his head away in startled frustration.

What the hell?

He stood up and saw Jordan's rapidly blinking eyes as she quickly pulled his shirt down to cover herself. She sat up looking at him questioningly. All he could do was shrug.

"I have no clue who that could be, but I fully plan on getting rid of them."

Of all the damn times.... Whoever was on the other side of that door was going to regret making a house call this morning. There were only a handful of people who could get past the front gate on their own without him buzzing them in. He reached over to pick Jordan off the counter and set her down, as the doorbell rang again.

He was stomping toward the foyer when she stopped him.

"Carter, you may want to cover yourself first!" she yelled.

He looked down at his hard dick still sticking straight up, though it was rapidly deflating now, and felt frustrated all over again. He was tempted to answer the door anyway, just to give the intruder a good lesson in showing up at people's homes unannounced. He thought of the headlines that would produce and instead sighed and jogged up the stairs to grab a stray pair of jeans to throw on. Jordan came behind him, realizing she was also in no condition to meet guests.

She was rifling through her suitcase and pulled out a pair of panties and skinny jeans to throw on underneath his shirt. The bell rang again. Whoever it was seemed to have no intention of giving up and just going away. He stormed down the stairs, Jordan followed more slowly.

He almost broke the door off of its hinges as he opened it.

"Ma?" he cried in shock as he saw Madison standing there.

She gave him a sweet smile—too sweet. She had a bag from Taco Cabana in one hand.

"What the hell are you doing here?" She was supposed to be in Palm Beach.

"What kind of greeting is that for your mother?" she asked, giving him a frown and walking in right past him. She stopped short when she saw Jordan standing at the bottom of the stairs.

His mother's hand flew dramatically to her chest as she eyed her, then over to her shirtless son. "Oh my, I didn't realize I was interrupting."

"Maybe you should have called first," he retorted.

She spun on him and glared. "Since when does your mother need to call ahead to visit her son?" she asked, putting her free hand on her hip.

"Since when does my mother visit me out of the blue?" he shot right back at her.

"Don't be mean," she frowned. "I come bearing gifts after all," she said, smiling brightly again and lifting up the bag.

She turned her head to glance at Jordan. "Fortunately, I brought plenty of breakfast tacos. I know how much you like to eat."

Jordan coughed a short laugh at that. Carter smirked, recalling the "breakfast" he had been in the process of indulging in before they were so rudely interrupted.

Madison looked back and forth between the two, frowning again. "Well, are you going to introduce me?"

"What are you doing here Ma?" he sighed.

"I'm Jordan Douglas," Jordan said stepping forward with her hand out.

"Madison Grant," his mother said, eyeing her up and down, then giving her son a glare.

"Well, shall we?" she said lifting the bag again.

"What are you doing here?"

"Of course we shall," Jordan said chirpily, giving him a look of disdain.

The woman had no idea what a can of worms she was opening.

"Great, I'll set up in the dining room," Madison said making her way there. "Why don't you get some coffee going."

Not five minutes and she was already giving orders. Jordan took his hand and led him back toward the kitchen. She was most likely under the impression that this was some happy little coincidence. She had no idea what his mother was like.

"Well, I guess we don't have to worry about cooking now," she said smiling at him as he pulled out the coffee maker and filled it with coffee grounds.

"Prepare to have your day ruined, sweetheart."

"She seems nice enough and she even brought food. I don't know why you're complaining."

"You heard that phrase, 'beware of Greeks bearing gifts'?"

"Don't you think you're being a bit dramatic?"

He just sighed as he watched the coffee pot fill up. When it was finished, he reached up and grabbed three coffee mugs to fill up. Jordan looked in the fridge and found the half and half and brought it out. She took one of the mugs as he grabbed the other two and they made their way to the dining room where Madison had already laid out the breakfast tacos, salsa and napkins.

Naturally, she was sitting at the head, so the two of them sat on either side of her. They each grabbed a taco and began unwrapping them.

"So, Jordan Douglas," she said looking up in thought. "You're that woman from the...*incident* with the ball?" Madison gave her son a brief look before turning to inspect Jordan.

Jordan twisted her lips in a smile and nodded. "Yep, I'm the woman from the incident with the ball."

"I had no idea you two had become so...*close*," she said giving her son another look.

"And yet, here we are," he responded.

Carter hadn't bothered to keep his mother up to date on what had developed between Jordan and himself over the course of a semester. The rare visits he had managed to make to Austin had stayed conveniently under her radar. Now he was damn curious as to what had tipped her off.

There was no way this visit was a coincidence.

Carter eyed Jordan. She was slowly beginning to see the light.

"Yes, here you are," Madison mused. "I can't say I approve—"

"There's nothing for you to approve or disapprove of," Carter interrupted, getting heated.

"I'm just thinking of your career."

"Really?" he said. "What exactly does my personal life have to do with—"

"Everything!"

"Don't start, Ma!"

"I should probably go and call my parents," Jordan chimed in, shutting both of them up as they remembered they had an audience. She grabbed her coffee mug and taco and tactfully ran upstairs.

Once she was out of sight, they were at it again.

"Okay, so tell me why you're really here," he demanded.

"When they told you to kiss and make up with her, they didn't mean *literally*," she hissed.

"I don't see the problem."

"You know full well what the problem is," she retorted. "This is Texas, Carter—not New York or LA or *Austin* or wherever this kind of thing flies."

"This is Houston, the 4th largest city in the country," he countered. "I've seen plenty of interracial couples here. For Pete's sake, we had a gay mayor."

"You may think we live in a post-racial society. Just because we have that *Obama* in office doesn't mean everything is a-okay. People are not going to like this."

"People? Or just you?"

"Okay fine," she said crossing her arms. "If you must know, no, I don't like it. I mean thank God she's not one of those—well you know the type."

"What type is that, Ma?"

"The type that likes to trap a man," she snapped. "But just because she's some fancy law student doesn't mean she's not trouble waiting to happen."

"So, is it her race you have a problem with or her intentions? Just so's I'm clear is all," he said trying to control his anger.

"Both," she shrugged. "Sorry if I'm not *politically correct*," she said sarcastically. "I just think people should stick to their own kind. And *you* need to be extra careful no matter what the race."

"Well, ma, as usual, it's been a pleasure," he said rising up. "But I have just this one week with Jordan before she goes back to school, so I'm going to have to ask you to leave."

"You're kicking me out?" she asked with genuine surprise.

"It looks that way. If you're going to continue talking this nonsense."

"It's not nonsense Carter, it's reality. You saw the comments online when this whole thing started. Think what it's going to be like when they find out you two are—well, whatever it is you have going on here."

"Which is my problem and Jordan's problem, not yours. But thanks so much for your concern."

He stopped short. "What made you show up today of all days?" he asked suspiciously.

She blinked at him. "I was just in the neighborhood—"

"Cut the crap, Ma."

"What exactly are you implying?" she asked sharply.

"Okay if you want to make me say it. Are you spying on me?"

Her mouth flew open. "Well, if you're going to accuse me of something like that, maybe I *will* leave."

She grabbed her purse and stood up. Carter offered no protest. She stalked off toward the front door and grabbed the handle. Before opening it, she turned to him. "I never thought I'd see the day my own son—who I pretty much raised, single-handedly—would choose another woman over his own mother."

With that, she opened the door, walked out and slammed it behind her.

Carter ran a frustrated hand through his hair as he breathed out all the fire that had been building inside of him. He had figured this point would come if he continued to date Jordan, but he certainly hadn't expected his mother to be so frank about it—or pick up on it so soon. That was a discussion to be had at some point.

He knew there were people who would take issue with the relationship he had with Jordan. But half the professional ball players in America were in interracial relationships. Granted it was usually a black man and white woman, but still. Why should Carter's be any different? He could certainly *personally* handle any idiot who made the mistake of taking issue with it to his face—or worse, to Jordan's.

He sighed. He wasn't going to let his mother ruin what had started off as such a good day. He headed toward the stairs to go up and get Jordan. He only hoped she hadn't heard any of that.

She was on the bed with the phone to her ear. She looked up when he walked through.

"Okay, Mom, I should go now. Uh-huh...love you too," she smiled at him and rolled her eyes, shaking her head. "Okay...gotta go...bye!"

She hung up and gave a big sigh, falling back on the bed. "Moms, huh?"

"You have no idea," he grumbled.

She sat up on her elbows. "So is yours still here?"

"Nope. The house is all ours again."

"Are we in trouble?" she asked teasingly.

"Only if you want to be," he grinned coming over to the bed and tackling her.

She yelped, laughing in his embrace.

"Speaking of which, you're violating the house rules," she said eyeing his jeans.

"Same goes for you, Ms. Douglas," he said eyeing hers.

With that, they tackled each others' jeans down their legs.

21

That night Carter was inspired.

It was nice having Jordan around the house, especially wearing nothing but one of his shirts. He finally had an inkling of what it might be like living with her and he liked it.

Still, they couldn't spend the entire week lolling around in domestic bliss, as pleasant as it had been so far. He wanted to take her out some place special. Someplace where they wouldn't be pestered by fans and fawning wait staff that completely ignored her. He also wanted to make up for that morning's intrusion. She hadn't said anything about it, so he wasn't sure if she'd heard the worst of it, but she had to have felt the tension in the room.

Jordan was cuddled in one of the comfortable chairs by the fireplace in his bedroom reading one of his favorite books she'd found in his library: *The Right Stuff* by Tom Wolfe, all about the first pilots selected for the space program.

"So, I hope you packed something nice to wear," he said taking a seat in the opposite chair.

Her eyes blinked rapidly as she was brought out of the story that she seemed utterly engrossed with. He could understand; Carter himself had read the book four times already.

She smiled as she registered his words. "Why is that? Are we braving the public again with a date?"

"This time I picked the place," he grinned. "Trust me, no interruptions tonight. Not if this place wants to stay in business."

"Wow, sounds like my kind of date," she smiled, setting the book on her lap.

~

It was a steakhouse with intimate seating and even more intimate lighting. They had a table near the wall in the oak-paneled, dimly lit room. There was a candle on their table which allowed Carter to view Jordan across from him in a sort of hazy, warm glow, which made her look stunning.

She was wearing a red sweater dress, belted at the waist, with black tights and ankle boots. He had enjoyed watching the figure-hugging outfit walk to the table ahead of him.

Now he was looking at her gorgeous face. Her full, sooty eyelashes contrasted against her bronze cheeks as she looked down to butter the warm bread.

She felt him staring at her and looked up, giving him a smile.

There were those brown eyes and dimples. He found himself wondering what their kids would look like. His intense green eyes, or her rich brown eyes? Maybe some interesting amber or hazel mix that fell somewhere in the middle. As long as they had her dimples. His son would be a definite lady killer with dimples like those. And a daughter —Jesus, he didn't even want to think about that.

Kids. Why the hell was he thinking about kids?

Looking at her across from him, watching her do something as ordinary as biting into a piece of bread, Carter knew why.

"So, I've been curious about something and I can't believe I haven't asked before now but, why Babe Ruth?" she asked as she finished her mouthful. "Ben tells me he doesn't even have the record for the most home runs."

"Well, first of all, the man is a legend, from the golden age of baseball, when it was America's sport. I wish I could have played then. Nostalgia has a way of making everything in the past seem better." He looked thoughtfully into the flame of the candle on their table.

He smiled and looked up. "On the other hand, I probably couldn't be sitting here across from you in those days."

She gave a brief laugh and gave a nod of agreement as she took another bite.

"They also played far fewer games per season back then, so he had fewer opportunities to score a home run, which makes his all the more impressive. These days they play you almost every night."

"But you enjoy it don't you?" she prodded.

"Baseball? Oh, hell yeah," he laughed. "I love it. I'll play as long as I can, then maybe be a manager for a team. I think I'd like that. Baseball will be a part of my life forever if I can manage it."

He leaned in toward her. "Now we just have to get you on board."

She smiled as she chewed and shrugged. "I'll have to actually pay attention when Ben's explaining the stats next time."

The waiter came by with their order. Steaks for both of them, his 12 oz and hers 8 oz. He watched with admiration as she eagerly dug into it. Definitely a keeper.

They talked about her life as they ate. He could tell she enjoyed law school but there were parts of it, like her job at the firm, which seemed more like an obligation rather than passion. It bothered him. He knew he was lucky working, and making a ton of money, doing what he loved. Most people couldn't. When Jordan finally realized she belonged with him, he'd make it a point that she only did what she loved.

"So, are we doing dessert or what?" he asked.

"Gosh I'm so full," she gave a guilty grin, "but that Chocolate Ganache cake is literally screaming at me. I know I'll regret it if I don't at least try it."

"Why don't we split it? I can't have you thinking about some chocolate cake you didn't get to try tonight when you're with me." He leaned in over the table and gave her a wicked grin. "Tonight I want you focused only on me."

She gave a bemused smile as the waiter came up right at the end of his sentence.

Carter didn't break eye contact with her and before the waiter could even ask if they would like anything else, he spoke up. "We'll have the Chocolate Ganache cake...and there's double the tip in it for you if you make it speedy."

"Yes sir," the waiter said deferentially, then made a quick getaway to get their dessert.

In less than a few minutes, the two of them were looking down at a decadent slice of rich, dark chocolate placed between them.

Good man, Carter thought.

He picked up his fork and dug in to break off a bite. He brought it up to Jordan's mouth and she smiled as she leaned in to taste it.

"Mmmm," she said sliding her lips off the end of the fork and closing her eyes to enjoy it. That expression was definitely doing things to Carter's cock.

He dipped in to take a bite for himself. It was a delicious cake, that was for sure. Not nearly as delicious as the woman sitting across from him. He watched as her mouth rolled around to enjoy the chocolate in her mouth. By now his dick was so hard, he was most likely going to embarrass himself as he walked out of the place.

Still, no sense in letting it go to waste. The next time the waiter came by, he offered triple the tip if he had the check on their table ASAP.

Two minutes later, Carter was a few hundred dollars poorer, and they were walking out the front door.

He made it back to his place in record time and they were through the front doors like a couple of teenagers trying to beat curfew. They both laughed as he messed up, punching in the wrong code for the alarm the first few tries.

"You better hurry it up," Jordan laughed, poking him in the back. "You seriously need to take care of unleashing that monster between your legs that terrified the entire restaurant as we were leaving."

He finally managed to successfully punch in the code, silencing the annoying beeping sound. Then he turned around to grab her, poking said monster into her stomach. "Are you making fun of me? This monster is about to give you the best orgasm you've ever had."

She looked up with a smile. "I don't know; that chocolate cake will be pretty hard to beat."

"*What* was that?" he growled.

He grabbed her in a bear hug and lifted her off the ground. She gave a surprised yelp, but then laughed and willingly wrapped her legs around his waist. Her arms went around his neck and they kissed passionately as he hurried up the stairs.

He threw her on the bed and scrambled to get his clothes off, peeling off his Paul Smith blazer and tossing it to the floor, like it hadn't cost the $1200 he'd paid for it. He watched Jordan as her body wriggled on the bed, while unwrapping the belt from around her waist.

Good God, if they didn't go at it soon he was liable to explode just watching her undress.

When he finished undressing he made his way over to the nightstand to pull out a condom. By the time he had it open, Jordan was down to her underwear. He excitedly stroked his cock, firming it up for the condom as he watched her unhook her bra and scramble out of her panties. He pulled the condom from his mouth and ripped it open.

Jordan licked her lips as she watched him roll it down the shaft. He reached out and grabbed one slender, perfect foot and dragged her to the edge of the bed. She eagerly moved into position, pulling her knees up on either side of his chest. Carter brought them all the way up to his shoulders. He planned on going in as deep as possible. He wanted to feel every inch of her surrounding his dick.

Jordan was so wet he didn't even have to guide himself in. The head slid between the slippery lips and eventually fell right into the inner depth. Still, he thrust himself forward to completely surround himself with that tight, wet warmth.

"Unh!" she grunted, then bucked her hips up to meet him, wanting all of him inside of her as much as he did.

Everything that had been building up inside of him on the drive over came out with full force as he fucked her, his hips pumping up and down with a powerful force. He felt her nails digging into his shoulders as he aggressively pounded into her.

He pressed forward until her knees were practically at her chest. He could feel her heavy breathing against his face and was certain she could feel his. The whimpering moans that escaped her lips were matched by his primal groans.

There were no words, just grunting and moaning and cries of pure, unadulterated ecstasy. This was the very definition of sex...pure and animalistic. They could be sweet and gentle during round two.

Finally, he felt the tell-tale clinching around his manhood that told him Jordan had reached her peak. It was accompanied by a guttural moan as she arched her back so hard she actually lifted him up with her.

He met her wave by releasing the dam holding his own climax back.

He gave one long deep thrust, going as deep as possible, as he emptied himself into the condom.

He fell limply onto her as he recovered, slowly releasing her legs from his shoulders. He lay there, still inside of her as her legs slid down his sides. He rolled himself off her, feeling his wet cock slide out of her.

The open air hit him immediately. Something wasn't quite right. He looked down with a frown.

What the hell?

The condom was a busted mess around the penis that lay limp against his thigh. A slick coating of cum shimmered in the light of the bedroom amid the ruins of latex. The only thing that was still intact was the top ring, still wrapped uselessly around the middle.

"Oh *shit!*" he uttered jumping off the bed. "Shit, shit, *shit!*"

"What is it?" Jordan asked, perking up at the outburst. Her eyes flicked to the direction his were looking, then grew wide.

"Oh my God!" she gasped.

"*Oh hell, oh hell, oh hell*" he muttered over and over, as a whirlwind of panic blew through his brain. "*Fuck!*" he roared.

Jordan cowered away from him, with worry in her eyes.

"Please tell me you're on the pill," he pleaded.

She looked up at him with what looked like shock. He stared back, waiting for her to say the magic words. Finally, she broke out of her frozen state and gave a stunted nod.

"Y-yes...I am. Of course," she stuttered, still cowering away from him.

He looked at her and realized how upset she probably was as well. They'd discussed STDs at some point during one of their rare in-person dates in Austin but had never quite made the leap to unprotected sex for some reason.

"Hey," he said, calming down a bit, now that it seemed his biggest concern had been dealt with. "I'm sorry."

He made his way back to the bed and was dismayed to see her flinch away from him. Then realized how terrifying it must have been to see someone his size get that upset. He'd make it up to her.

"I know I overreacted just now. It's just that...Jesus," he sat down on the edge, running his hand through his hair with relief, "neither of us is ready for a kid."

"Yeah," she said softly looking down at the covers of the bed.

"Hey," he said, reaching out one finger to lift her chin. Again she flinched and he wanted to kill himself all over again. Now that he knew the coast was most likely clear, he wanted nothing more than to go back five minutes and undo the way he'd reacted.

It had just been the shock of seeing the broken condom. Despite whatever thoughts he'd had over dinner, he was in no way, shape, or form ready to start that right now. He thought back to that morning with his mom. Then, there was his asshole of a sperm donor. Definitely no kind of situation to bring a baby into.

Besides, Jordan wasn't even done with law school. Just because Carter was making money and had a career, well...it just wasn't the time. They weren't even married, for crying out loud!

"Are we okay?" he asked looking at her with focused concern as he gently cupped her cheek.

She nodded under his hand, giving him a reassuring smile.

"Come here," he said, cradling her in his arms. He brought her head down against his chest and began stroking her hair.

"I'm so sorry, Jordan," he soothed. "I know I scared you, and I'd give anything to take that back. I—God, you're the only sane thing in my life right now, the *best* thing, and I don't want to lose you because I was stupid."

He felt her relax a bit in his arms. That was a good sign. He'd hold her like this until she was back to being his again.

"Can you imagine us with a baby?" he asked, giving a slight chuckle.

She gave a soft laugh against his chest. "Crazy, huh?" she said.

He held on to her, never wanting to let her go. At some point, he felt her begin to squirm.

"I have to pee," she said.

It reminded him that both of them were still covered in his semen.

"Of course," he said letting her go.

He watched her escape quickly into the bathroom. He sighed and followed her, heading toward the sinks. He grabbed a washcloth and ran it under the sink. He looked at himself in the mirror as he washed himself up. His eyes ran over his large, muscular body, covered in tattoos. No wonder she had been terrified.

He heard the toilet flush and she stepped out, blinking rapidly as she saw him at the sink. She slowly approached the space next to his to wash her hands. He looked at her naked body, tiny in comparison to his and felt like a monster.

When she was done, he reached out again. He brought her into his chest and stroked her hair.

"Let's go back to bed, okay?"

He felt her nod against him.

He walked the both of them back to the bed.

22

J ordan felt him fall asleep underneath her, then she shifted her body to stare at the ceiling.

There would be no sleep tonight.

Birth control pills.

She gave a silent, crazed laugh at the lie she'd so easily told. He had just been so *upset*. It terrified her to think what his reaction would have been if she had said no. So she'd told him what he wanted to hear.

She didn't think he'd actually hurt her. She had just wanted it to stop. The panic. The yelling. The cursing. The craziness.

She'd been on birth control pills in college. It had been horrible: the acne, the weird hormonal issues, the headaches. After realizing that law school would be an exercise in celibacy, she'd gone off them. After all, there were still condoms, which she and Carter had used during the handful of times he'd come out to see her. She'd thought briefly about going back on them before this week, but it didn't seem worth it for just the one week, especially since he hadn't complained about the condoms.

Maybe she had nothing to worry about. What were the chances that this one tiny little mishap would result in a baby?

It was morning and she was still staring at the ceiling, having not slept a wink. She felt Carter stirring underneath her. She was both relieved and scared. Relieved that he would be awake to comfort her again. Scared that she might give herself away.

She needed to get out of here. There was no way she'd last the week, looking him in the eye every day, not knowing if she was actually pregnant with his child or not. How long did you have to wait before you could do a pregnancy test anyway? She was almost certain it wasn't the very next day...was it?

No, she'd make up an excuse and go back to Austin.

"Hey, what's up?" she heard Carter's sleepy voice say.

It shocked her into paralysis. She let out a deep breath and tried to calm herself. Time to put on a poker face.

"Nothing," she said a small laugh coming to her lips. She stopped it before it became too hysterical. "I'm just cold."

"Well let's take care of that," he murmured, using his arm to curl her back into his chest and hold her under the covers. It felt wonderful, warm, and comforting.

It felt like a lie.

"So what are we gonna do about breakfast today? I think we might be stuck cooking. Frankly, I prefer it to yesterday's little family gathering," he laughed.

She joined with him, even though her heart wasn't in it.

His mother. There was another little tickle. *She* certainly wouldn't be happy about this.

She sat up and looked down at him, a bright smile masking the turmoil inside of her. "I'm famished, so let's dig something up."

He smiled up at her and shrugged, pulling himself out of bed. "Sounds good to me."

She snuck a look at the time on the phone. 9 o'clock. Too early to get an "emergency" call from someone at school about anything. She'd wait until after breakfast. Then she could at least have one last meal with Carter. She would miss him, but there was no way she could keep this up the rest of the week.

As they made their way downstairs, she tried to calm herself down at least enough to get through breakfast.

She was fine. Everything was fine. She'd go back to Austin. In two weeks her period would come. She'd laugh it off, breathe a sigh of relief, maybe go through a brief bout of disappointment at having left Houston so soon, then come back after graduation and the two of them could pick up right where they'd left off.

They were in the kitchen making scrambled eggs, the one thing Jordan could make with some proficiency. As she whipped the eggs and milk with a beater she actually felt a little better. She felt fine. Perfectly normal. No weird tingles or sensitivity or pain.

Of course, she wasn't pregnant.

She didn't bother to dwell on the fact that it was far too early to have any signs.

She poured the eggs into the buttered pan that was heating on the stove while Carter scooped coffee grounds into the pot.

"So what shall we do today, Ms. Douglas?" he asked looking over at her.

She hadn't thought about plans with him for today, having already made her alternate ones.

"Um, I don't know, you decide." She said shrugging as she began using a spatula to scramble the eggs in the pan.

"I have an idea," he said enthusiastically. "Let's visit the Museum of Natural Science. The IMAX there is showing a film on space. I've been wanting to see it for a while. It would be perfect with you there."

She smiled into the pan, scrambling away. It did sound nice, and he sounded so excited about it. It made her feel guilty and sad. Maybe leaving could wait....

No, she definitely needed to go. Time to think. Time to herself.

Time to find out the truth.

"Sounds nice," she said. She looked over at him with a bright smile. "It should be interesting."

He gave her a big grin and nodded, looking over as the coffee pot announced it was done. He pulled down two mugs and poured them each a cup as she finished up the eggs. She turned off the stove and scraped most of the pan into one plate and the rest into another. She was far too anxious to eat much.

They sat in the little kitchenette area overlooking the backyard. She stared out at the pool as she forked a little at a time into her mouth.

"Not hungry?" he asked, looking down at her half eaten plate.

"Still full from last night I guess," she said, shrugging with a smile.

She couldn't do this. Pretend everything was A-Okay when it wasn't. Once she was certain this had been nothing more than a stupid scare, she could come back to him.

"Hey, I'm going to go check my messages. I haven't since yesterday," she said, popping up.

He gave her a confused smile and shrugged, taking another bite of his eggs. "The eggs are great by the way," he said.

"Thanks," she responded as she walked quickly out of the kitchen and up the stairs.

Once in the bedroom, she fell against the door taking a moment to breathe. She waited long enough to make it seem like she had checked her messages, then she headed back downstairs.

Carter was finishing up his eggs and looked up questioningly. He saw the look on her face and frowned.

"I'm sorry Carter," she said. "There's a minor emergency with law review and it looks like I have to head back early to put out a few fires before school starts."

The frown turned into a look of disbelief. "What the hell?" he asked incredulously. "Can't it wait? We've only had two days here."

She had expected this and was prepared. "I wish it could, but if I don't handle this now, it's going to be an even bigger mess when I get back next week, and that would just interfere with school, so—"

"There's no one in Austin who can deal with this? Why does it have to be you?"

"Because I'm the Managing Editor," she responded testily.

"And you can't do it over the phone or by email or something?"

She shook her head. "No, you don't understand what goes into—"

"I understand someone is trying to lay all their mess on you and you're just letting them."

She was beginning to get angry now. "That's not fair. My position is important with a lot of responsibilities, and sometimes that means canceling plans. I'm sorry we have to cut our week short, but you know how important law school is to me."

"More important than me?"

"Are you seriously trying to make me choose?" she protested

"I guess I am," he said standing up. "I'm not asking you to drop out of school here, Jordan. I'm asking you to do a little compromising. Let someone else put out the fires for once. Does it really have to be you?"

She just stared at him, unsure of how to respond.

"I thought not. So *stay*, Jordan," he urged. "I have an idea there are ten people in Austin who could handle this, without you having to drive three hours back to fix it."

She finally found her voice. "What if I told *you* to stay? Skip a game? Do it over the phone or by email? How would you respond?"

He sighed. "That's different, Jordan."

"Why? Because you make millions of dollars a year? Because you have a gazillion fans cheering you on? Because you're famous? Don't belittle *my* responsibilities just because you want someone to *screw* all week long."

She hated herself the moment it came out, but her head was too filled with panic, and anger, and weariness, and God knew what else, to speak to him with anything even resembling calm rationality.

His expression was a mixture of shock and confusion. "That's not why I want you to stay and you know it."

She couldn't let him lull her into staying. "I'm sorry, Carter. I didn't mean that. But I do have to go," she said firmly.

She fled out of the kitchen and up the stairs before he could say anything else.

"Jordan!" he yelled after her. She could hear him following her up the stairs.

She slammed the doors to the bedroom after her and went to her suitcase. She stuffed the clothes from last night angrily into the bag just as he banged the doors open. She flinched at the sound and worked even faster to pack.

"Jordan, stop!" he pleaded. "Will you just talk to me?"

"Carter I just—I have to go!" she insisted.

He stared at her for a moment and she could see the confusion and pain and anger in his eyes.

She almost told him...almost. Then she remembered his reaction last night and her determination came back.

"Goodbye Carter," she said.

He stared at her. "So that's it, then?"

She paused before answering. "Yes."

"Goodbye then, Jordan," he responded, turning to look out the window as she left.

23

She was thirty miles outside of Houston, driving on pure adrenaline when everything hit her at once: the hyperventilating; the death grip she had on the steering wheel; the dizzy fog through which the road in front of her appeared. In a panic, she got off the highway and pulled into the nearest parking lot and turned off the engine.

She gripped the steering wheel so hard that her hands hurt.

That was good. Pain was good. It erased the panic.

Panic.

That wasn't good.

Breathe.

Breathe!

Breathe dammit!

She let out a loud, ear-piercing scream.

Then the tears came. Rivers of salty streams ran down her face. Uncontrollable sobbing erupted from her mouth. She brought her head against the steering wheel, nose running, eyes blurry, mouth hiccuping uncontrollably. She let it flow. There was no one here to see her. No one to witness her lose control. No one to see her fail.

No Carter.

No mom.

No dad.

No classmates.

No employers.

No one.

No Carter.

Why had she felt so conflicted hearing his words? Law school was her life. It was her future.

Compromise. That's what he had said. Compromise. How could she compromise when she'd spent so long focused on the ultimate prize? There was no such thing as compromise in her vocabulary. It was why she was top 10% in her class. It was why she had been offered a position at one of the top firms in Houston. It was why everyone was so proud of her.

Even the *slightest* chance that she was possibly....

Panic.

Breathe!

The exhales came harder and faster, and the turmoil built until—

She quickly opened the car door, jumped out and bent over to vomit, going until there was nothing left but dry heaving. She stayed there, hands on her knees, staring at the result of everything that had happened in the last 24 hours.

How the hell had her life gotten so turned upside down?

~

Once she was calm enough to drive without losing it, she started up the car and made the rest of the trip back to Austin, music turned up uncomfortably loud to drown out the crazed thoughts running through her head.

She was exhausted by the time she rolled her suitcase up the stairs and down the walkway to the apartment she shared with April. She barely had enough strength to put the key in the hole and turn the knob.

She was met once again with April and Matt going at it, this time on the couch. This time, early enough in the coitus stage for them to be only *half* naked. April was straddling a boxer-clad Matt while in nothing but a bra and underwear.

She was too tired to be startled. Instead, she was just angry. All she wanted to do was fall into bed and sleep away all her fears, and now this.

"Oh, for Pete's sake!" She exclaimed with exasperation. "You *do* have a bedroom. Have you ever tried, you know, *using* it!"

They both stared at her in shock, completely unused to a Jordan who was this mean and spiteful. Matt just scrambled from underneath April, while she stood up to confront her roommate, hands on hips, totally unconcerned with her state of undress.

"And you aren't supposed to be back until next week!" she exclaimed. "I'm beginning to wonder if you actually enjoy catching me and Matt going at it."

"Well maybe if you didn't feel the need to screw everywhere but your bedroom, I wouldn't 'catch you at it'" Jordan retorted.

Matt slowly and wisely made his way to the bathroom.

"Why are back so early anyway? Did Carter Fox finally dump you?" April spat.

Jordan stared at her with shock. She could see the immediate regret in her roommate's face at what she'd just said, but she didn't give her a chance to apologize. She angrily rolled her suitcase back toward her room and slammed the door behind her.

She had no idea what had caused such an outburst. Perhaps it had been catching April about to go at it, so carefree. April who was smart enough to be on the pill. April, who would probably never have a pregnancy scare.

Jordan had done Every. Damn. Thing. Right. She'd followed all the rules, worked her ass off. And finally, *finally* when it was all starting to fall into place....

She thought of that annoying proverb: We plan, God laughs.

Jordan certainly wasn't laughing.

～

It was an hour later when she heard the knock on her door. She sighed. At some point, they would have to kiss and make up. Better sooner than later.

"Yeah," she called out.

April walked in with two beers.

"Peace offering?" she asked, raising them up.

Jordan gave out a short laugh at the irony, as she sat up from the bed. April took it as a sign of goodwill and strode over to sit on the edge of her bed. She handed Jordan one of the bottles and Jordan shook her head no.

"Thanks, I'm not in the mood."

April gave her a strange look then shrugged. "More for me," she said taking a swig out of one bottle and placing the other on Jordan's bedside table.

"So what's up?" she asked, "I thought this was supposed to be the

Week de la Carter Fox? Did he fuck with you? Am I going to have to drive to Houston and kick his ass?"

Jordan smiled and shook her head. "Nothing like that. It just...it got complicated."

"Complicated good, or complicated bad?"

Jordan gave her a bewildered look. "What in the world is 'complicated good?'"

April gave her a conspiratorial smile. "Was he getting too serious for you?"

Jordan blinked at her, not responding.

"Oh come on Jordan," she said with a sigh. "You put law school above everything! Then Carter Fox of all people wants to spend a week with you, and for some reason, you come running back early. Did he mess with your little plans on being Houston's number one corporate attorney?"

Jordan shook her head and fell back against the headboard. Was she really that bad? April was pretty much mimicking what Carter had said, and *she'd* known Jordan for two years.

"It's complicated, *complicated*." Jordan said, not wanting to expound.

"I'll take that as a yes," April said taking another swig.

Jordan shot her an annoyed look.

"What in the world is our little Jordan going to do when she finally graduates and starts that job? Conquer Mount Everest? Run for President of the United States? First astronaut to Mars?"

That made Jordan think of Carter and his love of space. She didn't want to think of Carter. She looked longingly at the beer.

Surely she wasn't pregnant. She couldn't be. Not after one time. One time where she wasn't even trying. One time with a stupid broken condom. One time where *maybe* only a tiny portion of semen actually made it to home base.

There were women who tried for years to get pregnant. Women who planned and calculated their cycles, so they had sex at the optimum time to get pregnant. Women who couldn't get pregnant at all.

Why should she be the "lucky" one to get knocked up over a stupid mistake? Heck, it wasn't even a mistake, they had done everything right!

No, she couldn't possibly be pregnant.

❧ 24 ❧

Carter had no idea what had happened that morning. He had thought they were fine. She was making eggs, he was making coffee. They were fine.

Then they weren't.

It had started last night, right after the accident. Carter couldn't blame Jordan for being put off by his reaction. He had just been so damn panicked!

Rule number one for all professional athletes: protect your man juice. So many women out there used it as the perfect way to get you for the next 18 years. Carter had certainly had his fair share of women try it on him. After he'd caught the first woman retrieving a used condom out of the trash can on her way out, he'd switched to flushing them down the toilet.

When he'd seen that broken condom his mind had just snapped. He hadn't thought about Jordan, and how he had only hours before, been thinking about having kids with her. He'd just panicked.

He remembered the terrified look on her face as he'd gone on. It filled him with bitter regret. She had probably been just as scared shitless as he was—and if the worst happened, she'd be the one taking the brunt of it: getting pregnant, giving birth, raising a kid. Technically, all Carter would have to do was sign a check each month.

That thought put a bad taste in his mouth.

Obviously, if Jordan was pregnant he'd want to do more than sign a damn check. He would want to be a part of the kid's life. He sure as hell wasn't going to be like his own father. Now that the panic was over, now that the coast was clear, he had time to think about it. Even though he wasn't even remotely ready to be a father, even though he'd only known her for a short while, if there was anyone he had to have an unexpected baby with it was Jordan.

But she was on the pill, so the coast was clear as far as that went, right? They weren't 100% effective but pretty damn close from what he understood. A tiny, primal part of him was almost disappointed. He thought of Jordan pregnant with his baby. An animalistic pride ran through him. There was no one who could hurt or touch her—not when she was the mother of his child.

But Carter had been the one to hurt her. First, by terrifying her when she was probably at her most scared and vulnerable, then by attacking her with the one thing she was most proud about. Carter understood full well how much her accomplishments meant, that she had worked hard in law school and was ambitious. He just didn't understand how she could put that above what he thought the two of them were starting to have with one another.

If anything, this week had started to reveal that she was the one for him. He had an idea that she was going down that same path. Then bam, law school comes calling and she drops everything and runs off.

Would this be what it's like if they got married? Her putting her career above him? Above their kids? On the other hand, Carter had a grueling career as well, one that had him on the road half the year, but he would have dropped everything if she asked...if it came to family.

None of that mattered now. She was gone. He would give her time to cool off, then work on getting her back. He certainly wasn't giving up this easily.

It had been a miserable rest of the week. He'd found the present he'd purchased for her still in the bedroom. Obviously, in her hurry to get out, she'd overlooked it. Or maybe she'd purposefully left it behind?

He'd waited a day to call. She hadn't answered. She wouldn't respond to his texts. She wouldn't call or text him. She had completely shut him out.

Were things really that bad between them?

The fight they'd had in the kitchen didn't seem like something that they couldn't overcome. Maybe he should just drive out and face her in person. He had an idea that she would hate that.

He was irritable and frustrated with no outlet for his angst. The funny thing was, Jordan would be the one he'd pick up the phone and talk to about it under any other circumstance. There was no one else.

His teammates just wouldn't get it. Heck, they'd probably laugh at how whipped he was.

His manager, Miles, was great when it came to coaching baseball and even offering good life advice, but Carter wasn't sure he wanted to unload a bunch of relationship shit on the man.

His mother? That was a laugh. She'd probably be relieved.

He didn't even think about Bobby Joe.

No one.

Jesus, the thought was depressing.

25

S he had been living in denial.

Carter had called and texted. Of *course,* he had called and texted.

She'd been avoiding his phone calls and texts, not wanting to deal with him without knowing for sure. Could they go back to where they were? Would he even want to after she'd ignored him for so long? Would their lives be completely changed forever? She hadn't wanted to think about it. So she'd ignored him. Eventually, he had taken the hint.

And Jordan had waited.

She'd delayed confronting it. Jordan Douglas, who planned her life to a T. Jordan Douglas, who dealt swiftly and deftly with anything that got in the way of her goals. Jordan Douglas, who had given up a good man —a wonderful man—because she couldn't face the truth.

Jordan Douglas, who had dropped the ball.

She'd gone on too long, living on a hope and a prayer. Because fate couldn't possibly be that cruel. It wouldn't come along like a thief in the night and completely and totally blindside her and all her carefully laid plans...would it?

But now her period refused to come.

She had at first gone through a litany of ridiculous excuses for it. Maybe being sexually active after such a long dry spell had somehow messed with her hormones and caused her cycle to be re-wired. Maybe the stress of worrying had screwed things up down there. Maybe she was going through *really* early menopause.

Then the second day had passed. Nothing.

Now, it was officially two weeks after "the incident," and she was standing in a CVS drugstore staring at way too many options for pregnancy tests.

The incident.

She was laughing hysterically inside. "The incident" was what had indirectly led to this mess in the first place. Said "incident" being that damn ball. Once again she found herself wondering what her life would be like if she'd simply held her glove a bit lower, or higher. She could actually picture the ball falling onto the steps of the stadium, bouncing down to the crowd of hopefuls below her, and her, returning to her seat, giving a *mea culpa* shrug to Ben as she grabbed her hot dog and finished watching the end of the game.

But now she was standing in the middle of a CVS looking at pregnancy tests.

She picked up one. A plus sign. She didn't like that. Plus signs were good...hopeful. She didn't want hopeful. This was *not* a hopeful situation. She put it back.

She picked up another. It was generic, cheaper. After all, she had student loans to think about. And if it was indeed positive, she'd need all the money she could save. Diapers were expensive. She felt her breath coming in faster. Formula was expensive. She'd read somewhere that it cost almost $20,000 just for a baby to be born. That was almost as much as a semester of law school. *Breathe.*

On the other hand, did she really want to trust her entire future to a generic pregnancy test? *Breathe!*

She put it back.

This one. Two blue lines. That was good. Straightforward. Not hopeful. Not reproachful. Just one line or two. Basic math. One. Two.

One.

Two.

Breathe!

Good God, she was going to faint in the middle of CVS with a damn pregnancy test in her hand.

She put it back.

Breathe!

Come on girl.

She wanted to walk right out. Put it off for just a little while longer. School had started. She had cases to brief. She had an issue of the law review to put to bed. She had a class rank to maintain.

Pregnancy was not part of the plan.

Breathe!

She breathed. She grabbed it. The blue lines. That was good. Not hopeful. Not reproachful. Neutral. One. Two. No. Yes.

She marched it up to the cashier. No eye contact. Cash payment. Out the door. Into the car. Back to her apartment.

One. Two.

No. Yes.

~

She sat on her bed staring at it. April was in the living room, obliviously reading a casebook with her headphones on. Oh, how Jordan envied her.

It sat on the bed across from her like some nemesis. James Bond and Dr. No. Superman and Lex Luther. Holmes and Moriarty.

Mother and child.

She choked back a sob.

Don't go there, Jordan.

She didn't even have to pee! It was like life was taunting her all the more. She rushed out to the kitchen to fill a tall glass with water, chugging it down, then refilling it and chugging it all over again. She stared at April on the couch, completely unaware of the aura of chaos that was going on around her.

Then she felt it. She needed to go. Badly.

She ripped open the box. Christ, why hadn't she read the instructions before gulping down so much water! She rapidly ran through the instructions.

...Hold in stream...

...Tip pointed down...

...Wait three minutes...

Three minutes?!

Three minutes to find out if her life was ruined? It seemed unnecessarily mocking. On the other hand, hadn't she waited two whole weeks hoping and praying it wouldn't have to come to this?

Three more minutes wouldn't matter.

Her bladder was giving her no choice. She ran to the bathroom and read the directions on the box *extremely* carefully.

Then she waited.

Shit! Her phone was in her bedroom. She looked at the time as she raced back to the bathroom. 4:43. Okay 4:46. That's when she'd know for sure. Three minutes.

At exactly 4:46 p.m. her life could be changed forever. It was such an arbitrary time.

4:44

4:45

4:46

Maybe wait one more minute just in case.

4:47

She picked up the stick.

One.

Breathe.

Two.

Oh no.

Breathe!

Oh no, no, no.

Breathe dammit!

Breathe breathe breathe breathe breathe breathe breathe breathe breathe breathe!

She became aware she was hyperventilating.

She threw open the door and ran out to the living room where April was still studying. She looked up in surprise at Jordan racing toward her like a maniac.

April pulled the earbud out of one ear and gave Jordan a startled look. That's when she noticed the rapid rise and fall of her roommate's chest. She threw her casebook on the sofa, pulled the second earbud out and rushed to her.

"What's wrong, chica?" she asked, looking her in the face with concern.

Breathe breathe breathe breathe breathe breathe breathe breathe breathe breathe!

"Okay, okay," April said calmly, catching on. "Calm down. Breathe. *Breathe.*"

Breathe breathe breathe breathe breathe breathe breathe breathe breathe breathe!

"Just calm down," she coaxed. "What's going on?"

That's when April looked down and saw the stick.

"*Oh,*" she said looking at it. Then she looked closer. "Oh...*oh!*"

Not helping.

Breathe breathe breathe!

April realized she was making things worse and tried bringing Jordan back down again.

She mimed a calming breath, her hand waving in front of her chest with a flair.

"Whooo, Whoooo" She breathed, deep and slow, trying to get Jordan to follow her lead.

It was calming. Kind of what they might teach in lamaze class.

Not helping.

Breathe breathe breathe!

"Okay, just sit tight," April said, leading her to the couch as she ran into the kitchen.

Jordan could feel herself getting panicky and faint at the same time. Why couldn't she stop breathing so heavily?!

April came back with a plastic grocery bag.

"Breath into this," she said, placing it over Jordan's mouth.

Jordan watched the white plastic inflate and deflate, in front of her face. Her breathing slowed down. She felt herself relaxing. This was helping. Having April next to her, rubbing her back was helping. Slowly but surely, her breathing became regular.

Eventually, she was calm enough to remove the plastic bag. April sat next to her on the couch, looking at her with some serious concern on her face.

"Please, just don't ask," sighed Jordan, wanting to avoid the obvious question that they both already knew the answer to.

April just nodded, rubbing her back some more.

They sat there like that for a while until Jordan couldn't take it anymore. She had to spill the beans to someone. Obviously, it couldn't be her parents...yet. Obviously, it couldn't be Carter...yet.

"Okay, yes, it's Carter Fox's" she said. It felt good to let it out. Of course, it would have felt better to not have to say it at all, but now that it was out there she could deal with it.

"Hmm," April said, nodding. She waited a minute. "So...what are you going to do?"

Jordan gave a sharp laugh. "I have no friggen clue. I mean, I just found out!"

There was another moment of silence.

"I mean, I know I have to tell him," she said, sighing.

"How do you think he'll take it?" April asked curiously.

"I don't know," Jordan said frowning. "I mean he was just so...crazed when the condom broke. Like it's the last thing in the world he wanted.

"I mean, I get it." She turned to look at her roommate, getting heated. "Does he think *I* want a baby? I'm still in school for crying out loud. I'll be out to here"—she brought her hands out in front of her in a wide arc—"by the time I start at *Morris*. Pregnant and unwed." She started laughing.

"Then, after only a few months, I'll have to take time off to actually give birth. 'Oh hey, thanks for hiring me, sorry I have to take three months maternity leave...for a baby I didn't plan for...by a guy I'm not married to...a guy who's totally out of the picture.' "

"You don't know that," April said. "Maybe he'll step up to the plate."

"Yeah," Jordan said, staring at the wall in front of them. "A nice fat check every month." She gave a wry laugh. "I guess if I have to get knocked up, there are worse people in the world to have as a baby daddy."

"So...you're going to keep it?"

Jordan blinked. She'd been so focused on her current state she hadn't thought of her options. Of course, they weren't just *her* options. She couldn't do anything until she told him, but that was a conversation she wanted to put off. At least until she'd had time to process everything.

She shrugged. "I don't know. I have to tell him first. That's only fair."

April nodded again and resumed rubbing her back. "So when are you going to tell him?"

Jordan stared at the wall. "I don't know."

26

F inally, Carter had something to take his mind off Jordan Douglas.
Baseball.

It was late February and spring training had officially begun. The Sluggers were in the Grapefruit League, which meant he was headed over to Florida for the next month and a half. Tropical weather, beaches or lakes within driving distance, hot girls in bikinis even at this time of year. Normally, Carter would have eaten it up.

They were playing the Baltimore Orioles in Sarasota. Right on the beach. Last year this time he had been scoping out honeys in the stands who were a little too enthusiastic to simply have a love of the game. This year all he could do was compare them to Jordan.

He shook that thought off. For the life of him, he couldn't understand why she hadn't at least called or texted. He didn't want to think it was over between them, at least not without a formal goodbye. In fact, he *refused* to think it was over between them. When he got back to Houston, he would work on getting her back.

And he had every intention of getting her back.

For now, he'd let her have her law review duties and final exams.

For now, he would focus on his second love: baseball.

Truth be told he loved spring training better than the regular season. The pressure was off. No pennant to vie for yet, no in-division ranking to keep an eye on with anxious determination. Just pure baseball. He got a chance to nostalgically appreciate fresh blood trying to move out of the minors and into the majors. He could sympathize with their ambition.

Yes, a month away from Houston, from Texas, from Jordan, was just what he needed.

~

He had caved.

A few team members had booked a hotel room at the Ritz. Obviously, they had invited the Sluggers' famous home run hitter to join in the fun. It certainly helped entice the clique of New College of Florida coeds to join them for some after-game fun. After all, the Sluggers had won 4-2 against the Orioles today.

What better way to put Jordan out of his mind than loud music, free flowing booze, and distracting eye-candy? Carter had immediately been on board.

Now that he was there, the reality was far less appealing. In fact, it was damn depressing.

Carter sat in an armchair in the suite watching his younger, less inhibited, teammates play the mating game with a few girls who were just barely old enough to drink.

Right now, a size-2 brunette was making her way over to him. He was surprised to find himself eyeing that postage-stamped sized skirt and white halter top with concern rather than lust. How the hell old was she?

"So," she slurred, sitting on the arm of his chair, one hand holding a Heineken. "You're the big shot home run hitter, huh?"

He gave a perfunctory smile. What little there was of the skirt slid high enough up her thigh to give Carter a tiny peek of the hot-pink, lacy thing standing between her and the big bad wolves of the world.

"Yeah," he muttered. "How old are you?"

In the past, such a question would have been nothing more than a precaution. No sense in getting into trouble when you didn't need to. Now, he was honestly curious. He looked at the barely-there clothing, the facial features that still harkened back to teenaged innocence—and it bothered him. A *lot*.

"Twenty-one," she said with a smile and a wink, "Just turned legal one month ago!" She held her bottle of beer up in the air in salute.

It did nothing to quell the instinctive, paternal reaction that ran through him.

She leaned in and gave him a wicked grin that could only be read one way. "Wanna go back to the bedroom?" she purred. "I give the *abso-fuckin-loutely* best head *ever*."

Carter flinched at the boldness of it, still feeling rather fatherly—and just where the hell had *that* come from? The entire declaration had made his dick practically shrink back into his groin.

This was someone's daughter and here she was offering head to a man simply because he had the ability to hit a few home runs.

"I have a better idea," he suggested. "Why don't we take this to the balcony?"

Her smile indicated that she had a totally different interpretation of that suggestion than he had intended. All the same, if it kept her occupied until she could dry up—in every sense of the word—he figured it was worthwhile.

He took her elbow and led her out onto the narrow ledge, closing the sliding glass door behind them. His plan had been to enjoy the view, maybe talk for a bit as she sobered up and re-evaluated her life choices.

"So, what are you majoring in?" he asked, attempting to start off on an innocuous topic.

"You don't have to small talk me to get me on my knees," she purred with a smile. She came up close to him. "I've heard all about *you,* Carter Fox."

Before he realized what was going on she reached out and grabbed the crotch of his jeans. "Ohh!" she exclaimed, her eyes getting brighter. "Hellooo, *daddy.* It looks like the rumors are true."

Daddy?

Was he really that old? Looking at the fresh—if slightly sluggish with beer—face below him, he certainly felt old.

"Whoa, whoa, whoa, there darlin'," he said, quickly grabbing her hand and removing it. He used the other to gently push her away.

The beer delayed the reaction, but it came soon enough. Confusion. Hurt. Anger.

"You don't think I'm pretty?"

That look on her face almost killed him. An icy hot dagger of guilt went through his heart as he remembered all the women in his past who had probably also based their self-worth on whether or not their lips were wrapped around his cock.

"No," he began. Her face crumpled. "I mean of course you're pretty—"

"Then what?" she said, getting angry. "What's the matter with you? Do you know how many guys would jump at this opportunity?"

This was getting out of hand. "Listen, why don't we just sit and talk."

"Talk?" she spat back at him. "I didn't come to this party to *talk.*"

She headed back toward the sliding glass door. With one last look over her shoulder, she sneered, "seriously, what the hell is the matter with you?"

He sat down on one of the chairs and looked out at the water. He didn't have to ask himself the same question. He knew what was the matter with him. The only problem was, he hadn't called her in a long time.

He should probably do something about that.

❧ 27 ❧

"So this is the big reveal, huh?"

"Maybe we can use something other than 'big'," Jordan grumbled, "or reveal."

She looked down at her belly. According to her *extremely* accurate calculations, she was now a little over 10 weeks along. There was no actual bump, but boy was her body letting her know something was up. The sensitive breasts, the constant feeling of being bloated. She was also starting to get this weird thing for strawberry milk.

She'd had no morning sickness other than some mild nausea in the morning. She wasn't sure if she could handle throwing up her breakfast every morning and then heading off to class.

She mentally thanked her/him for that one. Small blessings.

"How do you think they'll take to being surprise grandparents?"

Jordan sighed. "Only one way to find out!"

She had decided to keep the baby. Once the initial panic of finding out had died down, she actually had time to think it over and discovered there was no reason not to...with or without Carter.

She would be out of law school by the time the baby was born and even past taking the Texas Bar. She had a well-paying, if extremely demanding job already lined up for her. She had always planned on having kids anyway. She even had grandparents living in the same city to maybe help her out every once in a while.

But first, she had to tell them.

She'd waited until Spring Break because she wanted to tell them in person. They deserved that much.

Frankly, she would be relieved to finally have it out there. April had been great, but she was just as clueless as Jordan when it came to what was coming down the line. Pregnancy? Birth? Afterwards?

April looked at her with wide-eyed empathy. Then she surprised Jordan by running over and hugging her. "Good luck, chica," she said. "Call if you need to."

It was a move that almost brought Jordan to tears, or maybe it was just the crazy hormones. They had been friendly roommates these past two years, in an Odd Couple sort of way. But April had completely stepped up to the plate since being the accidental witness to Jordan finding out about the baby.

"Thanks, April," she said, hugging her right back.

In her car, the first song that popped up on her playlist was *Me, Myself, and I* by Beyoncé. It seemed oddly fitting, despite the fact that she was about to bring two more people into the loop. However, it was true, ultimately it was all on her...and the little one growing inside of her.

But she totally had this.

Me, myself and I, that's all I got in the end. That's what I found out, and there ain't no need to cry....

～

She had them at the kitchen table. The ride in had steeled her nerves and seeing them in front of her had reminded her that, no matter what their thoughts on the matter, these two people more than almost anyone in the world would have her back.

"Well," she began, "Mom, Dad, I have something to tell you."

They stared at her expectantly and she could see the growing concern in their faces. Nothing good ever followed that sentence. Best to just get it out.

"I'm pregnant and I'm keeping the baby." She could hear the hint of pride in her voice, as if telling them that yes, something had gone awry in all their hopes and plans for her, but she still had things firmly handled.

As the statement hung in the air, she realized she did.

Carter...or no Carter.

But that was a confrontation for another time.

Her mother closed her eyes and held it in. Well, that was to be expected.

Ralph stared at her for a beat, then a small smile that was a mixture of sadness and pride came to his face, as though he was watching her grow up before his eyes, but way too fast for him to keep up.

Deborah, her eyes still closed, brought a hand up to her head, as though struck with a sudden migraine. Jordan heard a gasp that sounded like a sob escape her lips as she slid her chair back from the table.

"I'm sorry—I...I just...I need a moment."

Jordan's eyes blinked rapidly as she watched her mother head out of the kitchen.

Her father grimaced and looked her directly in the eye. "Don't you let that affect you, Jordan. She just needs a chance to adjust. You let me handle her."

"I can handle her, Dad," Jordan said, with a wry smile. "But right now, I need to know how you feel about this. I know this isn't what you expected from me but--"

He slid his chair around the table until he was right next to her before she could continue. He took her chin and lifted it up to face him. "Look at my face, Jordan," he said. "Do you see disappointment or judgement here? No, you don't, because you, sweetheart, will never, *ever*, disappoint me, you hear?" he insisted. "You are a smart, considerate, beautiful young lady. I couldn't be prouder of you if I tried. Whatever you decide to do, that baby is damn lucky to have you carrying it and bringing it into the world."

That was when the dam broke. She had built a barrier around herself on the drive into Houston, to counter any siege that might make her doubt herself, or shoot arrows at her own lofty ideas of going through with being a parent.

This was the one that caused her to crumble. He wrapped his arms around her, letting her release it all. Up until that point, she hadn't realized how heavy the load she'd been carrying was.

When the worst had subsided, he asked, "So, I'm assuming it's Carter Fox's."

She laughed. "Of course."

"Well hey, we might end up with a future athlete in the family."

That made her laugh even more, slightly rebuilding that wall of strength to hold her up.

"Does he know?"

"No," she stopped him when she saw his look. "I know he has a right to know, but this isn't something I can just text him or call him about. Especially since we haven't exactly been...well, since *I* haven't been talking to him."

"You're going to have to tell him, and the sooner, the better," he said.

"I know," she sighed, falling back into her chair. "He's at spring training, four states away. Then there's the start of the season. I don't want to mess up his—"

"Jordan," her dad interrupted gently. "There is no right time, as I'm sure you've figured out. The sooner you tell him the better."

Jordan nodded. Her dad was right. The sooner, the better.

He had a right to know he was going to be a father.

And she had a right to know if she was going to be on her own in this.

Her mother entered the kitchen ten minutes later, back to her usual calm, stoic self.

"I'll give you two a moment," her dad said, making his way out.

"I'm sorry for walking out like that," Deborah sighed. "It was inexcusable."

She reached out to take Jordan's hand. "I can't imagine what you've been going through these past months and here I am walking out after only a minute. I'm so sorry sweetheart."

She was going to make Jordan cry all over again.

"It's okay Mom," she said, giving a wan smile. There was no use holding the guilt over her head. Games like that were something she couldn't afford to indulge in these days. "You should have seen me. I think there's still a vomit stain in the parking lot of the Wal-Mart on the way to Austin."

They both laughed a little at that. The tension in the air eased.

"Best laid plans," Deborah said, and gave a brief smile.

"Yeah," Jordan said, giving her a soft smile.

"Have you told him yet?" Her mother certainly didn't need to ask whose it was.

"I will. Soon."

"Well, no matter what he says, you know your father and I are here for you." She reached out a hand to push a strand of hair from Jordan's forehead. "Being a mother? It's the most wonderful, and at the same time, the most heart-wrenching experience you can have." She gave a small, nostalgic smile. "It will emotionally drain you and make your chest explode with love."

Jordan felt herself softening, the tears starting to come back.

"I can already tell how much stronger this has made you. I am proud of you Jordan, and I love you something fierce, even if I sometimes have trouble showing it, this doesn't change a damn thing."

Jordan leaned over and hugged her something fierce.

Yeah, she had this.

28

Carter Fox...Doping?

With his mastery at hitting home runs, rumors of steroid use have followed Carter Fox, the Houston Sluggers' star batter, for most of his major league career. Until now, those rumors have remained just that—rumors.

In an exclusive, Lone Star State Baseball has obtained evidence that may lend credibility to those rumors. The evidence, which Lone Star State Baseball has strong reason to believe is credible, was obtained from an unnamed witness close to Carter. The witness has come forward with a syringe that contains traces of, what that our own experts have determined is a performance enhancing drug that is prohibited in major league baseball.

The most damning potential proof is the blood on the syringe that contains DNA evidence, which points the finger in the direction of Carter Fox. According to the unnamed witness, he has personally watched Carter Fox "use performance enhancement drugs since his first season with the Houston Sluggers." The combination of this eye-witness testimony and the blood on the syringe that is very likely a strong match to Carter Fox's DNA, doesn't look good for the Sluggers player.

Major league baseball players are tested every season during spring training, then again randomly during the season. Considering the fact that certain drugs can become undetectable in as little as three weeks, it's not unlikely that Carter may have, thus far, been lucky enough to avoid having his use discovered.

With so much damning evidence, it seems that Carter Fox may join the ranks of other beloved major league baseball players who have disappointed fans, such as....

Carter stopped reading when the punch in the gut hit him yet again. Doping? Performance-enhancing drugs? DNA proof? The whole thing was so absurd he couldn't even wrap his head around it. Carter would normally be inclined to dismiss any of Lucas Grabow's articles as nothing more than trash, but these were serious allegations. Even Grabow wouldn't dare print such a damning piece without at least *some* proof.

And apparently, he had proof.

How? Just, how the hell...*how?*

He hadn't been given a moment's peace since the article went live. Phone calls. Texts. Knocks on the door of his hotel room. Teammates. Miles Derrick. His mother. He had ignored them all while he sat in his hotel room, looking at his phone, re-reading the article.

Then came the call he couldn't ignore.

"We need to address this right, fucking, now!" Michael Snyder had literally screamed into the phone.

For once, Carter couldn't argue with the man.

Once again, Carter found himself sitting in Michael Snyder's office. They had immediately pulled him out of spring training and flown him right back to Houston. This time it wasn't just Snyder, it was the entire Sluggers' legal team.

Today, there would be no smart-assed comebacks. Today Carter was out for blood. This mess had to be cleared up, and cleared up soon.

Fortunately, Snyder was letting the lawyers take the lead. Carter was so wound up, he wasn't sure he could keep himself from leaping over the desk and breaking Snyder's goddamn neck if he heard one pretentious peep out of the man's mouth.

"Obviously, our first concern was libel," began Marc Scher, who seemed to be heading the group of business-suited clones sitting around the table next to Snyder's desk.

"Your damn right, libel!" Carter roared, standing up in anger. He pulled himself back down into his seat as the man flinched in response.

Keep it together.

"Well, it's only libel if it's untrue," Scher gave him an uncertain look as he said that, then continued when he saw Carter's expression. "Although *Lone Star State Baseball* refuses to reveal the source of their... evidence. They did realize that it would be in their best interest to allow an impartial party to have access to it," Scher gave Carter another slightly apprehensive look, "if only to test and see if the DNA actually matches yours."

Carter's green eyes turned to steel as he gave the man a measured look. "It won't."

"You'd better hope it doesn't" Snyder chimed in, shutting up when Carter turned the hard stare in his direction.

"Of course it won't," Scher said, flustered. "We already have the press release ready to go out to every news agency in the country," his look of apprehension deepened, "once we've actually performed the test."

Carter began rolling up the sleeves to his shirt. "Well let's go. Do it right now. I want this shit nipped in the bud—*today!*"

The table of lawyers blinked rapidly and looked at one another.

"We can't test you for drugs now, not when there is a chance you've had time to clean out your system. No one would trust it. We just have to make sure the blood on that syringe isn't a match."

"Then test my damn blood. I can guarantee you that won't point the finger at me either."

"The test won't be done here, Carter."

"Then why am I sitting here with my dick in my hands talking to you?" Carter got up out of his seat, causing the entire table of gray suits to collectively shrink back. "Let's get this rodeo going," he continued.

Scher looked around at the table. "We, ah...we just need to make sure—"

"They need to make sure the match to the blood will be negative, Carter," Snyder said, giving the table of attorneys a withering look of annoyance. "You know, before we *all* end up standing around with our dicks in our hands looking like a bunch of assholes."

"Don't worry, you can keep your zippers closed," he growled. "It won't match."

Scher continued. "Right now we have plausible deniability. They have an 'unnamed source,' which the public is bound to be suspicious of anyway. And they have a syringe that they claim has your blood on it, but have yet to come forward with *real* proof. They're just trying to force our hand. We can walk away, ignore it and still save a little face, basically treat it as something not worth responding to. Put the ball back in their court and see what they do with it."

"And have my fans think I'm doping, or worse, a coward?" Carter raged. "No fucking way. Let's do this—now!"

"Of course, of course," Scher said, giving his team a look that held some silent communication. Then he turned back to Carter. "In law, we like to deal with certainties. You know: don't ask a question you don't already know the answer to. Before we go ahead and do this DNA test, we need to know—*for certain*— that the result will be negative.

"Right now, you're just talking to us as attorneys. Everything in this room stays in this room as far as the press and the public goes. *We* can deal with *Lone Star State Baseball.*

"Once we do the test, the Sluggers would have no choice but to suspend you if it's positive. Granted, this wouldn't be an official league test. However, our priority here is to protect the team, specifically the team's image. It would mean an eighty-game suspension, the same as the league would give for a first offense. You, of course, would have your image to consider too."

How many ways did Carter have to clue them in?

He walked slowly to the table and leaned in, resting his body on his balled up fists. "I don't...fucking...dope."

Scher took a gulp and turned to Snyder for the okay.

Snyder just shrugged. "You better hope it's negative, Fox."

"It will be," he grumbled, not taking his eyes off Scher. "It will be."

Positive.

Fucking positive!

The test had been done privately. Despite Carter's assurances, the legal team wasn't stupid enough to make it public before the results came in. Now, they had snapped right back into C.Y.A mode, circling the wagons around the team and leaving Carter Fox to survive in the wilderness.

Carter had offered to drop his shorts right there and pee into a cup. It didn't matter, and he couldn't blame them. Of course his urine would be clean during the off season, and in preparation for any test they'd want him to take in light of this new development.

News of the test had somehow gotten out. Carter had been under a media telescope since the *Lone Star State Baseball* article had come out, so all anyone had to do was put two and two together. Or just grease the hand of a lab tech.

It didn't matter now. All that mattered was the test was positive, and now the media knew.

Once the leak in the dam had started with that first article, the entire thing had collapsed, leaving Carter Fox drowning in a river of shit. Suspected doping was news. Confirmed doping was front page, headline news.

Carter was camped out in his home. The crowd of reporters outside the fence to his property was probably giving his neighbors more of a headache than even his wildest parties ever had. He wasn't giving them the satisfaction of even making an appearance.

The Sluggers' had no choice but to give an official statement, the gist of it being exactly what they had threatened: out for 80 games. It might as well have been the whole season.

Hell, it might as well be his whole career. How on earth could he step up to bat in a stadium full of fans, when they thought he was nothing more than a dirty, rotten, juicer? He'd made the mistake of going onto one of the baseball forums. It took him less than 5 minutes to close it out. They had been brutal. Now at least he had a better idea of what Jordan had gone through.

The thought of her made him even angrier. No doubt she had heard about this. Who the hell hadn't? Did she believe any of it? That thought killed him more than all of his other fans combined.

And not a word of it was true.

Carter was still in a state of bewilderment. *His* DNA on a needle filled with steroids. How?

For the most part, he had avoided any and all forms of communication.

His phone once again lit up at the news. Teammates, corporate, his agent, his mother. He'd finally put it on silent. He couldn't face any of them. Not right now. He needed time to process, time to figure this whole thing out. Time to find out who the hell was out to get him.

In the meantime, he made full use of his bar. Watching the DVD set of *Cosmos,* while three sheets to the wind drunk was surreal—and he couldn't stop thinking about Jordan the whole time.

He'd picked up his phone, pulling her number up to call multiple times. She was the only one he could think of with no ulterior motive.

His teammates, most of them friends of his, had their own careers to think of. Carter couldn't taint them with his mess. They'd all be under suspicion by association.

Miles Derrick would be a voice of reason, but he was on the Sluggers' payroll, and ultimately had to fall in line with them.

His mother? Christ, he didn't even want to think about that. Especially not after their last meeting. He hadn't talked to her since she dropped in unannounced on Jordan and him. She was not the warm, welcoming into the bosom type.

At some point, Carter would be in no holds barred, warrior mode.

Right now he just needed someone to make him feel right...feel *normal.*

He fell into an alcohol-induced slumber in one of the seats in his home theater. As Neil's soothing voice droned on, he held a bottle in one hand, and his phone in the other.

He snapped awake sometime around noon the next day. His head was giving it back as hard as he had abused it the day before. Just one more notch on the belt he planned on using to whip the fucker who'd sullied his name.

Fortunately, bad boy Carter knew exactly what to do from past experience: eggs, coffee, and bit more liquor. Hair of the dog. It wasn't a cure-all but it would suffice.

He stumbled his way into the kitchen like the zombie he felt like. No time to cook the eggs; straight down his gullet, raw. Coffee...fuck it. He wandered back to the bar and grabbed a random bottle.

One swig.

Second swig.

He let the burn go down his throat, shaking it off physically.

He smelled himself. *Jesus.*

A shower would definitely help.

One more swig.

Up the stairs. Into the bathroom. Turn on the shower. Hot. Scalding. That should do the trick. Clothes ripped off. *Yikes!* Maybe not *that* hot, but it had certainly woken him up.

He stood there as water came at him from all sides, washing away the funk, the pain, the worries. That was good. So, so good....

He snapped awake. His body felt numb. The water had been hot. He turned it off, stepped out, grabbed a towel, managed to wrap it around his waist. Fell face first on the bed.

Sleep.

Two hours later his eyes blinked open. The room was darker, the sun on the other side of the house. His head felt surprisingly clear. He could actually think.

It was time to act.

He grabbed his phone.

That's when he saw the message.

❧ 29 ❧

S he was still stunned.

Jordan obviously made a point of never—*ever*—looking at LoneStarStateBaseball.com, but once the news hit the media at large, she was tuned in pretty quick to the fact that Carter Fox had somehow been suspected of steroid abuse.

April had at least had enough tact to leave it alone, though she did give the occasional surreptitious look her way. Thank goodness no one else at school knew about her and Carter, since they'd made a point of keeping it under the radar last semester. She couldn't take the entire school looking at her that way.

In the safety of her bedroom, she had opened up her laptop to read everything. A syringe with his blood on it?

She felt so hopelessly sorry for him. Sent back to Houston from spring training, with everyone most likely turning on him, thinking him guilty. His teammates. His fans. Based on what little interaction she'd had with his mother, she couldn't imagine there was much warm solace in those arms.

She felt angry. A surge of fiery protectiveness surged through her veins. This was Carter Fox, *her* Carter Fox. The man who had lain with her under the stars. The man who had told the world to keep their damn mouth shut when it came to her. The man who told her all about Venus.

The man who was the father of her baby.

Jordan had gone and abandoned him just like everyone else. After a few weeks of blocked calls and texts, he had eventually given up. By the time Jordan knew for sure, she had kept waiting for the right time. Now that she was ready, it most certainly wasn't the right time for him.

Ben had texted her: *Do you believe it?*

She had immediately responded. *No!*

One second later he had replied. *Me neither.*

So Carter had at least two people in his corner.

He had to know that she was here in Austin, thinking about him, caring about him...loving him?

Her heart stopped. There hadn't been a day that she didn't think about him, especially now. Whether it was some new, weird symptom of her pregnancy that made her aware that she was carrying a part of him inside her, or a random thing that brought his face to mind, clear as day: the something in royal blue; a truck that was the same make and model as his; looking up at the night sky.

She remembered how it felt to be in his arms, joking around with him, listening to him tell her some weird fact about space, trying to explain baseball to her, even carrying down the stairs against her will. God, how she missed all of that.

Even if she couldn't pick up and drive to Houston to be with him, she wanted—*needed*—to let him know she was his.

So she'd written a simple text:
Carter. I saw the news. I just want you to know that you have at least one

person who knows that it's all lies. I know Ben feels the same way. Call me. I miss you.

She was in the kitchen later that evening, wearing an old UT t-shirt and Victoria's Secret pajama shorts washing up the bowl of spaghetti she'd had for dinner.

Carter hadn't called or responded to her text. She was heartbroken, but she understood. The man probably had a million things on his plate. Playing make-up and break-up with a pigheaded Jordan Douglas was probably not high on the list of things he wanted to deal with right now.

How could she have been so damn stubborn? She'd left in a huff, not even giving him a minute of time. She hadn't returned any of his desperate phone calls or texts. She'd ignored him for months trying to wrap her head around this pregnancy, recognizing full well that he had every right to be involved so he could make a decision. It had taken a devastating knock to his career, his *life*, to actually get her to reach out to him again.

No wonder he was ignoring her.

April was in the living room, having taken over the coffee table with highlighters, pens, laptop, casebooks and more. Even over the music blaring from the earbuds, she started with surprise, just as much as Jordan did at the insistent knocking at the door. Since Jordan was the one already standing, she headed over and took a peep through the peephole.

Her heart exploded.

It was Carter.

She pulled back and stared at the door, jumping as he started in on a second round of knocking. She looked through the hole again and saw the angst on his face. It made her heart seize.

By now, April was next to her, curiosity and worry clouding her face. She mouthed the words *who is it?*

Jordan looked at her friend, bit her lip, then opened the door without responding.

April's eyes grew wide, blinking rapidly as she saw who it was.

"Carter," Jordan breathed.

He looked at her, blinked over at April, as if registering the fact that his unannounced visit might be impacting more lives than hers.

"Um, hey," April said thinking fast, "You know, I was just about to head over to Matt's tonight if you need the apartment." Her face went back and forth between the two of them.

Jordan gave her a grateful smile as her roommate turned to go pack up her stuff.

"Sorry," he said watching her roommate head back toward the living room. "I—I didn't realize—I just...you're the only one I could think of to talk—"

"It's okay Carter," Jordan shushed him. She grabbed his arm and led him inside.

April was finishing up stuffing everything haphazardly into her bag and watched as Jordan led him to take her place on the sofa. While his back was turned she gave Jordan an *are you going to tell him?* look.

Jordan quickly shook her head no.

April shrugged and left.

Now was definitely not the time. The last thing he needed was a surprise baby on top of everything else.

She sat on the sofa next to him, pressing her lips together with worry over the state he was in. The man looked a complete mess. Had he just hopped in his car and made the 180-mile trip on the spur of the moment? She supposed she should be glad he had made it in one piece, especially considering the haggard appearance, head in his hands, fingers grabbing his blond locks that looked like they hadn't been combed at all today. She also suspected there had been more than a bit of alcohol at some point.

He was wearing a flannel shirt, half buttoned. The jeans were loose and comfortable, and the usual, well-worn cowboy boots were on underneath. Every piece of clothing was wrinkled and disheveled as if he'd twisted and turned during his whole drive over.

"I just...I don't understand how this could be happening," he groaned with frustration.

She rubbed his back, not knowing what to say, just wanting to be there for him. She had read the original article. It was pretty incriminating. Then, the follow-up articles, where his DNA had matched. Jordan didn't understand it either. All she knew was there was no way Carter Fox, the man who loved baseball, the man who had so much respect for the game, would *ever* taint it by taking prohibited drugs.

Having him here like this, in person, for the first time since she'd left Houston made her want to hold him tight and tell him everything was going to be fine. She regretted the way she had left him. She felt a fierce need to comfort him well up inside her. Maybe it was the baby inside of her—*his* baby. Maybe it was because the hormones were really starting to kick in. Maybe it was because she was the first person he had thought of to come to for comfort.

All she knew was, this was *her* man and if he needed her to be there for him, she would be. She would shield him against all the negativity and hate being thrown at him. Soothe away all the pain and suffering he was going through. Calm his fears and worries. Just...be there. She would never, *ever* abandon him again.

Because she loved him.

She didn't realize it until she saw him at his most vulnerable. As much pain as he was in, her heart ached twice as hard, watching him suffer it.

She leaned over and wrapped her arms around the back that was hunched over on his elbows. Her head rested on his shoulder as she ran her hands soothingly over his hair.

"It's going to be fine, Carter," she soothed. "We'll figure this out together."

She could feel her body reacting to being in such close proximity to him again. The smell of him was so familiar and arousing. The feel of his hardened muscles, tightly wound under her soft cheek as he sat there, taut with frustration. She wanted to massage every bit of tension away, turn him back into the playful, teasing Carter who was always the one trying to make *her* let go and unwind.

"April will be gone all night," She murmured into his back. "Stay with me. Let me help you."

She felt a shuddering breath go through his body underneath her as he let it out. His muscles relaxed and he turned his face around nuzzling it into her neck. His torso followed as he wrapped his strong arms around her, embracing—*absorbing*—her into a powerful bear hug.

Her arms went around his neck, cradling the back of his head into her shoulder, kissing his temple, savoring him. Her legs naturally wrapped around him wanting every part of her against every part of him. She pressed herself into his embrace, letting him know that she was all his, in any way he wanted her.

She felt his hands slide up then work their way under the waistband of her shorts, seeking, massaging, grabbing. Squeezing. He groaned into her clavicle and she felt his manhood pressing into her, straining against the zipper of his jeans.

God, how she wanted him.

She leaned down to bite the edge of his ear, wanting nothing more than to taste him. Her fingers grabbed at the wool of his shirt, clawing it up his back. He released her so she could finish the job, helping her rip it off of him and cast it aside.

She sat back on his lap, her hands and eyes exploring every bit of tattoo-covered flesh with a hunger that only starvation could cause. God, how she missed him. His embrace. His mouth, his eyes, his hands, his hair, his everything.

They gradually tore away each other's clothes until they were both naked.

Carter didn't even pause; simply fell on top of her and thrust himself inside of her causing her to grunt with pleasure. She met him just as hard, pressing her thighs tightly against his waist, arching her back into him, digging her claws deep into his back, pressing him harder into her.

"That's right," she urged, growling in his ear. "Give it to me. Give it *all* to me."

The rabid yell of release that escaped his lips as he thrust into her, nearly made her deaf. He went harder, faster. It only made her want more. She bucked up against him, urging him to give it everything he had. He met her with an intensity she hadn't felt before and she knew he was finally letting go.

It went fast and dirty. The violent current of orgasms that raged through her body were nothing like she'd ever experienced before.

"Oh God, Carter!" she yelled with a primal fervor that harkened back to a distant past where civilities were left behind. This was pure, unadulterated fucking. And she wanted more.

Carter was beyond forming anything resembling coherent phrases, simply grunting and groaning and thrusting on top of her like a caveman.

She welcomed it, embraced it. If this helped him, she was a perfectly willing. She was his woman. He was her man.

She felt him stiffen, the final act commencing. She opened herself up to take it all. He released with a shuddering groan, unleashing inside of her.

When his massive body fell down on top of her, she curled around it, welcoming the familiar build. She stroked his hair and back, smiling into his head as he pressed it to her neck.

"Wow," he breathed. "That was...intense."

"Yeah," she said laughing a little.

He lifted himself onto his hands, looking down at her. "You okay?"

She gave a chuckle and reached up to cup his face. "Yeah, I'm fine."

After they had dressed again, he sat next to her on the couch.

"Where the hell did that come from?" he pondered. Then he chuckled. "I guess it's a good thing you're on the pill. I wasn't even thinking."

She gave a sardonic smile.

Oh Carter, you have no idea.

"Yeah," she said in agreement.

She snuggled in beside him and was pleased to feel the familiar arm go around her body, pressing her closer.

"Thanks for that," he said softly. "I...I have no idea where that came from...but thanks."

She could hear the mild self-reproach in his voice and she wasn't having any of it. She reached up to take his chin in her hand and turn his face toward her.

"Hey," she said. "This is what you needed. I'm here for you. I'll *always* be here for you. Got it?"

He looked at her long and hard. As the impact of her words hit him, she was almost certain tears were about to come to his eyes, as a crease dented his forehead. Instead, he just nodded wordlessly and pulled her in closer until his chin rested on top of her head.

~

They had escaped to the comfort of her bed and were now lying together, naked in an embrace that was warm and familiar to Jordan. She rested her head against the firmness of his chest and traced a finger over the tattoos on his body.

She didn't bring up the steroid accusation at all. If he wanted to talk about it, he would say something. She just wanted to be a comfort to him in his time of need.

"Thanks again for this," he said, staring at the ceiling. "For once I'm glad you don't live in Houston. You have no idea how hard it was trying to get rid of the press once I left my house."

"Well, thanks for not bringing them here," she laughed into his chest. She lifted her head to look at his face, the stubble on his chin was practically a small beard at this point. His sharp features were both more jagged, and yet softer, most likely due to a lack of food, and too much drink.

"I'm going to make you some spaghetti. You look like you could use something to eat."

"What I could use is you lying back down against my chest," he said pulling her down.

She fell back reluctantly but didn't give in. "I'm serious Carter," she murmured into his chest. "You need to eat. I think April has some Oreos I could steal. She'll understand."

Before he could argue again she jumped out of bed, jogged out to the kitchen, grabbed the Oreos and a large glass of milk.

When Carter saw what was in her hands, the smile that she longed to see graced his face. "Oreos and milk? I can't tell if you're my mother or my girlfriend."

The words made her stop short. Mother. Girlfriend?

Being the overthinking Jordan that she was, she immediately wondered if being pregnant had made her think of milk and cookies.

She shook her head of the thought. That was ridiculous. Besides, there was no point going down that mental path. She couldn't tell Carter about his baby...not yet. Not now.

30

He held the glass of milk in his lap so Jordan could dunk her cookies. Carter didn't have much of an appetite. His insides were riding an emotional roller coaster and he wasn't quite sure milk and cookies would survive the trip. But he was happy to watch her eat.

He closed his eyes and leaned back against the headboard, relaxing into the hand that was stroking his hair. This was all he needed right now. Peace. Quiet. A good woman by his side. A woman who had his back, no matter what. A woman who had faith in him, believed in him, despite everything being thrown her way telling her that she shouldn't.

His woman.

The woman he loved.

He'd known it since—he couldn't even say. Maybe since he'd first seen that face on the screen. Despite her stubbornness, which he occasionally found endearing, she was perfect. Her brains, her ambition, her devotion to her family, the way she looked, felt, smelled, tasted...

He could feel his cock start to twitch.

Although he would have loved another, less angst-filled session with Jordan, he forced himself to let it go. That first round had been a much-needed release, but right now he just wanted rest. He needed time to think, figure this mess out.

He appreciated the fact that she hadn't yet mentioned anything about the steroids, letting him open up when he was ready. He opened his eyes to stare up at the ceiling.

"I just don't have a goddamned clue how this could be happening," he sighed.

Jordan let it sit, waiting to see if he went on.

"I mean how the *fuck* did my blood get on a syringe laced with steroids?"

She pulled away, taking in the fact that he was ready to talk it out. He tried not to focus on the fact that they were both still naked.

"Okay, so let's work it out," she said, her face taking on a look of concentration. "Do you remember anyone sticking you? A pinch or something?"

He gave a soft laugh, "Trust me hon, I'd remember something like that."

"She fell back against the headboard, facing him. "Okay well, it's a bit outlandish, but maybe some employee at the doctor's office? Have you given blood recently? It would be a way to make a quick buck. Sell the story to LoneStarStateBaseball.com...?"

"Yeah, that's pretty out there, Jordan," he said shaking his head.

She nodded, concluding it was an unlikely scenario. "Well, how else could someone get your blood?" She gave him a sheepish look before going on. "I know you've gotten into fights on the field. Maybe...?"

He gave a hefty laugh. "Yeah, maybe one of them saved the blood from when they punched—"

It hit him like a sledgehammer to the chest, so hard he almost couldn't breathe. He sat straight up.

Holy shit!

He jumped out of bed and began to pace, ripping a hand through his hair.

"What is it?" Jordan asked, wide-eyed with apprehension.

"That goddamn motherfu-!" he roared, coming to a stop and digging his fingers into his palms so hard he could feel them breaking the skin.

Jordan flinched back against the headboard, bringing the covers up to her chest.

Carter saw her reaction and it quelled the rage instantly, or at least masked it. He had no intention of creating a repeat of his last bedroom freak out. He never wanted to see scared look in her eyes again.

He took long slow breaths, doing everything he could to calm himself down and focus on where to go from this point. First of all, he had to get out of here. He searched out his boxers and jeans.

Jordan watched him angrily heading toward the living room, and warily got off the bed. She grabbed a robe from a hook on the back of her door and came up to him gingerly.

"Where are you going?" she asked with a warning tone, following him.

"I'm going to deal with this," he growled, pulling up his underwear and following with his jeans.

"You're angry, and I know you haven't eaten," she pleaded, standing in front of him. "You're liable to run off the road Carter!"

"Jordan, I love you," her eyes fluttered in surprise at that, "but you need to get out of my way."

She stood firm and crossed her arms over her chest blocking his way. "No. Tell me what it is. I can help you!"

"This is my fight." He grasped her by the arms and physically lifted her up, eliciting a gasp. He placed her down next to the couch and out of his way.

She kept a healthy distance as he stuffed his arms into his shirt, and buttoned it up. Then, she grabbed his arm as he headed to the door and he tensed, instinctively wanting to pull it away and take care of business. He saw her face and momentarily relaxed.

"It's okay if you don't want to tell me," she said, "but please, just promise me you won't do anything that might...get you in trouble, or hurt."

He just stared at her. She stared right back at him.

He waited a moment then sighed and nodded. He couldn't make a verbal promise. He could only hope that the ride there would calm his nerves.

Because right now Carter Fox felt like murdering someone.

Jordan was probably right, he was too angry and worn out to be driving, especially all the way to Pasadena, Texas. He had basically tailgated, raced, lane-changed, and bogarted his way there. It was a wonder he hadn't got a ticket, or worse.

None of it calmed the anger that raged inside him as he pulled into the dark parking lot of Bay Vista Apartments. Carter had never been here before but he knew the address well. After all, he'd sent more than a few checks here.

Today, he was delivering something else...personally.

He thought about knocking, the split second before he kicked in the door to apartment #127.

Bobby Joe Fox tumbled off the couch in surprise. The legs that had been propped up on the coffee table twisted and he fell, face first, onto the floor. As he struggled to right himself and stand up, Carter took three steps in to grab him.

"Listen, son…I can explain," he sputtered.

That told Carter all he needed to know. He was so shocked to have his assumption—about which he'd still held a tiny, hopeful sliver of doubt —confirmed, that he dropped the man.

Bobby fell onto his ass with a thud. He used the momentary freedom to scramble away from Carter, well out of reach. As he backed into the kitchen, he looked at his son with a wary eye.

The movement created a fresh wave of anger in Carter and he rushed over to pick the man up again, banging him against the kitchen wall. Bobby Joe grimaced with pain.

Carter slammed him again. Then slammed him again.

A flash of anger went through the older man and he began to fight back. He took a swing and managed to connect with Carter's temple, causing him to loosen his hold on him. Bobby Joe gave in to the momentum, swinging and kicking.

Carter dropped him again and moved back a step, fists balled, ready to strike back.

"Come on then!" he raged. "Go for it, *Dad!*" He spat out the last word like a bad taste in his mouth. "You wanna try for some more? Pay off some more loans?" he roared. "Make sure you swing hard enough to draw blood. At least now we know how they could prove it was probably my DNA; they had the sperm donor ready and willing to match it."

"What the hell is going on over here?" screeched a woman's voice from the front doorway.

Carter didn't bother looking over; his eyes stayed locked tightly on the green irises that were mirror images of his own. Bobby Joe just waved an idle hand toward the front door, shooing the woman away.

"I'm callin' the cops!" the voice said warily.

"How the *hell* could you do something like this?" Carter asked.

Bobby Joe just sagged against the wall, breathing heavily, looking at his flesh and blood with a mixture of anger and resentment.

"You think you're such hot shit," he snarled. "Can't even take your old man's calls. Do you remember who the fuck taught you baseball in the first place? *Fuck you...and fuck your career!*"

The rage came back.

Bobby Joe saw it in his son's eyes and braced himself.

"Fuck my career?" Carter screamed, charging at the man and pinning him up against the wall. *"Fuck my career?!"*

"How much did you get?" Carter demanded, slamming the man against the wall again.

"Fuck you!"

"How much?!" he slammed him again.

"FUCK YOU!"

Carter let go of him and drew his fist back with a roar. He saw Bobby Joe's eyes light up with fear, realizing how massive and powerful that fist was.

Carter paused. He thought of Jordan sitting in bed with that same look of fear in her eyes. He thought of her parting words. Don't get in trouble. Don't get hurt.

He gave a frustrated roar and brought the fist forward, slamming it into the wall beside Bobby Joe's head. He flinched, twisting his head away from it. Carter pulled himself away from him, ignoring the fist-sized dent in the wall.

He could hear the sirens coming. He strolled over to the sofa and sagged down, resting his elbows on his knees, completely drained. He dropped his head into his hands.

"How could you do this?" Carter asked softly.

Bobby Joe walked over to the side table and picked up the pack of

Marlboros lying there along with the lighter. He lit the cigarette and took a deep puff. Squinting out of the ruined front door, he rested one hand in his jeans pocket thoughtfully.

Carter heard him give a soft cackle as he blew out a puff of smoke, and he looked up in disbelief.

"Assholes only gave me $5,000 for the story. You fuckin' believe that? Didn't even make a fuckin' dent."

Carter just shook his head and put his head back in his hands. His entire career. His *life*. For $5,000.

He lifted his head to look at the man. "Did you have it planned before you showed up at the party, or was it a spur of the moment idea?"

Bobby Joe twisted his lips with guilt before taking another drag, still unable to look his son in the eyes.

So it had been planned all along. Carter's head fell into his hands again.

"If it makes you feel any better, I waited a good while before going through with it. It wasn't an easy thing to do....What can I say? I was desperate." He shrugged and took another puff.

Carter could feel himself getting warm. The blood rushed to his brain, making him see red. He wasn't sure even Jordan's sweet voice in his head could stop him now.

"Alright everyone, freeze!" two cops came rushing into the room, guns drawn, taking note of the front door on its hinges.

They paused when they saw Carter, sitting like a boulder on the couch and Bobby Joe idly smoking a cigarette.

"What's going on here?" the first one asked, confusion in his voice.

"We're alright boys. Just a little accident there," he pointed the cigarette at the front door, with a wry smile.

The cop looked at the door then back at Bobby Joe, then over toward Carter. "Are you alright, sir?"

His eyes grew wide with instant recognition when Carter lifted his head from his hands.

"Yeah," said in a monotone voice. He looked up at Bobby Joe, who refused to look his way. "We're alright."

"Anyone want to explain this front door?"

"Like I said, just a little accident. Y'all gonna hang around here for a damn front door?"

That got their hackles up and Carter could just see trouble brewing.

"Shut the hell up, Bobby," he sighed. He stood up and walked over to the two men. "I'm sorry you had to come all the way out here for this. Like my—like he said, it was a simple accident. I'll be paying for the door in the morning with the management company."

The two looked at Carter, then at Bobby Joe, the front door, and then back to Carter. Probably sensing the headlines in the morning, they backed off.

"Just make sure you...you keep it down," the first one said, feeling the need to perform some sort of policing duty.

"Yes, sir," Carter said and then watched them go.

There was a crowd of curious onlookers outside. The combination of a police unit in the middle of the night and the Houston Sluggers' star hitter was enough to get the community grapevine running at lightning speed.

"Fix this," Carter said without turning back to Bobby Joe.

He heard his dad puff out another cloud of smoke.

Carter walked to the entrance and paused at the threshold. *"Fix. This."*

"Yeah, son," he heard his dad sigh.

He stepped over the entryway and began walking back toward his truck. He stopped when he heard Bobby Joe's voice.

"Carter," came the raspy voice, "I'm in a lot of trouble. I know I'll probably end up in jail or somethin' over this, but these people, they're gonna want their pound of flesh. If they can't get it from me..." he let the statement hang.

A wave of anger ran through Carter again. He let it crash and whither away. He was just too damn worn out.

31

Call me! Text me! Let me know ur ok!

Jordan had lain awake with worry. She had texted over and over begging him to call or text, just so she knew he was okay. She hadn't heard anything and it had been 5 hours already.

She had no idea what revelation had made him run out so quickly, and so angrily. She had just known whoever was on the receiving end of that wrath was in for trouble. She couldn't give two shits about them. If they had caused this mess, they deserved the mighty force of hell rained down up on them. But she didn't want to see Carter bringing himself down with them.

Finally, he had responded.

I'm fine. Everything is fine. Don't worry.

And that was it. She stared at the phone. At least he wasn't dead, and presumably not in jail.

She was anxiously curious to know what had happened, but the fact that he had simply texted instead of calling meant he didn't want to talk about it. She'd let him be.

At least she could rest easy tonight, somewhat.

~

One day later, she was woken up by the knocking on her bedroom door.

April burst in without waiting for a response.

Okay, we're like that now are we? Jordan thought irritably.

She looked at her friend with sleepy annoyance, tempered only by the mild curiosity of seeing the laptop in her hands.

"Holy shit, Jordan!" April gushed. "Have you seen this?"

Jordan wanted to remind her that just moments ago she'd been sleeping, so no, she hadn't seen "this." But now her curiosity was piqued and she was very alert.

April boldly sat on the edge of the bed next to Jordan and swiveled the laptop so they could both see it.

"They were talking about it on the radio this morning, so I went online to see," April said.

Carter Fox's Father Comes Forward, Confesses to Lying About Steroid Abuse.

Her eyes snapped wide open as she re-read the headline then scanned the article. So Carter was innocent. And his own father had done this to him? Her heart both leapt for joy at his cleared name, and clenched tight, realizing what a toxic relationship he with his own father. She thought of how wonderful her own dad was, a dad who would lie down in traffic before *ever* hurting her. Poor Carter.

"Jeez," April said looking at the screen. "And I thought *my* family was nuts."

Based on what she read in the article, the Sluggers were rapidly doing damage control. Their number one player was once again the Golden Boy. In fact, the story was so salacious they were going overboard, cashing in on the family drama aspect: boy somehow makes it big in the major leagues despite having an asshole for a father. Jordan had no doubt that the rest of the week would be dedicated to the Fox Family Saga.

She didn't care. All she knew was her Carter was back; maybe a bit emotionally bruised and battered, but nothing time and the love and care of a woman couldn't fix. She'd bring him back.

She thought back to when he left. It had been in the heat of the moment, but he'd said it: he loved her. She smiled thinking about it. Carter loved her. She felt like a silly teenager all over again.

She thought about the baby. Now was probably not the time—or at least not the *best* time—to tell him. She'd give him a few days to recover, then send him on yet another emotional spiral. Would he be happy? Mad? Supportive? Would he abandon her?

The thought sent her heart straight down to her stomach.

"So, I guess you two are back on again?" April asked.

Jordan snapped out of her thoughts and looked at her roommate. She shrugged, "I guess? It was a...revealing night."

April gave a sly smile. "Revealing *good* or revealing *bad?*" she asked.

Jordan rolled her eyes. "I don't know," she said with exasperation, not wanting to give too much away. "But I've got at least another hour of sleep before I have to get up for class so, thanks for the 411 but I'm going back to bed!"

She took a pillow and hit April on the side with it. Her roommate laughed and jumped off the bed, grabbing her laptop. "So that's the thanks I get for showing you the news about your boyfriend?" she laughed.

"Go away!" Jordan said falling back down on the mattress.

April left, closing the door behind her.

Jordan stared at the ceiling thinking. She had no more excuses. She had to tell him.

After he'd recovered a bit.

It was late afternoon, a few days after learning the good news about Carter. Her plan had been to drive all the way out to Houston that weekend and break the news to him. Classes were done for the day. She'd finished up a hand-holding session with a second year, who'd been a bit sloppy with her cite-checking for a law review article. Now she just wanted to go home and nap. She was so tired lately, and Jim Straton's aftershave next to her in her seminar class was literally making her want to hurl. She'd have to see about switching seats.

She turned the corner to her street...and saw her. Carter's mom. Jordan had no problem remembering her: those sharp features; that flaming red hair; that permanent look of disapproval.

What in the world was she doing here? How in the world had she found her? Did Carter send her? What did she want?

Jordan slowed her pace, warily eyeing the woman who was finishing up a cigarette, leaning against the hood of her white Mercedes-Benz. As she dropped the butt to the ground, twisting into it with one high-heeled shoe she caught Jordan looking in her direction and stopped.

Having both caught sight of one another, Jordan figured she might as well approach the woman. She slowly made her way toward Carter's mother, her senses on high alert for trouble.

"Hello," Jordan said guardedly. "Carter's mother, right?"

Madison made an attempt at giving a smile, but it never reached the eyes, which were watching Jordan like a predator. Finally, she closed her eyes, shaking her head a bit.

The eyes flew open again as she began. "I suppose there's no point in beating around the bush," she said, squinting in Jordan's direction. "Are you pregnant?"

Jordan gasped and her eyes grew wide. Instinctively she placed a hand on her belly.

Madison's eyes flicked to the hand movement and she pursed her lips. "I guess that answers that."

Jordan fixed her face, a curtain of impassivity hiding her emotions. "How did you know?"

Madison gave her a look of disdain. "Do you think I don't keep tabs on everything in my son's life? Of course, I know. It didn't take a calculator to put two and two together. The number of times my guy saw you heading to the free clinic and then the gyno's office. Either you've got a super case of the clap, or..." She waved a hand down towards Jordan's abdomen.

Madison gave her a speculative look. "Are you planning on getting rid of it?"

"What? No!" Jordan said shocked. Honestly, the thought hadn't ever crossed her mind. "They do other things at the clinic, besides..." She stopped herself. Why in the world was she spilling everything to this woman? She certainly wasn't about to reveal that she now had every intention of keeping it.

Madison gave a heavy sigh, then began digging around in her purse. "I'm guessing Carter doesn't know. I would have heard something by now, even if he still isn't talking to me," she said, giving Jordan a hateful look.

Jordan just stared at her, revealing nothing.

Madison snorted, pulling out a cigarette and sticking it in her mouth.

Jordan gave her a quick look of contempt as she took two steps back, her hand flying down to her stomach again.

There was a brief flash of maternal empathy as Madison's eyes followed

Jordan's hand. Then she gave an exaggerated sigh and took the cigarette out, placing it back in the carton in her purse. "I should give these things up anyway," she muttered.

Madison looked back up at Jordan. "So then you're going to have it?" Without waiting for an answer she continued. "If you think this is the way to keep him, you're mistaken. You aren't the first little butter tart to try, you know?"

Jordan's poker face melted into pure disdain, but Madison continued on, ignoring her.

"Carter is 100% baseball. It doesn't leave room for the next flavor of the week, no matter how long she's managed to hold on." Her eyes gave Jordan a once-over. "And certainly no room for a baby."

Jordan thought back to the night the condom broke. She wanted to believe it was the shock of the moment that had caused his reaction. Heaven knew she had been just as terrified.

Having a baby meant coming home at night, not out to a club. It meant being good, being a role model. It meant birthday parties with balloons and clowns, not booze and club girls.

It meant being tied to a woman for at least 18 years.

Sure he seemed like he was ready and willing to forget his playboy past and make it work with her, but was he really? Especially with a two-for-one deal?

"You have no idea how hard it is to raise a kid do you?" Madison gave a brief laugh. "The constant worry. The pressure you put on yourself to make sure they come out okay, or at least better than you did. The fierce desire to protect them from anyone who might want to hurt them," She looked Jordan square in the eye as she said this.

Jordan wasn't sure if it was her irritation that was starting to kick in or the firm knowledge that she would never—*ever*—do anything to hurt Carter but she gave it right back to the woman. Her eyes didn't fall even when Carter's mother began talking again.

"Besides," Madison continued, noting that she had managed to get a hook into Jordan's subconscious. "do you really want to bring a mixed kid into the world?"

Jordan was shocked out of her confidence.

"I mean, just think how hard they'll have it. White? Black? And don't you want a child who...looks like you? Doesn't *everyone*?" Madison dug the last point in, eyeing Jordan with the unspoken meaning: Carter Fox would want a child that looked like him.

Jordan pressed her lips together hard to keep from saying something she'd regret. She had figured out Madison was trouble from the first day she'd met her, now it was coming at her full force.

"I'm having this baby," she said firmly. "What *Carter and I* decide to do after that is between us...no one else. Not even you." She gave Madison her own meaningful look.

She walked away before she could listen to another hateful word from the woman. Her steps quickened as the panic set in. By the time she made it through the front door of her apartment, she was shaking.

She fell back against the door, making sure it was securely closed. Her bags slid down her arms in a heap to the floor. She balled her hands into fists and began hitting them against her thighs.

Finally, she let out an ear-piercing scream. "*Aaaaaaaarghhh!*"

Good Lord, was everyone in Carter Fox's family crazy?

First, his father turns out to be some sort of sick psychopath, who would happily throw his son under the bus for a measly $5000.

Now his lunatic, *racist* mother was spying on her. Madison showing up that morning at Carter's place back in January all made sense now. She'd probably had Jordan on her radar ever since.

She shivered against the door, still recovering. What the hell kind of family was she getting herself involved with?

She had a little over a month until graduation. Then she'd be back in

Houston. She could wait until then, tell Carter face to face, and see how he really felt about this. Besides, she needed time to process this new development. Having been raised by a mom like that, she wondered how he really *would* feel about having a child that wasn't a blond haired, green eyed replica of himself. She had to remind herself that his little declaration of love had been in the heat of the moment. Right before he picked her up to move her out of the way as he walked out the door to deal with his father.

What difference would one month make?

32

Carter had been riding a wave of optimism. Jordan was his good luck charm and as far as he knew, she was behind him 100%. One month into the season and he had already scored 10 home runs for his team, helping the Sluggers start out the season first in the National League West division.

He had no doubt that trend would not only continue, but accelerate once Jordan was back in Houston...back for good. Jesus, how he needed her!

Then the bad mojo came.

It was in the form of a text. He hadn't paid much attention to Bobby Joe's parting words after the fight. The man was, for once, sponging off of someone other than Carter. Actually, he was sponging off of quite a few someones, since he had room and board for the next year, courtesy of the tax payers of Texas. It seemed like a small amount of time to pay for almost destroying a multi-million dollar career—and of your own flesh and blood to boot. On the other hand, a year was long enough for Carter to put the man out of his mind forever.

The Sluggers corporate office had also done a number on

LoneStarStateBaseball.com as well. These days the URL led to a defunct placeholder. That was probably because the blog had been sued right into bankruptcy. As pissed off as Carter was about the way he had been treated after the accusation, he had to give it to the team of lawyers for immediately jumping into action to repair his good name. It wasn't lost on him that theirs was simultaneously buffed back to a nice healthy shine as well.

Now, everything was falling back into place as it should be. Jordan was back in his life. Baseball was back in his life. His mother was keeping her distance since the incident in January, which was fine by Carter. Bobby Joe was permanently out of his life. That was *certainly* fine by Carter.

Then he had received the text. It was short and to the point:

Your father originally owed $40,000. Interest has accrued. The current amount owed is $202,178.81. We would very much appreciate payment. You can send the funds to....

It had finished with a routing number, no doubt to a bank somewhere in the Cayman Islands or Switzerland or something. The amount was laughable. $40,000 had somehow ballooned into over $200,000. Mathematically, that was about 10% compounded weekly. Loan Sharks.

His first instinct had been to ignore it. He was under no obligation to pay these men off, at least not legally. But he knew the type of people Bobby Joe dealt with, especially if that interest rate was any indication.

So he'd gone to his attorneys and they'd taken it to the authorities. The phone was a burner, dumped after the message had been sent. They'd gone to Bobby Joe to try and press him for information about the men. He'd been predictably tight-lipped on the matter.

They had nothing more to go on other than an offshore bank account and a routing number. Both led to places that didn't have to play nice when it came to giving information to the United States. Since there was no *direct* threat, they put it in a case file and assured him they would be "looking into it."

He decided not to press it. It was just one more nagging reminder about Bobby Joe, and Carter had no interest.

Over the next month, he received two more texts, both dutifully passed on to the authorities. After that, it had died down. They had obviously taken the hint.

❧ 33 ❧

She had just finished the Sunflower Ceremony, put on specifically for the UT School of Law graduates. Everyone had driven up from Houston: her parents, Uncle Roy, Aunt Pat, and Ben.

She knew Carter had a game that day in Houston. Thus, she hadn't expected him to come out, despite their being back "on" again. They had kept it to phone calls since their reunion, mostly for the sake of Jordan's finals. The truth was, she just couldn't handle the pressure of studying and dealing with his reaction to the news. She was also still a bit apprehensive about what his mother had told her that day.

Part of her was glad he wasn't here at her graduation. Obviously, she would have loved seeing him here for one of the most important events in her life. On the other hand, it would have caused way too much of a commotion. April was still the only person in her class who knew the two of them were dating.

Besides, it gave Jordan an excuse to put off telling him about their happy little accident. Completely naked, it was more than obvious that she had a nice little baby bump in the making. Flowy dresses and baggy shirts had done the trick for the casual observer.

The tell-tale signs were there for anyone looking out for it. Zoe, the managing editor of the law review, had pointed out that she was "glowing." Fortunately, she had just teasingly attributed it to some secret boyfriend that Jordan had—and it was "about time, girl!" She didn't bother correcting her.

Morris & Gibson would be a different story. It didn't matter the circumstances, she would be nothing more than a statistic in some people's eyes. Hello! Pregnant, unwed, black woman reporting for duty! Oh, and by the way, thanks for hiring me, now I immediately have to take a few months off for maternity leave. It was the perfect way to start her legal career.

She'd worry about that when the time came. Right now her family was here, ecstatic about her success and ready to celebrate. They were at the reception taking pictures of Jordan with some of her fellow classmates.

She heard the ripple of whispers that ran through the atrium, where the reception was being held. Jordan was posing with Zoe for a photo when she sensed it. She held the pose until her father had snapped the photo. Just as she turned to see what the commotion was, Ben cleared things up for her.

"Carter!" he yelled.

Jordan saw him make his way through the crowd of surprised onlookers.

"What in the world is Carter Fox doing here?" Zoe pondered next to her, looking at the man with undisguised admiration as he made his way toward them, holding a large box.

It had been almost two months since she'd last seen him. She had nearly forgotten how handsome his face was, especially when it wasn't haggard with worry. She wanted to memorize it the way it was now, giving her that grin, his green eyes twinkling with delight. She wondered what it would look like after she told him the "happy" news.

She had turned in her robe and was wearing a business-like shift dress that, fortunately, was still loose enough to cover her smallish bump.

"You came," she said, smiling. "I thought you had a game. When did it end?"

Zoe looked at her, then back at Carter with surprise. When she saw the intimate way the two stared at one another she slowly backed off to join the rest of Jordan's classmates to revel in this bit of freshly brewed gossip.

"A couple of hours ago," Carter answered. "I tried to hightail it out here, but it looks like I missed the ceremony. Sorry about that."

Jordan just shook her head with wonder and delight. "Don't worry about it. I'm glad you're here."

There was a small lock of blond hair that fell on his forehead. She instinctively reached up to brush it back. The gesture was so minor but they both seemed to feel the instant wave of warm affection run through their bodies. His eyes softened with adoration.

She realized her family was standing there watching the two of them, and behind them her fellow alums and their families. She drew back self-consciously. She looked down at the large wrapped gift he had in his hands. It was beautifully wrapped with thick white handmade paper, a white crepe ribbon in UT orange, and white roses tucked into the bow on top.

"Not to ruin the surprise but it's something that is technically already yours." He leaned down to whisper in her ear. Her heartbeat intensified so much it nearly leapt out of her chest. She wanted him closer, so much closer. "You left it at my place."

He pulled away and that wicked grin that made her wild with desire returned.

"Hey, Carter," Ben said, reminding the two of them that they weren't the only two people in the room.

"Hey, Ben," he said giving him a fist bump.

"So are we still top of the division?" Ben asked.

"You know it. 5-2 today."

"Awesome!"

Jordan felt everyone else's eyes on her while Ben and Carter talked baseball. By now everyone in the family knew her little secret. Now that she was here, face to face with Carter she couldn't put off telling him anymore. It was late May. Five months was already too long...far too long.

Of course, right here, in the middle of a curious crowd of her fellow classmates, was no proper time and place either. She was headed back to Houston tonight to settle into her *own* apartment. She'd set aside a time to meet with him where they could talk privately and figure it all out, together.

Carter turned back to her. "So you're back in Houston tomorrow?"

She nodded. "Yes. Why?"

"Let me take you to dinner after the game tomorrow. We can make up for lost time."

So, tomorrow it was then.

Jordan wanted to laugh at the irony. They were at the same restaurant that they had eaten at the night she became pregnant. Full circle.

At least it was private and appropriately intimate. They could definitely talk here. She could also rest assured that he wouldn't have a total freak out since there were other diners around them.

She was thrilled to see him again after so long, but her excitement was overshadowed by the butterflies that were at it again in her stomach, and not in a good way. Her steak was half eaten and the garlic mashed potatoes had been picked over.

"You haven't touched any of your wine. That's a pretty good bottle there." He gave a small laugh, "It should be for what I paid for it."

Jordan looked at the untouched glass the waiter had poured for both of them. She supposed now was as good a time as any to tell him. He was still eating. She'd wait until he was done. One tiny little sip wouldn't harm the baby.

She smiled and took a small sip. "Mmm, you're right. It is good."

"So are you excited about finally having your own place?" He gave her a teasing grin.

Normally, she would say something sassy in response. Tonight, she just smiled and nodded.

He frowned a bit. "Are you okay?" he asked with a tiny crease in his forehead. "You seem a bit off tonight."

She brightened up, the mask coming down over her face. "Yeah," she said shaking her head. "I'm just thinking about all the studying I have to do for the bar, and then work."

He laughed. "There's the Jordan I know. No rest for the wicked." He gave her a devilish wink.

She gave a genuine laugh in response.

He put his knife and fork down, finishing his meal with a sip of wine.

Jordan braced herself. Now was the time. She looked over at his handsome face, oblivious to what was about to come. It pained her. But it needed to be done.

Just tell him!

"Carter, I'm pregnant," she blurted.

34

He had been so focused on the anxious look on her face that he didn't even register what she had just told him.

The look was not one of happiness from eating a fine meal (which he noticed she hadn't eaten much of), or being done with law school, or being together again. It was a look that registered bad news.

Then his neurons and synapses went to work.

Pregnant?

"Pregnant?" the word left his lips and sent his head spinning.

The anxious look transformed into worry, then panic. "Here, have some more wine," she said placing her—untouched!—wine glass in front of him.

He took the glass and drank, unable to make his mouth work for anything else.

"I know it's a shock and I know I should have told you months ago—"

Months?

It hit him. January. That's why she'd left.

He took another gulp.

"—but when it happened you were just so, *so* upset. So I told you I was on the pill, so you wouldn't get mad at me—"

That was a sharp, little dagger through his heart. He could have known this whole time. Been there to hold and comfort her from the very beginning, but his damn overreaction had kept her away. She'd had to deal with this on her own...for months.

He took another sip.

"—then it was just never the right time, what with"—she gave him a guilty look—"how I left you, and then I wanted to do it in person but you were away at spring training, and then the steroids thing and—"

Now she was babbling nervously, waiting for him to answer.

He took another sip, if only to loosen his tongue, or at least loosen his thoughts. Right now they were a tightly wound tangle of confusion.

"Then your crazy mother came to see me, and I just—"

"What?" That was the magic word that made his voice suddenly reappear.

Jordan stopped short and looked at him in confusion, as though questioning which part of her incoherent rambling he was asking about. Then the obvious hit her and he saw a gleam come to her eye that told him he wasn't going to like what he was about to hear.

"She's been spying on me!" she spat. "She came to see me a month ago and—and told me things." Her eyes fell to the table in hurt and anger.

Carter was still reeling from the sledgehammer that had just knocked him upside the head. But that look sobered him right up, taking front and center. His only focus was on making that hurt, that anger, disappear.

He reached across the table and took her hand. Her eyes flashed up to meet his.

"What did she say, Jordan?"

There was hesitation. He squeezed, letting her know she could tell him.

She seemed to be having some sort of internal dialogue with herself. Finally, she took a breath.

"Are you even ready for a baby?" she asked.

That wasn't what he was expecting, and he gave her a mild look of confusion. "Well, I just got the news, Jordan. I need time to process it."

"Because I know you've got baseball and the Sluggers are doing so well this season. And I've got the bar, and then my job. But I'm keeping it, Carter."

She looked at him with firm determination.

It hit Carter like a bullet to the chest as soon as she said it. From that second on, he didn't need time to process it. This baby...this baby that he was not nearly prepared for. This was *his* baby. His and Jordan's. *Theirs.*

"Jordan, if you're having my baby, I want it—I want you *both*—in my life."

A sob escaped her lips, as she broke down.

He quickly rushed around the table to kneel before her and wrap his arms around her. People were beginning to look, but he didn't care. He knelt there awkwardly until she had cried it all out.

"Shhh," he soothed, "It's okay, I'm here for you."

She was down to hiccups now. He blindly reached up to the table to grab a glass of water for her. He hurriedly set it down when he realized the one he grabbed held wine and not water.

That's when it hit him again; he was going to be a father.

He grabbed the water and held it to her. She took it gratefully and sipped between hiccups. They eventually died down.

When he felt she was ready to go on, he brought his hand up to her chin and lifted it to look at him. "Tell me what my mother said."

She gave a small sniffle, then tore his heart open. "She...she made it seem like you wouldn't want a baby with me because...well, because of how...I'm black and you're white. She said you'd—

He stopped her cold. "Jordan, I can't think of a woman in the world I'd rather have a baby with. Are you kidding me? With your brains and beauty and my...well, with *your* genes anyway. They'd be super-kid."

That got a smile out of her.

"In fact, I'm only worried about it being a girl. If she has your good looks I don't think I'd ever let her out of the house."

That made her laugh and made his heart soar.

He pulled her in for another hug. "You let me worry about my Ma. I'll make sure she gets the memo...signed, sealed, and delivered."

~

Carter looked at the ring again.

Five carats. It was a doozy.

"Cushion cut," the woman at *Intercontinental Jewelers* had said, whatever the heck that meant. All Carter knew was, it looked nice. Very nice. The kind of nice that would make heads turn. The kind of nice that would make other women jealous. The kind of nice that would make Jordan say yes.

Because, whether she knew it yet or not, Jordan was his. He had known that way back when he'd left Austin hell bent on kicking his father's ass. She had comforted him when he needed it the most. She had helped him work through the noise and figure out the truth. She had kept him from ending up in prison.

Now she was going to be the mother of his child.

He was going to spend the rest of his life doing his best to make sure she was happy. She would want for nothing. She would never be scared, or worried, or upset, or sad. Not if he could help it. She would lie in his bed next to him every night, and wake up to his face smiling down at her.

If this ring didn't do it, he wasn't sure what would. As completely uninterested as he was in jewelry, even he had been immediately drawn to it. The "cushion cut" was a large, roundish, squarish shape, surrounded by tiny diamonds, on a band covered in diamonds. Women liked diamonds, right? He sure hoped Jordan did, because she was about to be wearing a mine's worth on her finger.

As he pulled out his black AmEx to pay for the ring, he felt only a slight bit of apprehension. He was sure he wanted to make Jordan his wife. The baby had only made him wake up and realize that fact.

But Jordan was a plotter and a planner. Their roller coaster of a relationship only proved to Carter that she was the one; if they could survive all these huge ups and downs they could survive anything. Carter was down for embracing the rapids, her hand securely in his.

Jordan wanted a calm lake of smooth sailing. She would most likely see it as proof they needed to wait.

Now they had every reason in the world to be together. Surely even she could see that?

He had brought in one of Houston's top interior designers to get rid of his "sex room." Even now he cringed at the thought that she had ever laid eyes on it.

The designer had done her best to keep a poker face when he revealed it to her, but he'd seen the mild look of disapproval. He couldn't blame her. He'd literally taken the decor from a porno he'd watched right after buying the house.

"Make it...feminine," he'd said, leaving her to her own devices, money being no object. She'd certainly taken him at his word and he had the bill to prove it. But he had to give it to her, the result had been perfect.

That was the nice thing about money: it could buy you what you wanted.

But could it get him what he wanted most?

He looked at the ring again, imagining it on Jordan's finger...right next to the one that would make her his for life.

He would do whatever it took to make her his.

First, he had some business to take care of.

Jordan's words still filled his veins with fire as he recalled them. He took a day to calm down. Madison Grant may have fucked up big time, but she was still his mother.

It was time to do what he should have done long before he even met Jordan.

For the first time, it was Carter who was hounding his mother, and not the other way around. He knew full well that if she didn't want to be contacted, she wouldn't be. So he showed up to her place.

David, the doorman, recognized him and instantly picked up the phone to call her.

"Ms. Grant, your son Carter is here—"

The doorman paused as his mother was no doubt rattling off a list of excuses to relay to her son. Carter watched with a mixture of growing irritation and sympathy at what he was about to put the man through.

He hung up and looked at Carter, who stopped him before he could open his mouth. "Let me guess, she's not feeling well? Busy? Having the place fumigated?"

David gave him a look of consternation. "I'm sorry Mr. Fox but she—"

"Don't worry about it, David."

He pulled out his cell phone and dialed. It went straight to voicemail as he'd expected.

"Ma, we've got to address this at some point, and I've decided that today is the day. I'm going to give you exactly one minute to listen to this message, call me back and invite me up so we can deal with this... or I'll simply stand here in the lobby leaving another message detailing all your exploits for David, and any of your neighbors who might wander in, to hear. One minute."

He smiled at the doorman, whose face was a mixture of discomfort and mild curiosity. No doubt a delightful little scandal concerning one of the residents was a fun way to break up the monotony of the day. On the other hand, there was a certain propriety to maintain. They both waited there in silence.

After a minute, Carter made good on his threat, calling her back fully prepared to follow through.

She picked up after the first ring. "Carter Fox, you have no shame!" she said before he could utter a word.

"That's mighty *rich* of you to say, considering," he retorted. "Do you wanna do this here or send me up? David's looking mighty interested and I think I just heard the elevat—"

"Don't be crass, Carter," she spat. After a moment she sighed. "Fine, give the phone to David."

Carter handed the phone to David whose curiosity had diminished under the prospect of being thrown into the ring between Madison Grant and Carter Fox. He listened warily and then nodded. "Yes, Ms. Grant."

He handed the phone back to Carter. "You may go up now," he said hurriedly.

"Thank you, David," Carter said graciously. He'd have to remember to send him an expensive bottle of whiskey for Christmas.

Madison opened the door already on the defensive. "You should be ashamed of yourself bringing David into this!"

"There wouldn't be a 'this' if you hadn't completely crossed the line."

"I don't know—"

"Don't!" Carter roared, causing her to flinch with startled eyes.

"Don't lie," he said in a calmer tone, which was somehow even more intimidating.

She pressed her lips together and crossed her arms not saying a word.

"I suspected, after that day in January, maybe you were keeping tabs on me. But *Jordan?*"

She broke her silence. "Well, it's a good thing I did, Carter! Who knew what she would have tried with that baby—"

"So you *knew?*" Even though Jordan had said it, his mother confirming it made it hit home. "And you didn't tell me?"

She gave a defiant laugh. "Of course not! What would you have done? Something stupid like run off and buy a ring?"

He laughed at the irony.

"I don't see what's so funny about it Carter. It's 18 years she's got you trapped."

"I did buy a ring, Ma," he told her matter-of-factly.

She gasped. "Carter, no!"

"Hush Ma!" he shouted. "Listen to me. I love her."

"Carter—"

"And I'm going to ask her to marry me." He gave her a direct look, "because you know what? I want her for more than 18 years. I want her for life. And I don't care what our child looks like...in fact I hope it does look like her. I'll love it all the more."

"Carter you don't know what you're—"

"From now on, if you want to be a part of my life, you have to accept Jordan...and our baby."

He came in closer and she shied away from the look in his eyes. "Either way, I have two rules. One, no more spying, or detectives, or whatever it is you're doing to keep tabs on us. You wanna know something you pick up the damn phone."

She pursed her lips but nodded.

"And two, don't you ever—*ever*—talk to Jordan that way again. I swear I'll cut you off for good. Do you understand?"

She gave him a look of indignant disbelief.

"Do you understand?"

She looked out the window as her lips began to tremble. "I was only trying to protect you Carter."

"I don't need your protection, Ma. Not from Jordan."

She continued to look out the window and gave a deep breath, but didn't say anything.

"I'll give you time to think about that. If you do decide to come back, I expect you to apologize to her, or no deal."

He waited for an answer, then left.

35

Jordan looked around at the apartment with a satisfied huff.

The decor was a motley mix of the low-end Ikea furniture that was still stable enough to survive the trip from Austin, and slightly less low-end Ikea furniture which she had splurged on in Houston. It didn't matter that she had this fancy new job with *Morris & Gibson*, complete with a fancy new salary, she still had almost a hundred thousand in student loans to pay off. No sense going too crazy with the money.

Besides, it was hers...all hers. Finally!

Houston had been going through a bonanza of luxury apartment building. She had snagged a place only a few blocks away from the light rail. She wouldn't even have to drive into work. Sure, the place was a cookie cutter "luxury" apartment, with boring beige walls she wasn't allowed to paint, and boring beige carpet, which she could at least throw a rug over. But it was hers.

She smiled thinking of how she could walk around naked, eating peanut butter straight from the jar, while belting out Katy Perry songs...or Kanye West songs...or even the *Sound of Music* at the top of her lungs, and no one would be there to stop her.

It was a stupid thought to have. With the bar, and her job, and the growing bump in front of her, she had far bigger things to deal with. But it was still nice to think about.

She could also come in late at night, after a date, without another certain someone staying up to wait for her.

She thought about Carter and her heart practically doubled in size. It had been a week since she'd revealed the truth. He'd been so perfect, so *damn* perfect, when she'd told him about the baby. This was her baby. Hers and Carter's. Theirs.

And he'd stepped right up to the plate—and hit a perfect home run.

She rubbed her belly looking around at her place.

"Well, baby," she mused, "It's not as grand as your daddy's place, but we'll make it work."

Carter was coming by later to "take her out some place special."

Baseball season was in full swing again and his free nights were few and far between. So she was anxiously awaiting their date. She looked at the time and got a move on. She had to take a shower and get ready. Now that she no longer had to worry about hiding the little one, she happily embraced her small curve.

The dress was floral and sleeveless with an empire-waist that ended in gauzy handkerchief layers around her knees. The beauty of it was that she could wear it even after the baby was born.

The intercom buzzed and she pressed the button by the door to let Carter into the building. A few minutes later he was knocking at her door and she opened it, and taking a good look at him. As usual, she was amazed by his sheer size. He practically filled the doorway and was dressed especially well tonight with a crisp white dress shirt, perfectly tailored slacks and a matching jacket. He was even in dress shoes instead of his trademark cowboy boots.

Carter looked down at the dress, and she was pleased to see his eyes linger at her center with a mixture of awe and joy. God, she loved this man!

She opened the door wider to let him in and see her place for the first time.

"So this is the official Casa de Jordan?" he teased, looking around. "Did you buy out the entire Ikea store?"

"If you're going to make fun of it, then you can go and have dinner alone," she retorted.

He threw his hands up and laughed. "Okay, okay. Sorry."

He walked over to where she was and wrapped his arms around her. "I know how much you've been looking forward to having a place all to yourself." He pressed his body against hers, "I know how much I've been looking forward to it too." He purred.

She laughed and threw her arms high around his neck standing on her toes. "As much as I like where your mind is going, I'm really hungry."

"Well, I can't have my woman going hungry. Let's get this night started."

Dinner had been delicious, Latin American. They had even made a virgin sangria for her. Now she was completely stuffed, and Carter was driving her back to his place. He apparently had something to show her. She couldn't even imagine what it might be.

He opened the front door and took her hand. As soon as she walked through and saw what was inside she understood.

Oh!

There was a path cleared through a winding stretch of rose petals, straight to the living room. The lighting inside was dim and she could see that the coffee table was covered in candles.

Oh yes! Yes, Carter, yes!

"You didn't leave these burning all night did you?" she asked suddenly.

He looked back at her with a laugh. "That would be a no, Jordan. I may not be a rocket scientist but I know basic safety. I had Ms. Stewart, my housekeeper, set this up right before we came. She was pretty excited about it. I guess throwing rose petals is a nice change from making beds and filling the fridge."

She felt silly for having ruined the mood with such a dumb question.

The petals led directly to the sofa where Carter sat her down.

"I'll be back in one moment," he said, then jogged upstairs.

She knew exactly what he was off to do and her insides were nearly exploding with excitement. To the side of the coffee table was an ice bucket that held what looked to be sparkling cider. She smiled and rubbed her belly. This was so, *so* perfect. Carter was perfect.

The circumstances could have been a bit more...planned. She shook her head. The old Jordan needed to take a seat—two seats. If anything, this little bun in her oven showed her that life's detours could lead to something even more wonderful than all her perfect little plans.

She heard him coming back and turned to see him holding one hand behind his back. She sat up straighter to prepare herself.

He approached her and knelt on one knee in front of her, taking her hand.

"Jordan, ever since that day I saw you—"

"Yes!" she said, unable to contain herself.

He gave a startled pause then grinned, "If you had any idea how long I spent on this speech—"

"I'm sorry," she babbled, "I just...oh Carter, yes! Yes!"

"There you go again!" he bellowed, with a laugh.

She leaned down to kiss him as a form of apology. He leaned into it, and she forgot all about the proposal. She felt a warm wave of euphoria run directly from his lips to hers and straight through her body. She physically shuddered as it hit her. Man, this guy—*this guy*. He was hers.

His mouth still firmly on hers, he pulled himself up to join her on the couch. She brought her arms around his neck and shifted over to straddle him. Suddenly she broke the kiss, pulling away.

"Wait a second," she laughed. "Do I actually get to see this thing?"

He joined her laugh as he pulled the hand, placed awkwardly behind his back, out and revealed the little, black, velvet box. She bit her lip and held her breath in anticipation as he brought it between them and opened it.

"Oh, Carter," she breathed.

It was stunning. Obscenely stunning. Even in the dim, candlelit, room it sparkled like a giant...star. She reached out to touch it and he slammed it shut on her, making her jump. One hand swiftly reached around protectively to the small of her back to keep her from falling off his lap.

"Whoa there, filly," he said. "First, let me do this properly—no interruptions!"

Jordan grinned and nodded obediently.

"I would get back down on my knee but I kinda like this position better," he grinned back at her.

She wriggled impatiently on his lap, wanting to see that glorious ring again.

"Not helpin', sweetheart."

She laughed. "If you don't get on with it, I'm going to grab it right out of your hand and stick it on my finger myself!"

He raised it over his head, knowing that, even propped up on his lap, she wouldn't be able to out stretch him.

She gave a loud huff and then settled down. "Okay, go ahead."

He looked at her for a beat then brought the box down between them.

"Since you preempted my pretty little speech I'll just do the quick and dirty version," he said, giving her a mocking look of disapproval. He opened the box to reveal the perfect ring once again.

"Jordan Douglas, will you do me the honor of giving me your hand in marriage?"

She brought her arms back up around him and looked him in the eye. "Yes, Carter Fox, I will."

He plucked the ring out of the cushion and she dutifully held out her left hand. The feel of the band and his fingertips on her finger sent shivers through her body. They kissed and again it was like a lightning bolt of euphoria running through her.

She came in closer toward him, pressing as much as her tummy would allow. He moved his body so that he was lying on the couch underneath her. She slid a hand down the front of his shirt, working a button loose.

"So," he said, underneath her lips, "you can move in anytime you want."

She paused and pulled away from him, registering what he said.

"What?"

"Move in," he said shrugging against the seat of the couch. "Obviously."

She sat up and looked down at him with a wary smile. "Why would I 'obviously' move in? I have an apartment, on which I *just* signed the lease."

He sat up and her body slid further back on the couch away from him.

"Yeah but, don't you want...?"

"Want what?" she prodded.

"Don't you want to be a family?"

"Of course I do, but that doesn't mean moving in with you tomorrow just because we're engaged."

"Well what *does* it mean?" he asked, his voice getting heated. "I mean, I'm here offering you my house, my rather *large* house, so that we can be together—as a family—but here you go being stubborn again—"

"*Stubborn?*" she exclaimed. "Why is it that every time I do something for myself I'm 'stubborn?' You just don't get it Carter...and to think I thought *you* of all people *would.*"

"What is it I'm not getting?"

"For once I *finally* have a place that's all mine. No, it's not a big, impressive River Oaks mansion," she waved her hand around the room, "but it's all mine, that I earned with my own money. No parents, no roommates, no one except me."

"Well it's more than just *you* isn't it," he retorted, looking pointedly down at her stomach. "Maybe you want to think about that."

"I *am* thinking about that. I want to be a role model, not some silly girl who went straight from her parent's home to her husband's like a piece of chattel. I want to be someone she can look up to."

"She?" Carter started at that. "It's a girl?"

It took a moment for Jordan to process the non sequitur. "What?"

"You know it's a girl?" he pressed.

"Well...no but—"

"So it could be a boy?"

She gave him an irritated look. "Or it could be a girl. What? You only want to be involved if it's a mini-me? A Carter Jr. you can play catch with?"

He gave her a confused look and shook his head. "What? No, it's just... Jesus, a *girl.*" He ran a hand through his hair as his eyes grew wide at the prospect.

"For Pete's sake, Carter!" she said lifting herself off the couch. "What does it matter if it's a boy or a girl? What does it matter if I move in today or after we're married? I knew you were...I don't know, maybe a bit alpha, but I never figured you for a complete caveman."

"Caveman?" he repeated, his jaw hardening. "That's kind of a low blow."

She blinked at that, remorse coming to her face. "That's not what I—"

"Never mind," he sighed.

They waited in silence for several moments, both of them processing the 180 that the night had taken.

"I should go home," she said softly.

Carter sucked his lips in and nodded. "Yeah, I suppose so."

As he sighed and got up off the couch, she looked at the ring. After a moment she pulled it off and handed it to him.

"I think we should hold off on this," she said.

The look of shock and hurt nearly caused her to slip it right back on her finger. Her more rational mind prevailed.

"No, Jordan, don't," he insisted. "We'll work through this."

"Perhaps, but now...I just don't think it's right for me to take it." She kept it held out to him.

"At least hold on to it," he insisted. "You don't have to wear it, but it's yours, whether you take it today or 10 years from now. It's yours."

She shook her head and placed it on the coffee table. "I'm not saying no, but I can't say yes...not like this."

❧ 36 ☙

The Sluggers were in San Francisco to play the Giants this week. Not a horrible place to be in mid-June, especially in comparison to the blanket of humidity settled over Houston. Carter had heard down the pipeline that he might be a candidate for the Home Run Derby and the All Star game.

It was shaping up to be one of his greatest seasons ever.

Right now he had one thing on his mind, and it wasn't baseball. Ever since Jordan had placed that ring back on the coffee table his emotions had been a complete surprise, even to himself. From the moment it touched the table he'd felt a strong sense of determination.

This wasn't over.

Because she was his.

He couldn't say why, but he just knew it, ring or no ring. Maybe it was because she was carrying a part of him inside of her. Maybe it was because she "wasn't saying no." Maybe it was because he just knew.

They belonged together. The baby, even if it was unplanned, only cemented that fact.

She was his. Eventually, she'd figure that out.

It was this determination that was running through his head as he stood there at bat, with a man at second and third. He was up against Bradley Waltman. The man had five good pitching styles so it was a toss up as to what he'd get thrown at him.

The first pitch was positionally perfect, at least as far as height...then it curved away, just as Carter swung. Strike one.

Bradley had gone with a cutter. He was unlikely to try the same pitch twice. That left four others.

Carter saw the next pitch heading out of the strike zone just as his shoulder gave a twitch. Ball one.

The next two pitches were out of the strike zone, which left it at three balls, one strike.

Come on Bradley. Carter wanted to actually feel that ball connect with the bat. He also didn't want to be walked, especially as it wouldn't move any of his teammates forward.

The next pitch looked outside, *really* outside. So far outside, Carter was certain he had a walk. As soon as it hit the Catcher's mitt he actually dropped the bat in disappointment and actually began to walk.

"Strike 2!"

Carter spun around in outrage. *Are you kidding me?* There was no way that ball was over the plate. He thought about arguing with the umpire, but that would only get him kicked out of the game. Carter calmed down and shrugged it off, picking his bat up again.

Determination.

The next pitch was a slider, usually pretty good for hitting a home run...but not when they were that low. Too low. Low enough for Carter to be lucky if he hit it as far as the outfield.

He swung.

Both Carter and Bradley gaped in surprise as the bat connected the ball arced high. Really high. High enough to...score a home run. Three points for his team.

Determination.

Jordan was going to be his.

M*orris & Gibson* had given the associates the summer to take the bar before they had to show up for work. They had even paid for the absurdly expensive bar course just to seal the deal. The deal being: make sure you pass.

They'd all been warned that they had exactly two shots to pass. Jordan had no intention of going for round two. It was bad enough trying to study with a rapidly expanding middle and her hormones raging. She couldn't imagine what it would be like trying again in the winter with a newborn, and a stressful job, not to mention the embarrassment of everyone knowing you hadn't passed the first time around.

No, she was sealing the deal this summer. Then she could relax. Sort of.

She'd taken a wee break to watch the Sluggers play the Giants.

When Carter hit that home run, instinct took over, and her heart swelled with pride. She knew nothing about baseball, but the swing had seemed incredibly awkward. She hadn't been sure that he would even hit it. Which made it all the more impressive.

She wished she could talk on the phone with him after the game to congratulate him like she used to.

Why had she given him back that ring?

The rational part of her brain knew it was the right thing to do. They obviously had issues to work out and needed to be on the same page before they even thought about marriage. On the other hand, she loved him, he loved her, they were a family. Everything could work itself out. Couldn't it?

Why the hell had she given him back that ring?

By the end of the week, her mind had returned to studying for the bar. Naturally, she was cognizant of the fact that the Sluggers were flying back into Houston today. In between torts and contracts, Carter popped into her head.

Today he was coming back.

It had been a tedious day of lectures, and note taking, and she desperately needed to eat before taking practice tests tonight. She pulled into the parking garage of her apartment building and parked in her spot. She opened the back passenger side door to reach in and pull out her bag full of study materials, and the Chipotle salad bowl she'd picked up. Just as she pulled herself out, she turned around and, with a yelp, immediately dropped the bag that held her dinner.

It was a man, or at least she thought it was a man. He had a man's build, but his face was covered with a plain white mask. Her heart stopped...right before it began beating in a panic.

Before she could so much as scream, he brought a phone up to her face and snapped a photo of her.

"Tell Carter Fox we said hi," the man's voice said.

The next moment he took off running on foot.

Jordan let the shock subside, then fell back against the car with a sob. Her mind was a blur of what to do next. Run inside her apartment? Hide in her car? Call the police?

Her eyes fell to the Chipotle bag on the ground and something about it made her fall into the passenger seat shaking convulsively.

Minutes later, she cried out in surprise as her phone rang in her purse. Her body was so shaky that it slipped and fumbled out of her grasp. By the time she managed to pull it out, it had gone to voicemail. She looked at the screen and saw that it was Carter.

Before she could call him back, he called again.

"C-Carter?" she asked with a shaky voice.

"Jesus Christ, thank God you're okay," she heard him breathe out with relief in his voice. "Where are you?"

"I-I'm in my car, my garage—

"Okay, Jordan I want you to go into your apartment right now, do you hear me?" he demanded. "I'm on my way over."

"What's going on Carter?" she cried.

"Just do it Jordan!" he yelled, making her jump. "I can explain later, but stay on the phone with me, okay?"

She nodded dumbly into the phone, not registering that he couldn't see her. She had the wherewithal to grab her things, pick up the bag from the ground and rush to the entrance to her building.

"Are you still with me?" he prodded. "Say something, sweetheart."

"I-I hear you. What's going on Carter? That man he—he—"

"What did he do to you?" Carter growled.

"He said to say hi to you," she responded, getting on the elevator.

The call broke up and then died. Jordan felt like her lifeline had been cut and she began to tremble as the elevator took her to her floor.

As soon as the doors opened she jumped out, looking up and down the hallway with her heart in her throat, waiting for another masked man to assault her. The phone rang in her hand startling her. She pressed the button to answer it.

"Jesus Jordan, don't hang up on me!" Carter shouted before she could answer.

"It was the elevator," she trembled.

"Ok, baby, I'm sorry," he said in a calmer voice, realizing that his shouting wasn't helping. "Are you in your apartment? I'm almost there."

She fumbled with the keys, still looking left and right as she nodded into the phone again. "Yeah," she said realizing yet again he couldn't see her. She finally got the key in the lock and opened it quickly. She rushed inside and slammed the door shut behind her.

It wasn't until she was inside that she let loose again. She fell back against the door with a whimper.

Carter heard it through the phone and began to soothe her. "It's okay Jordan," he cooed. "I'm right here on the phone with you, almost there, sweetheart. Just hang on okay?"

"Mmm-hmm" she said nodding, hanging on tightly to his voice.

"Okay Jordan, I just parked the car on the street outside. Buzz me up sweetheart."

She heard the call come through and his voice in the speaker. She pressed the button and waited. Her body was so taut that she jumped when he pounded on the door. For a brief hysterical moment, she assumed it was the same man in the mask coming for her. Then Carter's voice boomed on the other side of the door.

"Jordan," he called. "It's me, let me in babe."

She reached out to unlatch the door and open it.

He rushed in and immediately snatched her into a bear hug. "Oh man, thank God," he breathed into the top of her head. "I'm so sorry, Jordan."

She let the seconds pass as she acclimated herself to the fact that Carter was here and she was safe. Then she pushed away from him. He held on tight but eventually gave in to her pressure.

"What's going on?" she demanded, getting angry now that the scare had passed.

"It's a long story—"

"Tell me!" she insisted.

"It—It's my dad. He owes money—"

"Your dad?!" she said in surprise. "Isn't he in jail?"

"Yes but—"

"But he's still screwing up your—*our*—lives!"

"Jordan, right now we need to think about your safety, yours and the baby's."

She stared at him for a few beats, not knowing what to say. Finally, she shook her head. "I can't believe this is happening." She walked over to her sofa and fell into it.

Carter stared at her giving her a moment.

"You have to move in with me Jordan."

She looked up at him with disbelief.

"It's for your own safety," he said before she could voice any complaints.

She put her hands over her stomach remembering that she had someone besides herself to consider. His eyes followed and a look of pain came over his face.

"Jordan, my house is just safer. I've got the alarm system, the gate out front, it's River Oaks for Christ sake! We've got our own security. I'm hiring guards first thing in the morning."

She stared at him, wanting to hate him for bringing this in to her and their baby's life. But she knew it wasn't his fault. Now he was trying to do the right thing.

She couldn't let her ego or need for independence get in the way of their safety.

"Okay," she sighed, and saw him relax with relief.

This wasn't at all how he wanted her back in his life.

It was almost as though these people had timed it so that Carter received the message as soon as the plane landed bringing the Sluggers back to Houston. Carter found himself high-tailing it out of the parking lot and straight to the woman he loved. Only this time there were two lives at stake.

The message had again been minimal, and straight to the point: a picture of Jordan's startled face and one line reading: $248,593.

Carter had immediately rung Jordan's phone and thought the worst when she hadn't picked up.

Now she was here living with him, just as he'd wanted. It felt wrong, like he'd cheated somehow. Either way, he would work on making this right. She was sleeping in the transformed downstairs guest room...as far as possible away from him.

The police and his lawyer had come and gone. They'd put a trace on the call, but everyone in the room knew it wouldn't lead anywhere. These people weren't stupid.

Carter would have paid the damn money, but who knew where it would end? Besides, now that they had involved Jordan, had involved his unborn child, his mind wasn't exactly on making things square; it was on something far more vicious.

There was only one person who knew who and where they could be found. Until now, he'd kept his mouth shut. Until now, Carter didn't have a reason to press the issue.

That moment had come and gone.

He was sitting in a plastic chair in the visitors' room of the prison. He ignored the blatant stares of the other visitors and prisoners. His mind was far too preoccupied.

He saw Bobby Joe swagger in with a look of smug curiosity. For once, Carter needed something from *him*.

"Well *Son*, to what do I owe the pleasure?" he asked, mockingly.

"Who are they?"

"You plannin' on paying my debts? That's mighty—"

"Cut the shit," Carter growled.

Bobby Joe shut his mouth and pondered his son for a moment. Finally, he sighed. "You know I can't tell you that. I'd be lucky to make it out of here in one—"

"I've got a baby coming," Carter said, using the only card he could think of. "They threatened the woman I'm going to marry and *your* grandkid." The word sounded every kind of wrong coming from his lips, but if it helped even a little it was worth it.

Bobby Joe twisted his mouth to the side, letting what he'd just heard marinate.

"For once in your life, do the right thing," Carter pressed.

Bobby Joe looked toward the tiny window in the visitors' room, his face contorted in thought. Carter didn't hold out much hope. The last thing Bobby Joe ever did for him out of selflessness was buy him a baseball and a bat. He could only hope that the years of bailing him out of trouble had added up to a modicum of decency.

Just as Carter was about to get up and leave the man spoke.

"You got a pen and paper?"

It had been two weeks since he'd met with Bobby Joe. Carter had thought long and hard about handling things himself, medieval style. One thought of leaving Jordan and their baby in the lurch as he finished his days in prison had made him think more rationally on the matter.

The police had been notified of the names and whereabouts of the people Bobby Joe had dealt with. It was a somewhat well-known group out of Laredo, Texas. Carter being a big fish had made them sloppy. The texts Carter had received—the last one being the nail in the coffin —were enough for at least a warrant. Arrests had been made, evidence gathered up, at least enough for charges on the blackmail and loan sharking. Carter planned on making sure the D.A. tacked on a few more charges just in case.

He was tempted to tell Jordan that the coast was pretty much clear, but she had been so distant since moving in. He couldn't blame her. He was indirectly responsible for the threat to her and the baby's safety. It would take some time to thaw from that.

Besides, she seemed to have enough on her plate with the bar studying. She had taken over the dining room table as Command Center One for Texas State Bar Study. There were large paperback books laid open on the table with a rainbow of highlights covering each page. Practice tests, notebooks pens, highlighters were scattered as though a localized hurricane had taken place on his dining room table.

Tonight had been another successful game, securing the Sluggers' lead in their division. Carter took it as a good sign.

Determination.

Jordan was his.

Carter walked through the front door, turning off the alarm. He saw the light was on in the dining room. He approached cautiously, not wanting to interrupt a late night study session. Frankly, he couldn't wait until this damn bar was over and done with. Then maybe Jordan and he could focus on repairing their relationship.

He saw the usual pile of books, papers, pens, and highlighters. Added to the mix were crumpled tissues and wrinkled balls of paper scattered on the floor. In the center of it all was Jordan, with her head planted securely in the crook of one arm at the head of the table, sound asleep.

He approached the table and looked down at the mess. It was like trying to decipher hieroglyphics, but there were a few clues to help him out. Foremost was what looked like a practice multiple choice test with a big red 52% scrawled across the top. He picked up one of the crumpled pieces of paper and saw that it was yet another practice test with a 51% scrawled across the top. He looked around at the tissues scattered across the table and then back at her face, resting on her arm. It was puffy and smeared with tears.

"Oh Jordan," he sighed.

From this vantage point, he had a clear view of her stomach, which was glaringly pregnant by now. Carter Jr. or Jordan Jr. He thought of a mini version of Jordan and the steel vice grip that squeezed his heart caused his breath to catch in his throat. A daughter. God help the man who ever broke her heart.

He was probably better off having a boy.

Jesus...he was going to be a father.

He reached down to push away a strand of hair that had fallen in front of Jordan's face. She was *his*. This baby was *his*.

Tonight she was sleeping with him, in *their* bed.

He gently pushed the chair back. She stirred with complaint but didn't come fully awake. He brought one strong arm under her legs and placed the other around her back. He shifted his weight so that she fell back onto his arm. She became groggily conscious.

"*Wha...?*" She mumbled, the sleep still overpowering her.

"Shhh," he cooed in her ear.

He lifted her out of the chair and her head fell against his chest. At this angle, her body was cradled protectively around the baby inside of her, and it caused his heart to stop again. They both felt as light as air in his arms. He was the last layer of protection. Carter would use every ounce of his strength keep either one of them from harm.

The three of them against the world. He would make this work.

By the time he made it to his room—*their* room—she was asleep again. He placed her gently on the bed and began the process of undressing her. He smiled to think about what a fuss she'd put up if she were awake. Eventually, he had her down to her underwear and brought the covers down. He slid her smooth brown legs underneath them.

He couldn't keep himself from placing one hand on the bump that was more obvious now that it was fully exposed. He waited and was rewarded with a tiny little kick. He gasped audibly, as his heart caught in his throat for the third time tonight. Jordan shifted underneath him with a small moan.

So this was what it felt like to be a father. A love so powerful it literally knocks you out. There was no way he was going to fail at this.

"I'm going to get you to marry me if it's the last thing I do, Jordan Douglas" he whispered as he brought the covers over her. He leaned in to kiss her forehead.

39

She woke with a start.

Something was nagging at her and it had snapped her out of her slumber. She looked around and was momentarily disoriented. This wasn't the guest room in Carter's house. It was his room, his bed. She quickly turned her head and saw him lying next to her.

She put it all together and wanted to jump out of bed with outrage. She just couldn't. She was tired of being angry at him. Tired of not talking to him. Tired of seeing him come home from a game and make wide circles around her while she studied.

She wanted him back.

Jordan looked down at his face while he slept. The comforter was only up to his mid chest, revealing his naked, tattooed muscles. She reached out a hand to stroke his hair. He was so perfect. Well...in his own way.

He stirred underneath her fingers and his eyes blinked open.

She smiled down at him and was rewarded with a sleepy grin in return.

"Hey beautiful," he murmured. His eyes blinked with alertness, realizing that she was actually acknowledging him and he came fully awake.

He pulled himself up into a sitting position and looked at her.

"How are you?" he asked with concern. "I saw the table last night and...."

She frowned. Yesterday had been a simulated practice exam for the multiple choice section of the bar.

"I scored a 52%," she said miserably. "That's *horrible*. I'm going to fail, I know it. Then *Morris* will take back their offer, and then I'll be a mom with no job and—"

"Hey, hey, Jordan," Carter said, pulling her into him and stroking her hair. "Jordan, you're the smartest person I know, hands down. If you can't pass this thing then no one can."

"But—"

"But nothing," he insisted, squeezing her tighter. "You got this, sweetheart, you hear me?"

She let it sink in for a moment, then nodded into his chest. In his arms, she felt so secure, as though everything would be okay. She relaxed into it and let the calm overtake her.

"I'm sorry for being so distant," she mumbled into his chest. "It's just with the bar, and this baby, and that horrible man—"

"Shh," he said. "It's all over. You're safe here with me."

"What about the thing with your father?"

He paused for a moment. "They found the guys and brought them in."

She wondered how long he'd known, but found she didn't care. She didn't want an excuse to leave.

After another moment he asked, "So, are we good here?"

She nodded into his chest.

"Even with your whole deal about the apartment? And your desire to live alone, be a good role model?"

She poked him in the ribs, making him flinch and laugh.

"When she's grown, I can tell her I had a full week on my own."

"Or *him*," he suggested.

She poked him again but laughed. "Fair enough, or *him*."

"If it makes you feel any better, I don't think he, or she, could ask for a better role model." He kissed the top of her head.

"Speaking of boys and girls, what are we going to do about names?" he asked.

"I've been sounding it out and I like...Bree?"

"Sounds good."

She pulled away from him. "Just like that? You don't want to talk about it?"

He shrugged. "I like the name. Bree Fox. Simple. Cute. What's to discuss?"

"Carter! We're supposed to—"

He laughed. "Why are you always looking for an argument, woman?"

She looked at him for a moment, then laughed, ceding the point to him. Then she squinted giving him a sly look. "And if it's a boy?"

He put his hands behind his head and shrugged again. "That's easy enough. Carter Jr."

"What?" she yelped. "No way."

"Why not?"

"Because...it's so...I don't know."

"See, you can't even think of a reason. Carter Jr." he said firmly.

She frowned at the name again. Then she let it roll around in her head. Carter Jr. It would do. She fell back against his chest and he brought an arm firmly around her.

"You have no idea how much I care about you, Jordan," he said almost idly.

"That's sweet," she said, giving a small nudge with her elbow. "But I've already agreed to stay here. You don't need to butter me up."

Carter released his arm and brought her around to face him. She looked back at him with wary curiosity.

"No, seriously Jordan. You listen to me because I want you to get it. *You* are my life, my heart," he pressed her hand into his chest right over his heart and tapped once. "You," he tapped again, "and her—or *him*," he smirked at Jordan, "you both are what makes this right here, beat." He tapped twice again, for good measure, then brought her hand up to his lips.

It was so damn romantic it brought tears to her eyes. "When did you get so poetic?" she asked.

"There's a lot you have yet to learn about me, sweetheart," he said smiling.

She pulled her hand out of his and brought it up to his face for a kiss. God how she missed the taste of him, among other things.

"Mmm," he said under her lips.

She pushed herself up against him, closer and closer. The months of avoidance caught up with her and she eagerly straddled him, abandoning any ideas of foreplay. She reached behind her back to unhook her bra. As she pulled it off her arms, Carter looked at her warily.

"Are you sure this is okay?" he asked, looking down at her belly.

"Um, it better be," she laughed. "This pregnancy has been making me horny as hell. Besides, we've got a few more months to go. Do you really want to wait that long?"

He nodded his head to the side acknowledging the point. "In that case, you don't have to ask twice."

She laughed. "Great, now get me out of these panties, Slugger."

🎋 40 🎋

EARLY OCTOBER

Once again Jordan found herself back in her old room at her parents' house. This time, it didn't matter. This time, it was for a good reason. The best possible reason. The Sluggers had made it to the postseason.

On top of this, Carter had also scored exactly 60 home runs, tied with Babe Ruth. They both decided that was good enough.

The first division series game with the Braves was actually supposed to be on her due date in Atlanta.

"Say the word, and I'm off that plane, right here by your side," he had insisted.

"First of all, Ben would kill me," she had chided. "Second, I wanna see my man make it to the World Series. Now go get 'em Slugger." She had said, leaning into him, kissing him on the lips.

The next best people in her life were taking his place to get her to the hospital when the time came. By now her parents had adjusted to the idea that they would be grandparents. In fact, both of them, in their own ways, seemed to actually be looking forward to it.

The first indications hit her right on schedule the night before the game. After sleepless hours *(this is it!)* of pacing her room and breathing, mostly to calm her nerves, she made her way down to her parents' room once it was obvious that things would be moving along. She hadn't wanted to keep them up all night just to watch her pace. Now, she was tired of being alone. At exactly 8 a.m. she knocked on their door.

It was as though they had been waiting up. Her mother answered after the first knock. She took one look at Jordan's face and her hand flew to her mouth with anxious joy.

"Alright," she said, hugging Jordan into the room. "Ralph!" she called.

"I'm here, I'm here," he said making his way out of the bathroom with a toothbrush in his hand. He looked at her questioningly, then put it together running back in to put his toothbrush away and get ready.

"Okay, so we have your bag for the hospital. We have your doctor's name right? Oh, we need to call Roy and Pat and your grandparents. Ralph, don't just stand there, get the car ready."

"Mom, *Mom*," Jordan smiled. "Calm down. They said it would take a while. Breathe!"

Her mother looked at her for a moment, then nodded, visibly relaxing.

"I'm going to call Carter and let him know. You guys just get ready, okay?"

She made her way back to her room and picked up the phone.

He picked up after the first ring.

"It's time?" he asked anxiously before she could even say hi.

"Almost."

"Wow...*wow!*"

She laughed. "I know right?"

"I'm sorry I couldn't—"

"Stop," she chided. "You just make sure y'all win out there."

He laughed on the other end. "Aye, aye, captain."

"I love you, Carter."

"I love you too, Jordan."

∾

It took eight more hours before all was said and done. Her mother was right there by her side the whole time.

❧ 41 ❧

I *t's a girl.*

The first text had hit him like a splash of cold water, waking up all of his senses at once, forcing him to face his new reality.

He was a father.

A father to a girl.

Now Carter stood in the hotel room looking at Jordan holding his daughter, and it all made perfect sense. Of course, it was a girl.

He wouldn't have it any other way.

"Hey, Daddy," Jordan sing-songed on the other side of the facetime they were having via iPhone. "Say hello to Daddy, Bree." She held the baby up in her arms.

The emotional bomb in his head exploded as he saw the tiny, wrinkled face as she discovered the new world around her. He brought one large hand up and placed his thumb and two fingers over his eyelids trying to press the tears that began to flow back in. It was no use.

"Aww," Jordan said on the other end. "It's okay, you should see the waterworks that went on over here. I think even Ben got a few in."

"*Jor*-dan!" he heard Ben's voice protest from somewhere in the room.

Carter gave a sharp laugh which made him have to sniffle.

Jesus, he hadn't even met her in person yet and already his little girl was doing a number on him. Of course, it was a girl. How could it be any other way?

He laughed again.

"Well, we know you have to get to practice so we'll let you go. You'll have plenty of daddy daughter time when you get back."

He couldn't even speak, just nodding in response.

"Say goodbye, everyone!" The camera panned around the room, where the rest of her family—*his* family—waved excitedly congratulating him and wishing him good luck tonight, Ben being especially exuberant about the latter.

The phone came back to Jordan and Bree.

"Bye Carter, and good luck!" She mimed a kiss toward the phone and he instantly screen captured it. It was perfect. Jordan kissing him and Bree looking straight up at him.

He sat there staring at in wonder for a moment; perhaps a bit longer than a moment.

Then it hit him that he had the rest of his life with these two.

He shook his head. If he kept having these kinds of deep thoughts he'd never get out of here.

As soon as he walked through to the visiting clubhouse he was shocked yet again. A spray of champagne cascaded over his head as two of his teammates aimed the bottles his way.

"Congratulations Daddy!" everyone screamed.

What he thought at first were pink and blue balloons were actually blown up condoms bouncing around on the floor. He laughed at the irony. Even Miles joined in on the fun as he came forward to stick a cigar in his mouth.

"So, are you gonna leave us all in suspense?" he asked.

"Well, guys...it's a girl!"

A mixture of laughs, cheers and "*uh-ohh's!*" filled the room.

"Man, I don't know who's in more trouble now, you or anyone she dates!"

Carter had no idea either.

❧ 42 ❧

Her family had gone home to watch the game, giving Jordan and Bree a blessed moment of peace. It had been wonderful having them there, especially as she facetimed with Carter, but she was completely worn out.

Now it was just the two of them, Bree and Jordan.

Bree had thankfully latched on easily enough. Jordan had worried it would be just one of many failings she'd have as a mother. But there she was, sucking eagerly enough at her breast.

It gave Jordan such a warm and happy feeling watching her.

"Hey there green eyes," she cooed down at the face.

That had been the biggest surprise. Carter's eyes.

The hair was light brown and wavy, the skin was surprisingly pink. He mother had taken one look at the top of Bree's ears and pointed out the exact shade of *cafe au lait* she'd probably end up being. Her dad had criticized that that was just an old wives' tale.

As she looked down at her, Jordan realized she didn't care. Bree was perfect.

Jordan looked at the time and saw that the game had already started. She turned on the TV in the room, putting it on mute and watched the game unfold. She wanted to watch her man beat the Braves.

Besides, she—and now Bree—were his good luck charms. She smiled down at the fuzzy head below her, oblivious to the screen above them.

A few players in and Carter was at bat. She wasn't aware of her body tensing until she heard and felt the mildly irritated whimper at her breast. She kissed the head to calm Bree a bit and looked back up at the screen.

"There's your daddy," she whispered with a smile.

The camera zoomed in on his face for a moment and she was instantly taken back to the very first day she met Carter Fox. That face....

"Go get 'em Slugger," she whispered and smiled up at the screen.

The first pitch was thrown and even Jordan could see it was a ball. She started with satisfaction before remembering that Bree was still in her arms. She could feel the earlier eagerness slowing down. Pretty soon, she'd probably be asleep.

She couldn't tell if the next pitch was a ball. It didn't matter, Carter swung...and missed. Her heart fell with disappointment. It was crazy how emotional she got when her guy was at bat!

Strike one, ball one.

The next came so close to hitting Carter in the crotch she actually gasped. Even the crowd in Atlanta gave a ripple of shock. She tensed, waiting to see his reaction. Would he get upset? She didn't want to see him sitting out a game this close to making it to the World Series. She saw him grimace, step away from the plate, shake his head vigorously then step right back.

She let out a breath, rubbing Bree's soft head to calm herself.

She saw the look of determination on his face just as the next pitch was thrown. She knew even before the bat connected with the ball. The camera followed it up...up...up...and over the stands.

The camera switched back to Carter and that's when her heart burst into a million pieces. As if fully aware that she was looking at him through the TV screen, he double-tapped his chest, right above the heart, with his fist then brought two fingers up to his lips.

"We love you too Carter Fox," she whispered with pride.

She looked down and saw that her nipple had no little mouth attached to it. Bree was sound asleep. Jordan just chuckled.

The hospital had a policy of keeping babies in the room with their mothers instead of the nursery. The literature said it was to help form an attachment between the two. Jordan had an idea it was also to enlighten new moms to what it would be like once they got home, so it wasn't too much of a shock to the system.

Jordan was most definitely enlightened. The nurses could send her home today knowing that she was fully aware of what she had gotten herself into. Carter was the one who was now in for a surprise.

She smiled at the thought as she got out of bed to check in on her daughter, who was suspiciously quiet.

"They, um...said it was okay for me to come by since it was visiting hours."

She turned in surprise at the voice that was permanently embedded in her memory.

Madison Grant, in all her flame-haired glory, was standing in the doorway of her hospital room.

The two blinked at each other awkwardly for a moment, then Jordan swallowed.

Madison glanced past her toward the bassinet where Bree was staring up idly out the window. "Can I see her?"

An instinctively protective force ran through Jordan. She let it subside.

The woman was Carter's mother. She was here to see her granddaughter. That said something.

Jordan nodded.

Madison gave a brief, grateful smile. She held up the tiny pink bag, which Jordan noticed for the first time.

"Carter texted me," she said pursing her lips at the impersonal nature of the notification. "I suppose I should be grateful he got in touch at all," she said, making her way to Bree.

She handed the bag to Jordan and peeked down at her granddaughter. Bree stared up at her with that newborn look of wonder and surprise, most likely at the strikingly, flame-colored halo surrounding the woman's face.

"A girl, huh?" she said smiling down. "That probably gave Carter a nice little heart attack."

Jordan couldn't help herself, and she laughed. Madison looked up at her with surprise, then joined in. Another female to wreak havoc on his life.

Seeing that the ice had been somewhat thawed between them, Madison pressed on. "May I?" she said reaching her hands down to Bree.

Jordan nodded again.

Madison reached in and picked the tiny bundle up, cradling the head expertly and bouncing her lightly. "Hey there, little girl," she cooed.

She peered closely and her eyes blinked in surprise. "She has green eyes!" she said, astonished.

Jordan tensed, remembering full well their one-time conversation on eugenics.

Madison's slight smile faltered as her eyes rolled over to meet Jordan's and she saw the expression there.

"I—I didn't mean," she stammered. "It's just…she reminds me so much of him."

Jordan's tension level decreased by exactly one notch.

Madison looked down at Bree with a somber expression. "What I said that day…I…you just have no idea what a mother pours into her child."

"I think I have a pretty good idea," Jordan said testily.

Madison gave her a wry smile. "Oh, you're just beginning," she mused. "Wait until she breaks your heart for the first time."

"Those things I said, I…I honestly don't know what I think anymore. Everything changes with a baby." She turned to look down at Bree again with an almost nostalgic smile. "I know Carter loves you. I hope you love him just as much."

"I do," Jordan confirmed.

Madison brought her eyes back up to Jordan. "I wanna apologize for that day. No matter how I feel—*felt*—you didn't deserve it, especially considering your situation. It was mean and spiteful of me. I was just so scared of losing Carter. He's all the family I have."

Jordan thawed. This was progress at least.

She reached down into the bag and dug through the pink tissue paper. Jordan pulled out three little onesies, pink, lavender and white. All Sluggers' gear.

She laughed as she held them up.

Madison looked up. "Might as well start her early," she shrugged with a grin, then she began chuckling as well.

43

C arter stopped the truck down the street from his house, pulling over in idle.

He grabbed the steering wheel and stared straight ahead. This was it. The moment he entered his house, his life was changed forever. Heck, it was already changed, it just hadn't caught up with him yet.

His daughter was in that house waiting for him. Today she was three days old. Three days he had missed of her life already.

That lit a fire under him.

He put the truck back into drive and sped the rest of the way home. He pulled into the driveway and wasn't a bit surprised to see multiple familiar cars there. It gave him a feeling of pride. Jordan's family had come out to greet him, to welcome him into the fold.

No sooner had he opened the door, than he heard them yell out "Congratulations!"

It was the second time he had been greeted that way. This time around, in lieu of the condom balloons and cigars, the foyer was covered in pink streamers balloons and a large sign congratulating him once again.

In the back of his mind, it occurred to him that all he'd really done was break a condom. Maybe everyone should wait 18 years to see if congratulations were actually in order. That thought sank in as he realized the gravity of it.

Then Jordan appeared in the middle of the group, holding Bree. As small as Jordan was, at least compared to him, his daughter looked tiny in her arms.

"Hey, Daddy," she said bringing Bree to him. "Say hello to Bree René Fox."

He just stared down in wonder, terrified to touch her. Then Jordan held her up to him, urging him to hold her. She must have seen the look of trepidation in his face because she smiled in assurance.

"It's okay," she whispered.

That was all the encouragement he needed. She helped place Bree in one arm and brought his hand around to support the head. He was in awe at the fact that it was no bigger than his palm. She stared up at him with a confused and slightly unfocused look. That's when he saw the twinkle in her eye and peered in closer.

"Huh," he said, noticing the specks of green.

"Yep, definitely yours," Jordan teased as if reading his mind.

That's when everyone came forward to join in the moment. Jordan's parents, her aunt and uncle, and of course, Ben were all there. They had set up a small buffet in the dining room, which had also been decorated.

The doorbell rang. Carter saw Jordan skip out to go answer it.

He went back to staring down at his daughter, taking in every tiny little detail. He saw Jordan coming back in out of the corner of his eye. Then he noted the flicker of red and his head shot up.

"Ma," he said in surprise. His body tensed.

She looked across at him, her eyes blinking as she took in the picture of him holding Bree in his arms. She gave a teary smile.

Jordan brought an encouraging hand up to her back, urging her toward her son.

He relaxed a bit at the gesture but still gave his mother a wary look.

"Hello Carter," she said smiling first up at him then down at Bree.

Carter looked past her to Jordan who gave him a smile and a nod letting him know everything was just fine.

It was late at night and Jordan was sound asleep next to him. The bassinet was on her side near the fireplace and armchairs. He gently removed himself from the bed and walked over to it. He could just make out the outline of Bree's head in the shadows of the room.

He reached a hand in and reflexively brought it back out, scared to wake her. So he just stood there and stared. He wished one of the lamps next to the bed was on so he could see her. Right now Bree just looked like a tiny, helpless little nugget in the dark.

Would it be okay to hold her? He longed to experience it again.

He saw movement as she stirred. There was a small whimper that grew into a cry, then a wail. He froze, thinking somehow he'd caused it.

The bedside lamp nearest him switched on. One second later, he felt Jordan's hand on his back as she came up behind him and he flinched in surprise.

"Welcome to your life for the next several months," she said sleepily into his back.

"How do we know what's wrong?" he pondered.

"Well, it's either one end or the other," she laughed softly, reaching in to pick Bree up. "Or she could just be in a cantankerous mood.

"Only one way to find out, isn't that right, sweetie?" she cooed into Bree's screaming face, surprisingly calm in the face of that torrent. "Although I suspect this one is hungry."

She walked over to one of the chairs and settled in, tucking her legs up into the chair. Carter watched with interest and curiosity, as she unbuttoned the top of her nightgown and pulled out a breast, directing it with one hand toward Bree's screaming mouth. It took a moment but as soon as the nipple popped in, an instant calm fell over the bedroom.

"Voilà!" she sang out softly.

She looked up and saw him staring. She gave him an amused smile. "You can sit down, you know," she said, nodding toward the other chair opposite her.

He blinked as if realizing it was there and walked over to settle into it. It was mesmerizing watching Bree quietly suck away while Jordan stroked her hair. Now that it was quiet, it was actually calming. He had a chance to embrace it completely. And he loved what it revealed.

Jordan and Bree. They were his. He was theirs. A family.

It reminded him of the day's events. Now that everyone had gone home he could broach the subject of his mother.

"So," he segued, "you and my mother...?" He let the question hang.

"She visited in the hospital," Jordan said, still smiling down at Bree. "We...came to an understanding. I think she's come around."

She finally looked up at him. "Some people are allowed second chances. Heaven knows *we* of all people should know that," she said, giving him a wry smirk.

He smiled in return.

She looked back down at Bree. "I will say this though...." She brought her head back up. The smile was gone. There was a flinty stare in her eyes. "However you work things out with your father, that's on you. But he's never getting anywhere near my daughter."

Carter looked down at the tiny figure in Jordan's arms and couldn't have agreed more.

Jordan saw it in his face and her expression softened. She looked down at Bree again.

"I think she's done here," she said, pulling the nipple out with a pop.

Carter waited for the cries to come but none did. Apparently, Bree was sated. He watched as the tiny eyelids blinked slowly until they stayed shut.

"There we go," Jordan said. She looked over at him thoughtfully then slowly untucked her legs and got out of her chair. She brought Bree over to him.

"Here," she said, placing her into his totally unprepared arms.

It was the second time today he held her. This time it felt a little more natural. He looked down at her small, sleeping form and knew that his heart was forever hers.

Jordan went back over to sit in the chair she had just vacated to watch him with a smile on her face. "Is your heart breaking yet?" she teased.

He chuckled softly. "A million times already."

They sat like that for several minutes, Carter embracing every detail of his daughter, and Jordan embracing the picture of them together.

"Hey, Slugger," she said softly. His eyes shot up to her.

She walked over and knelt on the floor beside him. "Will you marry me?"

It threw him. In the past several months the ring hadn't come up. What with Jordan taking the bar, then starting work, then taking her maternity leave. Then, he was constantly away for games, then on to the post season. It had been a whirlwind.

But he didn't need a ring to know she was his. By now, he knew she felt the same way. Obviously, he would be giving it back to her...but they would do it right. It certainly wouldn't be Jordan on her knees asking for it back.

He leaned over to her and whispered. "No" He bopped her on the nose, just for good measure.

"What?!" she yelped, flinching away from his finger.

"Shhh!" he chided, giving her a scornful look and eyeing Bree still asleep in his arms.

"What?!" she repeated in an outraged whisper.

"Calm your panties, Jordan," he teased in a whisper, grinning down at her. "If anyone here is going to be doing the asking...it's going to be me."

She gave him an indignant frown, torn between wanting to have a discussion about this and not wanting to wake Bree. He was enjoying every minute of it. This wasn't payback, but hell if he wasn't going to follow through on the plan he'd had ever since she'd decided to come back into his life.

He winked down at her. "Trust me, sweetheart...it'll be worth it."

❧ 44 ❧

It was the first home game of the season for the Sluggers. Jordan's family had decided to make a family day of it in honor. Naturally, they all had season passes, but it was rare to get them on a day when they could all make it.

Bree was now six months old and seemed to be a good luck charm for both her parents. A month after she was born, the Sluggers had won the World Series. Jordan was pleased to find out that Bree's college would be more than paid for when she learned what Carter's player's bonus share was—which was nothing compared to the Sluggers more than doubling his salary. Jordan's own little accomplishment of finding out she had passed the bar seemed minor by comparison, but Carter had gone over the top with the congratulatory gift, replacing her 5-year-old Honda with a "more lawyerly" white Lexus SUV.

She had thought for sure that ring would make an appearance at some point. At first, Jordan was a bit disappointed, but as their life together continued on in familiar comfort, she found it bothered her less and less. She knew she was his, and he was hers.

Jordan's job at *Morris* was going...well, it was going. She was doing everything she had done during the summer, and then some. The late nights were starting to wear on her. Worst of all, she missed Bree and Carter terribly. Now that he was starting up baseball again Bree would be missing both her parents a good chunk of the time. It was something Jordan would have to come to a decision on.

She looked over at her little good luck charm, who had been happily passed around from family member to family member during the game. Right now she was with her designated favorite, Ben. She cooed happily up at him with a smile as she tried to grab his lower lips with her tiny hand.

Considering he was now 14 years old, it amazed Jordan that he even had the patience or tolerance for dealing with a baby girl, but he reveled in it. Based on the way Bree laughed and gurgled in his arms, she obviously felt the same way. Jordan was almost jealous, and she couldn't put her finger on which one of them it was that she was jealous of.

The jealousy was most definitely supplanted by the hot dog—extra mustard—that she had in her hand. Let Ben and Bree play grabbsies with one another. Jordan was more than happy to indulge in her second favorite part of being at a Sluggers game. The first being quite obvious.

They were at the bottom of the 7th inning against the Los Angeles Dodgers. The Sluggers had been killing it and the score was now 7-2. Jordan couldn't help but smugly attribute it to Carter Fox's own good luck charms being securely in the stadium with him.

"Ms. Douglas?" a voice behind her said, just as she was about to take a second bite of her hot dog. There were at least three Ms. Douglases in the vicinity but she looked up all the same. It was a young woman, semi-professionally dressed in a pencil skirt and a short-sleeved blouse with an official Sluggers' badge around her neck.

The woman smiled down at her. "Hi," she said brightly. "I was wondering if you wouldn't mind coming with me. The Sluggers' are planning a small ceremony during the 7th inning stretch to honor Carter for his outstanding home run performance last year. They really wanted you to be out on the field for it so I was tasked with getting you down there in preparation."

Jordan started for a moment. Her heart burst with pride that the Sluggers would be acknowledging the man that she loved like this.

Of course, they wanted to honor him!

"Now?" she asked, looking longingly at her hot dog. "Do you think I have time to finish this thing first?"

The young woman was apparently low enough on the totem pole to blink her eyes in a panic instead of insisting her going down to the field.

"Oh go on Jordan!" her dad urged.

"Yeah, just go!" Ben pleaded. "Take it with you and finish on the way."

Eventually, everyone joined in the prodding, bringing an expression of relief to the poor woman's face.

Jordan decided to throw her a bone and got up out of her seat, still holding on to her hot dog. The woman's eyes flicked towards it, but she eventually seemed to think better of saying anything about it. Jordan took another bite as she followed the woman up the stands. It would be long gone by the time they made it down.

She could still see the action from where they ended up, standing near the field, in an entranceway. It was actually a pretty good vantage point from which to view the game. Unfortunately, the Sluggers had managed to get one out while she was en route to this location.

She happily munched on her hot dog as she watched the Sluggers at bat. Bobby Ramos hit a double and got one more point for the team. Jordan cheered as she took another bite of her hot dog.

She was cognizant of the woman eyeing her hot dog while they waited. She finally turned to her.

"Trust me," she mumbled, the fresh bite warbling her words. "I'll be done with this"—she lifted what was left of the bun in the air—"by the time I have to be out there."

Based on the woman's confused expression, she obviously had no idea what Jordan was saying.

Jordan turned her attention back to the game. She nearly choked as a pop-up ball was caught, unfortunately Bobby decided to try and advance anyway and was tagged out. She yelled in frustration as the two outs ended the inning, before realizing that she had one bite of hot dog left.

The poor woman next to her was about to faint, so Jordan stuffed the whole thing quickly in her mouth, giving her a reassuring smile that she didn't really feel. It was a lot of food.

She chewed as fast as she could, all the while smiling reassuringly at the woman. Eventually, she just swallowed in one painful gulp, readying herself for her field appearance to support her man. That seemed to calm her somewhat.

"You have mustard on your lip," the woman said, pointing to her face to show her where it was.

Jordan ran her tongue over her upper lip, lapping up the tangy smear. She smiled as she remembered the first time she had done the exact same thing at a Sluggers' game.

Her thoughts were interrupted as the woman startled her. "Okay! It's time," she yelped, giving Jordan the once over and apparently not entirely approving of what she saw

Jordan was wearing a Sluggers' Jersey, #47 obviously, and a pair of cut-off shorts that were practically hidden by the baggy top. A Slugger's cap shielded her eyes. If she'd known there was going to be a ceremony she would have dressed accordingly.

As Jordan was led onto the field she became gradually aware that there was no one else there. There was no grandstand or trophy or anything.

It was just her.

She looked around at the empty field and the filled stadium with a growing sense of extreme self-consciousness. Eventually, she saw Carter Fox walk out towards her with a smile on his face.

What was going on here?

When he approached her and bent down on one knee, it all came together. She brought one hand up to her mouth in surprised joy. She had another fleeting moment of regret that she hadn't worn something a bit more...special. Then she thought better of it. What better attire than her guy's—*fiancé's*—number on her back for the world to see?

"Jordan," she heard it reverberate around the stadium and saw the microphone clipped to his chest. So everyone here would be a witness. "It was at this very stadium almost two years ago that I first saw your face on that screen. From that moment on, no other woman could compare. You've stood by my side through my ups and my downs. Now I'm asking you to stand by my side forever. Jordan Douglas, will you marry me?"

Tears immediately sprang to her eyes. Her bursting heart overtook her capacity to even breath the words. She saw the flicker of panic in his eyes and she immediately reached out a hand to cup his face...his perfect face.

She nodded vigorously to reassure him. She loved him and wanted to spend the rest of her life with him. He gave a smile of relief.

"Yes!" she finally blurted out. "Oh yes!"

It was caught on his microphone and she heard her voice echoed back to her. A second later a cheer went through the crowd in support of the couple.

This had definitely been worth it.

EPILOGUE

"So today's the big day?" April asked.

"Maybe we can use some other word besides big," Jordan said, smirking at her friend.

April just laughed.

They both worked at Houston Legal Aid Society, which was a much better fit for Jordan that *Morris & Gibson* had been. She had given her notice to the firm almost a year ago. Between Carter's hectic in-season schedule and missing all of Bree's life events, it was a no brainer.

Now, she worked part time at the legal aid clinic, which gave her the flexibility to take off when she needed to. Like, for example, going for her ultra sound.

"You guys didn't have to do the cupcakes," Jordan said, eyeing the tray of treats, half of which were blue and half pink.

"Well, you wouldn't let us throw you a baby shower," said Carla, the administrative assistant. "We had to do something to pay you back for all those breakfast tacos you bring in practically every day."

"So what are you guys hoping for?" asked Emily, another attorney.

"I don't care, as long as it's—"

"Yeah, yeah," said April, "as long as it's healthy. Now what do you really want?"

Jordan laughed. "Well, you know Carter. He loves Bree to death but, and he certainly hasn't said anything, but I'm pretty sure he wants a boy."

"Speaking of which..." April looked past her shoulder.

There was a definite buzz of electricity in the air as Jordan heard the bell over the front door ding. As usual, when her husband made an appearance, there was a shift in the atmosphere. The combination of his celebrity status and imposing size was enough to stop all conversation and have all eyes focused on him.

He had Bree, who was now a little over two years old, in one large arm. She was wearing a coral sleeveless dress and white sandals. Her light brown head of curls was up in a pony tail.

"There's my little kitten," April gushed, walking over to tickle her.

Bree laughed and shrieked away from her favorite person in the world, second only to Daddy. Then her eyes caught the tray of cupcakes and she reached for them, nearly toppling out of Carter's arm.

"Whoa sweetie," he said, quickly reaching around to secure her with his other hand.

"*Unh,*" she protested, straining in his embrace, until Carter finally grabbed one for her.

"Pink!" she insisted and, being permanently wrapped around her little finger, he happily switched out the offending blue cupcake for pink.

"You're going to regret that, I guarantee it," Jordan said coming over to him and reaching up on her tip toes to kiss him.

"Mmm, that's the kind of sugar *I* prefer," he said against her lips.

Jordan smiled, then leaned in to her daughter. "Hey there, baby."

"Cupcake!" Bree said, holding up her recently acquired treat to show her mother with a broad smile on her face. Jordan wanted to eat it up.

"Yes, it is! Are you ready to go see your little brother or sister?"

She was patently ignored in favor of the pink frosting.

Jordan turned her attention to Carter. "I guess that answers that," she said with a laugh. "Are *you* ready?"

Carter blew out of his mouth, looking at Bree's frosting covered chin. "As ready as I'll ever be."

"Uh oh," Jordan said, looking in the back seat.

Bree was already fast asleep in the car seat. Obviously being fawned over in the office was very tiring business. The half eaten cupcake had fallen out of her hand, leaving a nice pink frosting stain on the seat.

"What is it?" Carter asked, looking in the rear view mirror of his truck.

"You don't want to know."

"She dropped it didn't she?"

"I told you you'd regret it,' Jordan chided, laughing. "Still want another?"

"A bit too late now, sweetheart," he said with a smirk. "Besides, I kind of like being a daddy. In fact, I think we should keep doing this, you're kinda sexy when you're pregnant."

She slapped him on the arm, chuckling. "You're hopeless."

"We have a healthy heartbeat," said the doctor. "Two arms, two legs, and lookie there, even a head!" he went on, teasingly.

Jordan liked him. He countered her obsession over every detail of the pregnancy with a calm reassurance that was neither patronizing nor critical and often quite humorous.

"So, do we want to find out if we're painting the nursery blue or pink?"

Jordan looked up at Carter with her eyebrows raised. She truly didn't care, having been honest when she told her friend she just wanted a healthy baby.

Carter looked down at Bree who was curled against his shoulder, still sleeping, two fingers stuck firmly in her little mouth. Once again he blew out his mouth and nodded down at his wife

"Let's hear it, doc."

"I guess that's a yes," Jordan said, smiling at her doctor.

"Okay then, prepare yourselves...."

A very healthy, 8 pound, 1 ounce Carter Fox Jr. was born at 2:47 on a perfectly lovely day.

The parents and big sister are all doing fine.

❧ I ❧
COMING JULY 2017

HIGH STAKES
A Texas Heat Romance

PREVIEW CHAPTERS

HIGH STAKES

A TEXAS HEAT ROMANCE

COMING JULY 2017!!

A Poker Professional who plays it by ear. A Professor who plans every detail. Will love win...even when the stakes get too high?

CHANCE

His name is no coincidence. All his life he's taken chances.

Chance is how his days of playing poker came to an end.

Chance is how Juliet first came into his life.

She's one risk that's paid off, even though they are as different as oil and water.

Now he'll risk it all to keep her by his side...even when his past catches up with him.

JULIET

Rhyme and reason rule her life.

Everything from her commute to work to her choice in men, is carefully analyzed for the best possible outcome.

Then Chance storms into her life like a hurricane, throwing all caution to the wind.

With him, nothing is predictable...and it's perfect in every way.

But can two people who are as different as night day make it work?

For him, she's willing to risk it all to find out...no matter how high the stakes are.

This is a **Stand Alone**, BWWM Romance in the *Texas Heat Romance Books*.

WARNING: Due to steamy, graphic adult situations and language, for 18+ only!

Continued....

1

L eft or right.

Like the flip of a coin, it really had boiled down to chance.

Mixers & Elixirs.

Chance McCoy thought it was a clever enough name for the event put on after hours at the *Houston Museum of Natural History*. He'd only heard about it the day before, and what better last hurrah before returning to two weeks on an oil rig than drinking beer and admiring pretty women in pretty dresses?

He'd done the meandering around thing, finally making his way to the second level, since the band on the first floor playing 80's pop music hadn't really done it for him. At the top of the stairs, he'd paused for exactly half a second before coming to a decision.

Left or right.

Left were the wildlife exhibits, which had always fascinated Chance as a kid. It would have been his first choice, if not for the quartet of admirable pairs of legs that had just exited the ladies' room. Normally, that too would have been his first choice, but he had little desire to play eeny, meeny, miny, moe tonight. It was a delicate dance, focusing on the woman who held most of your interest while charming her friends just enough to keep from being cock-blocked.

At least those mascaraed and eye-shadowed gazes looked him up and down appreciatively enough to let him know that he cleaned up quite nicely.

If they had been just a wee bit closer, they would have seen the wear and tear. There was the tiniest bit of grime under his fingernails that he couldn't quite get out, short of a bona fide manicure, which was not happening for various reasons. He also carried with him the slight residue of unfinished re-acclimation into polite society. Two weeks in the testosterone-driven stronghold that was his day-job didn't rinse off all that easily.

But Chance had always been a chameleon. Thanks to his unconventional upbringing, he could kick back with the goodest and ole'est of good ole' boys, or sip champagne with the creamiest of the *crème de la crème*. So the comfortable t-shirts and worn-out jeans had been replaced with a decent, black dress shirt and a nicer pair of jeans.

All the same, those four subtle nods of approval put a nice little bounce in his step when he swiveled right instead, straight into the gems and minerals exhibit.

That's when he saw her.

It didn't matter that her back was to him, something about those straight shoulders drew him in. The dress was one of those halter-back deals that left plenty of flawless skin on display. Her shoulders formed a perfectly horizontal line, not too wide or too narrow. Just perfect.

She was standing in front of a display, rigid as a statue. Chance made his way over toward those smooth, brown shoulders. There wasn't the faintest movement on her part; whatever she was absorbed in held her captive.

As he came in closer, he had a strong feeling that just maybe his luck was about to change.

About damn time.

Chance came around until he could see her in profile: full lips that held the promise of a brilliant smile, but were now slightly parted in awe; a small, round chin that stuck out almost stubbornly; a pointed, round-tipped nose that was overshadowed by the very pronounced cheekbone he had a glimpse of; long lashes that framed eyes that gradually slanted into something approaching almond-shaped.

She didn't even register him in her periphery, which gave him pause. He certainly didn't want to interrupt her intense concentration on— he shifted his gaze to the object of her focus—the geode in front of her. One look at that shoulder, which had a rich, warm glow even in the darkness of the room snapped him right out of that lapse in judgment.

"Amazing isn't it?"

She jumped in surprise, turning to him with all her internal bells and whistles going off at once.

"Oh my God!" she gasped, placing a hand to her heart.

Chance's brain instinctively went to work.

The body's physical reaction to all forms of surprise was pretty much the same, whether it was the thrill of winning the lottery, or the shock of running into a grizzly bear during a nature hike. The sensory receptacles all opened up at once, absorbing data to send to the brain at lightning speed: dilated pupils set in eyes that opened wide; flared nostrils; lips parted to form a semblance of an O; ears perked up and alert. Even the blood vessels expanded, allowing for that rapid flow to and from the heart, which would be pumping double-time in an adrenaline-fueled rush.

Interpreting these signals was practically second nature to Chance. It was a perfect cliché, but he could literally read people like a book.

It was what came next that Chance was most interested in.

The human body was also quick to recover from that initial shock, once the brain determined whether the surprise was appreciated or not.

The "not" would be obvious to all but the most blind observer as the body closed in on itself: the brow crinkling; lips pursed or pressed in a straight line; eyes narrowing or looking elsewhere; arms folded over the chest. Taken together, they might as well have been a neon sign flashing: CLOSED FOR BUSINESS.

Fortunately, her open mouth breathed out a small, relieved laugh. That was the first good sign. The rest of her face remained open, taking him in with acute interest. Those pupils stayed dilated behind lashes that subconsciously blinked prettily. The nose flared once again, inhaling those pheromones. Her body subtly twisted his way, letting Chance have a better look at her.

Then that smile appeared. Oh, that smile. It was the kind that took over the entire bottom half of her face, revealing her teeth all the way to the gum line. Chance had always been a sucker for exaggerated smiles like this, which came so naturally to some women.

"Sorry, you just scared me," she breathed, giving him another small laugh. She had a nice voice, feminine with a slice of huskiness to it that was like that splash of Tabasco sauce in a Bloody Mary.

Her slim hand rested against the chest that Chance could practically feel her heart beating inside of. A sudden premonition hit him that one day it would be his hand feeling that *lub-dub, lub-dub* underneath his palm. It made his own heart beat a little bit faster.

Cool it, Chance. The last thing he needed right now was to get seriously involved with a woman. His circumstances were complicated enough.

"It seems I'm the one who should be doing the apologizing. I didn't mean to interrupt your concentration." He nodded toward the large geode on display.

Her eyes followed his. "Oh, that. It's just fascinating, isn't it?"

"I agree. Something that looks so ordinary and even a bit rough on the outside. Most people wouldn't look twice at it. Then you crack it open and your mind is completely blown by the wonders inside."

The slight comparisons to himself weren't an accident. In fact, they were subtle hints in her direction.

She gave a light laugh again, before pressing her lips back together as though she was self-conscious about her smile. "Actually, I was just trying to find patterns in it."

"Patterns?"

She pointed one delicate finger at the glass. Her nails were short and perfectly shaped, with black nail polish. Definitely no grime underneath those nails. In fact, everything about her, from the hair twisted in some intricate knot at the nape of her neck, to the sleek heels she wore, signaled sophistication.

"I was just wondering if there was a reason why one crystal should be bigger or darker than the one next to it. Is it a matter of how close it is to the hollow center? Is it determined by how the geode rests on the ground? Gravity? The heat from the sun? Air? Water?"

"Maybe it's just a random act of nature?" he offered, now truly interested. The conversation had taken a turn he hadn't expected, but he was fascinated all the same.

"Random hardly ever happens in nature. Usually, if you search hard enough, you can find a reason and rationale for everything."

"Is that so?" he replied with a grin.

She looked over at him and immediately matched his grin with one of her own, this time a little more restrained, now that she was in control of herself. Still, it was another good sign. "Trust me, I'm an expert."

"Is *that* so?" he added, chuckling.

She gave another one of those femininely husky laughs. "Before you start trying anything on me, I should let you know I'm here on a date with someone."

"Me? I'm just admiring not so random acts of nature."

Now those gorgeous lips were twisted in a smirk. "Well, I suppose I should move out of the way, and let you observe the geode unobstructed."

Chance moved one slight step closer to her, noting how her face and body remained open in response. She leaned back a bit, but her feet stayed in place. All very good signs.

"Who says I'm talkin' 'bout the geode?" he said in a playfully exaggerated drawl.

This time that slightly raspy laugh was deeper, as she twisted her head down in a bashful, but flirtatious way. Then she shifted her gaze to face him with a subtle uptick of one eyebrow. "He'll be back any moment now."

She probably wasn't even fully conscious of the challenge her voice and expression held. But Chance was more than happy to pick up the gauntlet.

"Now what sort of man is crazy enough to leave a woman like you all alone, even for a moment? I feel it's only right that I do him a favor by keeping you company so no man tries to step in and start making the moves on you."

This time, she couldn't keep the smile from her face. "You're awfully bold."

"Well, as you said, there's a reason and a rationale for everything in nature," he replied, raising an eyebrow with his own challenge.

Her body language was very OPEN FOR BUSINESS. Chance almost felt bad for her date. Then again, it couldn't be going all that swell if the woman in front of him was so amenable to other suitors.

"What am I supposed to tell him when he comes back and you're standing here flirting with me?"

"We're just two people who happen to be admiring the same thing," he said, letting his eyes wander down her body to clue her in on exactly what display he was admiring.

Her eyes responded in kind, though less blatantly: a quick scan of the goods, an even quicker dart in another direction, all while she tried to hide her smile.

Now he was curious about this date of hers. "Was this place your idea or his?"

"Hmm?" she asked, her eyes widening in surprise at the change in topic. "Oh, mine. I love the museum. Especially the Butterfly Center."

"Butterfly Center," he echoed.

"Mm-hmm," she said nodding and returning her gaze to the geode. "I escape there practically every—"

She instantly stopped talking and flashed her eyes back to him, as though she had almost said something she shouldn't have.

Chance's smile assured her it was already too late.

The lips pressed firmly together did a poor job of hiding her pleasure. The eyes that fell to the floor demurely, and the dimple forming in one cheek told him that she had no problem with him maybe knowing too much of her business.

Before he could proceed they were interrupted by the "someone" she was here on a date with.

"Red wine, as requested," said the voice, a little to adamantly.

"Someone" was a man who was quite a few inches short of Chance's 6'3". He was a bit softer under that, admittedly, much more impressive suit and tie. His dark hair, styled and coifed, was a perfect contrast to Chance's finger-raked, dark blond hair, which grew a little too far past his collar. "Someone" wasn't unattractive, Chance would give him that much, but there was an undercurrent of desperation and petulance Chance didn't much care for.

He shifted his gaze to watch her reaction to the reappearance of her date. Her body signals were practically flashing signs as the glass was presented to her: perfunctory smile (the teeth and gum line were noticeably absent), a single blink that lasted just a bit too long, eyes that were just a bit too bright, the slight sigh, the body that remained facing in Chance's direction.

Sorry pal, she's taken.

Now all Chance had to do was figure out how to make that a reality.

He held up a finger to the man. "Actually, if you could just give us one minute. I was this close to getting this gorgeous woman's name."

"Her name is, here-on-a-date-with-someone-else, pal."

"Hmm, that seems like a mouthful," he grinned at her. "If I were you, I'd think seriously about changing it to something a bit...easier on the lips."

The twitch of her mouth told Chance that she, one, got the joke and, two, appreciated it. The gleam in those eyes also indicated his reference to his lips—and what he was interested in doing with them— wasn't lost on her.

Her "someone" most definitely did not appreciate it. He placed the glass holding red wine directly in the line of sight between two of them, following it with his body.

Chance waited, watching, as her lips parted, a heavy inhale preceding....

....a resigned exhale. She diverted her eyes to her "someone," and that was the end of that.

"Thank you, Simon," she said, taking the glass.

Chance bowed his head graciously.

"Chance is *my* name. Long story there. I'd love to tell you about it sometime."

That got a small smile behind Simon's back as he gave Chance a hard stare. "Like maybe when she isn't on a date with another guy?"

Message received.

But Chance was never one to go down that easily. He gave his best conceding smile, making a show of back walking. "Fair enough."

Then he stopped, his smile becoming a bona fide grin. "But I do have to say, if I was out with a woman who could put most of the gems in this room to shame, I wouldn't leave her side for one second."

And there it was, all her sensory receptacles opening up again. One... two...three...

"Juliet," she said, just as Simon was about to give Chance another what for.

Chance just gave her a grin and a wink, nodding his head at the two of them, then leaving them to it.

Tough luck Simon, she's definitely taken.

2

"*It's gots to be real! It's gots to be real!*"

The words didn't quite match the lyrics sung by Cheryl Lynn, but Kenny had a way of making each song his own. Despite having raised the level of their bikes to "nine," a few snickers echoed around the spin class.

As usual, Juliet was at her Saturday morning spin class, which was no surprise should anyone have done the math. And Juliet most certainly had.

This specific class, at this specific gym, at this specific time was the deliberate result of a number of factors, each contributing to the probability of her actually attending on a regular basis.

Arranged in order of weighted importance:

- Proximity to her apartment
- Proximity to a Starbucks with plenty of seating
- Specifically being located between said apartment and said Starbucks

- Likelihood of actually getting a bike without being wait-listed
- Starting late enough for her to wake up, get ready, and make it to class
- Starting early enough so she didn't laze the morning away and eventually decide not to attend
- Liking the instructor

It was a good thing that the instructor was weighted less heavily than the others, since Juliet normally didn't care for Kenny's rather flamboyant way of guiding them through the class.

However, today even Juliet managed a chuckle.

"And release! Back down to two, for a *verrrry* short recovery!" he yelled in his exuberant way, as *You're the One that I Want* from *Grease* came on. "Okay, everyone...it's race time! Y'all know what to do! Get them legs pumpin'!"

Juliet took a deep breath and began to pedal faster. It helped that her heart was one step ahead of her the whole time. As she thought about last night's date, her legs pedaled faster, trying to catch up with her rapidly beating heart.

Sadly, it wasn't because of Simon.

> *I got chills, they're multiplying, and I'm losing control*
> *'Cause the power you're supplying, it's electrifying*

Chance.

What a name. A name with a story. A name that had disappeared almost as soon as it had been uttered.

Her legs faltered and her bike shoe snapped out of its lock.

Dammit!

Juliet snapped it back in, and began peddling faster again. As her pace increased, so did her optimism for some reason.

"Okay, now I wanna hear y'all sing along!" Kenny urged as the song got to its chorus. "Get that air into y'all's lungs!"

You're the one that I want...

"*Ooh ooh ooh,*" Kenny crooned. "I don't hear y'all!"

As usual, only a few spinners joined in. Normally, Juliet wouldn't have in a million years.

Today was different.

You're the one that I want...

"*Ooh ooh ooh,*" she belted out, earning her a surprised look of respect from Kenny.

"That's *it,* girl!"

For some reason that got more people in the class going. By the end of the song, everyone was "*Ooh ooh oohing,*" and laughing as they raced.

"And....done!" cried Kenny, clapping his hands.

"What got into you today?" Shayla Sweeny looked at Juliet with an amused smirk as they wiped down their bikes.

After spin class, showering and doing her hair at the gym, Juliet's next item on the agenda was always a trip to Starbucks, where she put all the calories she had just burned right back on with a grande caramel macchiato.

Without fail.

Shayla and she were what they termed "weekend friends." Months ago they had found themselves standing next to each other in line at Starbucks. After recognizing each other from class, they decided to sit at the only available table together. Now it was their regular Saturday routine.

Without fail.

Juliet just shrugged. "I'm just feeling good, I guess."

"The date went that well?" Shayla asked raising her eyebrows suggestively.

Juliet just laughed. "Not quite. Long story."

"Ooh, now I'm really looking forward to my after-spin Starbucks."

"And then he just took off?" Shayla asked, sipping her latte.

They were relegated to the patio outside Starbucks, and enjoying it, despite the late summer Houston heat.

Once again, Juliet admired how well her friend put herself back together again after spin class. Her hair was natural, in a cute little afro, so that helped. But the once sweat-drenched, makeup-free face was now like something off the cover of *Essence Magazine*. She wore a bright orange tank top that showed off her dark skin beautifully, and a fun, colorful African print wrap skirt.

Juliet's typical style was carefully curated, based on plenty of research, for the strongest possibility of attracting the kind of man she wanted... or thought she did. After last night she wasn't so sure. All the same, she had officially crossed that dreaded threshold firmly into her 30s and she couldn't afford to take chances with her appearance.

She had washed, blow-dried, and flat ironed her own relaxed hair into something resembling "straight," down past her shoulders, curling the ends for good measure (most men preferred straight, long hair). Her make-up was the usual mascara/eye-liner/lip gloss simplicity she limited herself to (men hated too much make-up, at least too much *obvious* make-up, and her face worked well enough without needing too much help in that department). She wore a sleeveless, knee-length sundress in white eyelet fabric that showed off her brown skin perfectly (men definitely preferred dresses to shorts and pants, and a little bit of skin —not too much though!—helped).

"Yeah. Gone, just like that," she said, shrugging. "But, I don't know. For some reason it just felt like that wasn't the end of it."

"Whoa, whoa, whoa," Shayla said, lifting her sunglasses up on her head. "Is this our Juliet? The one who doesn't believe in chance, or luck, or fate? Praise Jesus, we've finally found a man to convert our little analytical cynic," she said, falling back in her chair with a laugh.

Juliet just kicked one sandaled foot out at her friend. "Don't be ridiculous. It was just a fun detour on a so-so date." She frowned, remembering how disappointing Simon had been. "A *really* so-so date."

"And here you are, *ooh, ooh, oohing,* during spin class." Shayla leaned in closer to Juliet. "Girl, if you don't put whatever's going on with you out into the universe then you don't deserve this guy."

Her friend fell back and brought her sunglasses down again. "At least tell me he was hot enough for the spank bank."

"Shayla!" Juliet yelped with a laugh, nearly spitting out her macchiato.

Shayla just laughed. "Oh come on. Dish! I need something to distract me from the neanderthal waiting back at home for me, no doubt still in his boxers and unshaved face, drinking milk straight out of the carton. And before you say anything, I love him to death despite that."

Juliet took one look at the ring on Shayla's finger and felt that familiar pang of envy. At 31, it seemed like Juliet was a walking, talking cliché: smart, attractive, successful, nice...yet no man to show for it.

Not that it should matter. Or so all the magazines, books, and websites had informed her.

Juliet wasn't desperate for a man, she just felt like she should have met someone she was comparable enough with to marry by now. It was getting to the point where she had to analyze what was wrong with her, and not the men she was dating.

"Well?"

Juliet was brought out of those sobering thoughts and taken back to last night. She recalled the man with the recklessly styled hair, the eyes that sparkled with an interesting hue even in the darkness of the museum, and that killer smile.

"I guess if you took...the voice of Matthew McConaughey, the attitude of that guy from *Suits*—"

"Gabriel Macht?" Shayla interrupted, leaning in and pushing her glasses back up again. "Now I'm really intrigued."

"Yeah, but he *looks* more like a mix of..." she thought about it, "50% Jensen Ackles, definitely in the eyes, 30% Bradley Cooper around the mouth, and...maybe 20% Paul Walker?"

Shayla stared at her for a beat. "Leave it to you to boil him down to the world's hottest formulaic equation."

"It just fits," Juliet said, the picture of Chance etched so deep into her brain that he might as well have been standing in front of her once again.

"Of course the question still remains...."

Juliet bit, rolling her eyes, even though she damn well knew where Shayla was going. "What?"

"How the hell are you going to run into this Casanova again?"

Now it was Juliet's turn to fall back into her chair. "I don't know. All he has is my first name and..."

She recalled the slip-up with the mention of the Butterfly Center. At the time she had been appalled at how easily she had revealed her guilty pleasure to a perfect stranger. She often escaped to the Butterfly Center during the week, which was only a hop, skip, and a jump from where she worked at Rice University.

"And what?" Shayla asked idly.

"I mentioned the Butterfly Center."

Shayla raised an eyebrow. "Well, there you go."

Juliet wrinkled her brow. "I didn't even tell him when or where or—"

"So what?" Shayla sighed and put down her cup. "Juliet, not everyone in the world operates by a perfect analysis of likelihood and probability and whatever else it is that goes on in your brain. Some people just throw caution to the wind and follow their gut."

Juliet frowned.

"Don't you dare give me that look. After all, what the hell has eHarmony gotten you so far? You wanna talk odds, how about I bet you that this guy is sitting in that Butterfly Center right now, damn sure you'll show up?"

Juliet laughed.

"Laugh all you want, but next week it will be you buying me my latte, girlfriend."

~

Juliet had a membership to the museum. Considering how often she made her way across Main Street from Rice University to the museum on a weekly basis, it made financial sense.

As soon as she entered the Cockrell Butterfly Center, a mostly black butterfly with white streaks landed on her dress. Juliet was thrilled; the butterflies never landed on her.

She made a point to note, not only the species of butterfly itself, but exactly where and when it had landed, what part of the center she was standing in, what lotion and soap she had used earlier today—speaking of scent, did the caramel macchiato play a role?—what time of day it was, how long since she had washed this dress....

"Well, hello there stranger."

Every bit of analysis in her head evaporated upon hearing that voice.

Juliet turned to see her JensenBradleyPaul hybrid with a Matthew voice and Gabriel attitude strolling toward her. He was dressed in a simple black t-shirt that showed off his admirable build, and a pair of jeans that revealed something even more impressive.

Upon closer reflection, none of those men had anything on this one.

This one was his own man.

ALSO BY CAMILLA STEVENS

WRIGHT BROTHERS NOVELS (NEW YORK)

Mr. Wright & Mr. Wrong

Mr. & Mrs. Wright

So Wrong

CALIFORNIA NOVELS

One Night

Sweet Seduction

Made in United States
North Haven, CT
07 March 2024

49605964R00182